CHRISTOPHEF
THE CASE OF THE
THREE STRANGE FACES

CHRISTOPHER BUSH was born Charlie Christmas Bush
in Norfolk in 1885. His father was a farm labourer and his
mother a milliner. In the early years of his childhood he
lived with his aunt and uncle in London before returning to
Norfolk aged seven, later winning a scholarship to Thetford
Grammar School.

As an adult, Bush worked as a schoolmaster for 27 years,
pausing only to fight in World War One, until retiring aged
46 in 1931 to be a full-time novelist. His first novel
featuring the eccentric Ludovic Travers was published in
1926, and was followed by 62 additional Travers mysteries.
These are all to be republished by Dean Street Press.

Christopher Bush fought again in World War Two, and was
elected a member of the prestigious Detection Club. He
died in 1973.

By Christopher Bush

CHRISTOPHER BUSH

THE CASE OF THE THREE STRANGE FACES

With an introduction
by Curtis Evans

DEAN STREET PRESS

Published by Dean Street Press 2017

Introduction copyright © 2017 Curtis Evans

All Rights Reserved

The right of Christopher Bush to be identified as the
Author of the Work has been asserted by his estate in
accordance with the Copyright, Designs and Patents
Act 1988.

First published in 1933 by Cassell & Co.

Cover by DSP

ISBN 978 1 911579 83 0

www.deanstreetpress.co.uk

INTRODUCTION

THAT ONCE vast and mighty legion of bright young (and youngish) British crime writers who began publishing their ingenious tales of mystery and imagination during what is known as the Golden Age of detective fiction (traditionally dated from 1920 to 1939) had greatly diminished by the iconoclastic decade of the Sixties, many of these writers having become casualties of time. Of the 38 authors who during the Golden Age had belonged to the Detection Club, a London-based group which included within its ranks many of the finest writers of detective fiction then plying the craft in the United Kingdom, just over a third remained among the living by the second half of the 1960s, while merely seven—Agatha Christie, Anthony Gilbert, Gladys Mitchell, Margery Allingham, John Dickson Carr, Nicholas Blake and Christopher Bush—were still penning crime fiction.

In 1966--a year that saw the sad demise, at the too young age of 62, of Margery Allingham--an executive with the English book publishing firm Macdonald reflected on the continued popularity of the author who today is the least well known among this tiny but accomplished crime writing cohort: Christopher Bush (1885-1973), whose first of his three score and three series detective novels, *The Plumley Inheritance*, had appeared fully four decades earlier, in 1926. "He has a considerable public, a 'steady Bush public,' a public that has endured through many years," the executive boasted of Bush. "He never presents any problem to his publisher, who knows exactly how many copies of a title may be safely printed for the loyal Bush fans; the number is a healthy one too." Yet in 1968, just a couple of years after the Macdonald editor's affirmation of Bush's notable popular duration as a crime writer, the author, now in his 83rd year, bade farewell to mystery fiction with a final detective novel, *The Case of the Prodigal Daughter*, in which, like in Agatha Christie's *Third Girl* (1966), copious references are made, none too favorably, to youthful sex, drugs and rock and roll. Afterwards, outside of the reprinting in the UK in the early 1970s of a scattering of classic Bush titles from the Golden Age, Bush's books, in contrast with those of Christie, Carr, Allingham and Blake, disappeared from mass circulation in both the UK and the US, becoming fervently sought (and ever more unobtainable) treasures by collectors and connoisseurs of classic crime fiction. Now, in one of the signal developments in vintage mystery publishing, Dean Street Press is reprinting all 63 of the Christopher Bush detective novels. These will be published over a period of months, beginning with the release of books 1 to 10 in the series.

Few Golden Age British mystery writers had backgrounds as humble yet simultaneously mysterious, dotted with omissions and evasions, as Christopher Bush, who was born Charlie Christmas Bush on the day of the Nativity in 1885 in the Norfolk village of Great Hockham, to Charles Walter Bush and his second wife, Eva Margaret Long. While the father of Christopher Bush's Detection Club colleague and near exact contemporary Henry Wade (the pseudonym of Henry Lancelot Aubrey-Fletcher) was a baronet who lived in an elegant Georgian mansion and claimed extensive ownership of fertile English fields, Christopher's father resided in a cramped cottage and toiled in fields as a farm laborer, a term that in the late Victorian and Edwardian era, his son lamented many years afterward, "had in it something of contempt....There was something almost of serfdom about it."

Charles Walter Bush was a canny though mercurial individual, his only learning, his son recalled, having been "acquired at the Sunday school." A man of parts, Charles was a tenant farmer of three acres, a thatcher, bricklayer and carpenter (fittingly for the father of a detective novelist, coffins were his specialty), a village radical and a most adept poacher. After a flight from Great Hockham, possibly on account of his poaching activities, Charles, a widower with a baby son whom he had left in the care of his mother, resided in London, where he worked for a firm of spice importers. At a dance in the city, Charles met Christopher's mother, Eva Long, a lovely and sweet-natured young milliner and bonnet maker, sweeping her off her feet with a combination of "good looks and a certain plausibility." After their marriage the couple left London to live in a tiny rented cottage in Great Hockham, where Eva over the next eighteen years gave birth to three sons and five daughters and perforce learned the challenging ways of rural domestic economy.

Decades later an octogenarian Christopher Bush, in his memoir *Winter Harvest: A Norfolk Boyhood* (1967), characterized Great Hockham as a rustic rural redoubt where many of the words that fell from the tongues of the native inhabitants "were those of Shakespeare, Milton and the Authorised Version....Still in general use were words that were standard in Chaucer's time, but had since lost a certain respectability." Christopher amusingly recalled as a young boy telling his mother that a respectable neighbor woman had used profanity, explaining that in his hearing she had told her husband, "George, wipe you that shit off that pig's arse, do you'll datty your trousers," to which his mother had responded that although that particular usage of a four-letter word had not really been *swearing*, he was not to give vent to such language himself.

Great Hockham, which in Christopher Bush's youth had a population of about four hundred souls, was composed of a score or so of cottages, three public houses, a post-office, five shops, a couple of forges and a pair of churches, All Saint's and the Primitive Methodist Chapel, where the Bush family rather vocally worshipped. "The village lived by farming, and most of its men were labourers," Christopher recollected. "Most of the children left school as soon as the law permitted: boys to be absorbed somehow into the land and the girls to go into domestic service." There were three large farms and four smaller ones, and, in something of an anomaly, not one but two squires--the original squire, dubbed "Finch" by Christopher, having let the shooting rights at Little Hockham Hall to one "Green," a wealthy international banker, making the latter man a squire by courtesy. Finch owned most of the local houses and farms, in traditional form receiving rents for them personally on Michaelmas; and when Christopher's father fell out with Green, "a red-faced, pompous, blustering man," over a political election, he lost all of the banker's business, much to his mother's distress. Yet against all odds and adversities, Christopher's life greatly diverged from settled norms in Great Hockham, incidentally producing one of the most distinguished detective novelists from the Golden Age of detective fiction.

Although Christopher Bush was born in Great Hockham, he spent his earliest years in London living with his mother's much older sister, Elizabeth, and her husband, a fur dealer by the name of James Streeter, the couple having no children of their own. Almost certainly of illegitimate birth, Eva had been raised by the Long family from her infancy. She once told her youngest daughter how she recalled the Longs being visited, when she was a child, by a "fine lady in a carriage," whom she believed was her birth mother. Or is it possible that the "fine lady in a carriage" was simply an imaginary figment, like the aristocratic fantasies of Philippa Palfrey in P.D. James's *Innocent Blood* (1980), and that Eva's "sister" Elizabeth was in fact her mother?

The Streeters were a comfortably circumstanced couple at the time they took custody of Christopher. Their household included two maids and a governess for the young boy, whose doting but dutiful "Aunt Lizzie" devoted much of her time to the performance of "good works among the East End poor." When Christopher was seven years old, however, drastically straightened financial circumstances compelled the Streeters to leave London for Norfolk, by the way returning the boy to his birth parents in Great Hockham.

Fortunately the cause of the education of Christopher, who was not only a capable village cricketer but a precocious reader and scholar, was taken up both by his determined and devoted mother and an idealistic local elementary school headmaster. In his teens Christopher secured a scholarship to Norfolk's Thetford Grammar School, one of England's oldest educational institutions, where Thomas Paine had studied a century-and-a-half earlier. He left Thetford in 1904 to take a position as a junior schoolmaster, missing a chance to go to Cambridge University on yet another scholarship. (Later he proclaimed himself thankful for this turn of events, sardonically speculating that had he received a Cambridge degree he "might have become an exceedingly minor don or something as staid and static and respectable as a publisher.") Christopher would teach in English schools for the next twenty-seven years, retiring at the age of 46 in 1931, after he had established a successful career as a detective novelist.

Christopher's romantic relationships proved far rockier than his career path, not to mention every bit as murky as his mother's familial antecedents. In 1911, when Christopher was teaching in Wood Green School, a co-educational institution in Oxfordshire, he wed county council schoolteacher Ella Maria Pinner, a daughter of a baker neighbor of the Bushes in Great Hockham. The two appear never actually to have lived together, however, and in 1914, when Christopher at the age of 29 headed to war in the 16th (Public Schools) Battalion of the Middlesex Regiment, he falsely claimed in his attestation papers, under penalty of two years' imprisonment with hard labor, to be unmarried.

After four years of service in the Great War, including a year-long stint in Egypt, Christopher returned in 1919 to his position at Wood Green School, where he became involved in another romantic relationship, from which he soon desired to extricate himself. (A photo of the future author, taken at this time in Egypt, shows a rather dashing, thin-mustached man in uniform and is signed "Chris," suggesting that he had dispensed with "Charlie" and taken in its place a diminutive drawn from his middle name.) The next year Winifred Chart, a mathematics teacher at Wood Green, gave birth to a son, whom she named Geoffrey Bush. Christopher was the father of Geoffrey, who later in life became a noted English composer, though for reasons best known to himself Christopher never acknowledged his son. (A letter Geoffrey once sent him was returned unopened.) Winifred claimed that she and Christopher had married but separated, but she refused to speak of her purported spouse forever after and she destroyed all of his letters and other mementos, with the exception of a book of poetry that he had written for her during what she termed their engagement.

Christopher's true mate in life, though with her he had no children, was Florence Marjorie Barclay, the daughter of a draper from Ballymena, Northern Ireland, and, like Ella Pinner and Winifred Chart, a schoolteacher. Christopher and Marjorie likely had become romantically involved by 1929, when Christopher dedicated to her his second detective novel, *The Perfect Murder Case*; and they lived together as man and wife from the 1930s until her death in 1968 (after which, probably not coincidentally, Christopher stopped publishing novels). Christopher returned with Marjorie to the vicinity of Great Hockham when his writing career took flight, purchasing two adjoining cottages and commissioning his father and a stepbrother to build an extension consisting of a kitchen, two bedrooms and a new staircase. (The now sprawling structure, which Christopher called "Home Cottage," is now a bed and breakfast grandiloquently dubbed "Home Hall.") After a falling-out with his father, presumably over the conduct of Christopher's personal life, he and Marjorie in 1932 moved to Beckley, Sussex, where they purchased Horsepen, a lovely Tudor plaster and timber-framed house. In 1953 the couple settled at their final home, The Great House, a centuries-old structure (now a boutique hotel) in Lavenham, Suffolk.

From these three houses Christopher maintained a lucrative and critically esteemed career as a novelist, publishing both detective novels as Christopher Bush and, commencing in 1933 with the acclaimed book *Return* (in the UK, *God and the Rabbit*, 1934), regional novels purposefully drawing on his own life experience, under the pen name Michael Home. (During the 1940s he also published espionage novels under the Michael Home pseudonym.) Although his first detective novel, *The Plumley Inheritance*, made a limited impact, with his second, *The Perfect Murder Case*, Christopher struck gold. The latter novel, a big seller in both the UK and the US, was published in the former country by the prestigious Heinemann, soon to become the publisher of the detective novels of Margery Allingham and Carter Dickson (John Dickson Carr), and in the latter country by the Crime Club imprint of Doubleday, Doran, one of the most important publishers of mystery fiction in the United States.

Over the decade of the 1930s Christopher Bush published, in both the UK and the US as well as other countries around the world, some of the finest detective fiction of the Golden Age, prompting the brilliant Thirties crime fiction reviewer, author and Oxford University Press editor Charles Williams to avow: "Mr. Bush writes of as thoroughly enjoyable murders as any I know." (More recently, mystery genre authority B.A. Pike dubbed these novels by Bush, whom he praised as "one of the most reliable and resourceful of true detective writers"; "Golden Age baroque, rendered remarkable by some extraordinary flights of fancy.") In 1937 Christopher Bush became, along with Nicholas Blake, E.C.R. Lorac and Newton Gayle (the writing team of Muna Lee and Maurice West Guinness), one of the final authors initiated into the Detection Club before the outbreak of the Second World War and with it the demise of the Golden Age. Afterward he continued publishing a detective novel or more a year, with his final book in 1968 reaching a total of 63, all of them detailing the investigative adventures of lanky and bespectacled gentleman amateur detective Ludovic Travers. Concurring as I do with the encomia of Charles Williams and B.A. Pike, I will end this introduction by thanking Avril MacArthur for providing invaluable biographical information on her great uncle, and simply wishing fans of classic crime fiction good times as they discover (or rediscover), with this latest splendid series of Dean Street Press classic crime fiction reissues, Christopher Bush's Ludovic Travers detective novels. May a new "Bush public" yet arise!

Curtis Evans

The Case of the Three Strange Faces (1933)

AS CHRISTOPHER BUSH attained greater stature in the early 1930s with his Ludovic Travers detective fiction, the author began a period of publisher-hopping in both the United Kingdom and the United States. With *The Case of the Unfortunate Village* (1932), Bush changed his UK publishers from Heinemann to Cassell, purveyors of mystery fiction by such British and American heavyweights as G.K. Chesterton, E. Phillips Oppenheim, William Le Queux, Sax Rohmer, Baroness Orczy, Erle Stanley Gardner, Ellery Queen, S.S. Van Dine, Rex Stout, Dashiell Hammett and Mary Roberts Rinehart. In a series of splendidly jacketed editions, Cassell would publish all of Bush's detective novels in England until the end of the Second World War, when for one last time he again switched companies, this time to Macdonald.

Slightly earlier in 1932, with the detective novel *Cut Throat*, Bush had moved, among American publishers, from Doubleday, Doran to Morrow, whose mystery stable also included Erle Stanley Gardner, as well as Carter Dickson (a pseudonym of John Dickson Carr) and R.A.J. Walling, another once quite popular British author of classic crime fiction. Morrow evidently declined *The Case of the Unfortunate Village*--is it possible that that novel, which included among its characters a woman artist who began painting orgiastic "ultra-impressionist" paintings as a subconscious expression of her sexual awakening, was too racy for Morrow?—though the company accepted Bush's next four novels, which appeared in 1933 and 1934. The next year Bush changed publishers once again, this time switching to Henry Holt, where he was their big name in the mystery field, along with, to be sure, Brett Halliday (David Dresser), whose sleuth Michael Shayne in the 1940s would become one of the best-known tough guy detectives in American crime fiction. Holt would publish all eight of the Bush detective novels that appeared in Britain from 1935 to 1939, after which Christopher Bush, in response to the outbreak of the Second World War and drawing on his own military experience, sent Travers into the army for six years and made most of the sleuth's adventures military themed, a decision which, I presume, did not sit well with American publishers. No additional Bush detective novels appeared in the US until 1947, when Macmillan issued two Bush titles, one of them the rather ironically named *The Case of the Second Chance*.

As the above title hints, with *The Case of the Unfortunate Village* and *The Case of the April Fools*, Christopher Bush began giving his novels uniform "The Case of..." titles for the rest of his long writing career. Fully 54 Ludovic Travers detective novels would carry such "Case" appellations. It is an interesting exercise to compare the chronology of Bush titles with the very similarly styled titles by Erle Stanley Gardner, who, as the creator of dogged defense attorney Perry Mason, became, for many years, the bestselling American crime writer in the world. Both the first Perry Mason novel, *The Case of the Velvet Claws*, and Bush's *The Case of the April Fools* were published in the US by Morrow in March 1933. Did Bush inspire Gardner's titles format, or Gardner Bush's, or was it all simply coincidence?

Bush's last Ludovic Travers detective novel, *The Case of the Prodigal Daughter*, appeared in the United States in 1969, while Gardner's final Perry Mason detective novel was published, posthumously, in 1973. All of the Mason mysteries were published by Morrow, while Bush, as explained above, left Morrow after just a couple of years. Could this be seen as the case of the redundant titles? Certainly Christopher's son, Geoffrey Bush, thought as much, suggesting in his autobiography that "the choice of the same title format as that of the rather more successful Erle Stanley Gardner" undermined the sales of his father's books in the US. Admittedly the similarity in format seems to have led to changes being made to the titles of most of the Bush mysteries published in the US in the 1930s. Of the dozen Bush titles published in the US in that decade, only four appeared in the US under their original names. The other eight Bush novels all had altered titles, usually rather worse ones. Holt even took trouble to shear three words from *The Case of The Leaning Man*, leaving, simply, *The Leaning Man. The Case of the Three Strange Faces* became *The Crank in the Corner*, surely an unprepossessing title for an exceptional murder mystery.

* * * * *

...this is the story of the three men; one whose face was spotted, one whose face was brown, and one whose face became a most extraordinary red. There is also the fourth man whose face was altered, but he comes into the story much later.

So intriguingly begins Christopher Bush's *The Case of the Three Strange Faces*, wherein Ludovic Travers is returning by train from Bandol, in the south of France, having been sent there on doctor's advice after an attack of influenza brought on, in part, by too much work. ("That enormous and ramificatory business of Durangos Limited, of which Travers was an exceedingly live director, had made a lot of demands. Then there was that revised and cheap edition of *The Economics of a Spendthrift*, on which its author spent the time that should have gone to outdoor leisure.") Train mysteries and thrillers were quite coming into their own by the mid-1930s, what with not only the award-winning British film *Rome Express* (1932), which Bush wryly references in his novel, but Agatha Christie's *Murder on the Orient Express* (1934), American Lawrence Blochman's *Bombay Mail* (1934) American Todd Downing's *Vultures in the Sky* (1935), Jefferson Farjeon's *Holiday Express* (1935) and Ethel Lina White's *The Wheel Spins* (1936) (the latter of which was filmed by Alfred Hitchcock in 1938 as *The Lady Vanishes*). Christopher Bush's *The Case of the Three Strange Faces* preceded all of these classic train tales, though it followed Christie's *The Mystery of the Blue Train* (1928), Farjeon's *The 5.18 Mystery* (1929), and Graham Greene's *Stamboul Train* (1932, retitled *Orient Express* for US publication, which is why Christie's *Murder on the Orient Express* was lamely retitled *Murder in the Calais Coach* upon its US publication). Certainly contrasting with Christie's perennially popular 1934 tale of wealthy cosmopolitans embroiled in a claustrophobic though tony murder investigation conducted by the world-famous mustachioed Belgian detective, Hercule Poirot, *The Case of the Three Strange Faces* takes place in a decidedly unglamorous second class carriage on a French train bound from Toulon to Paris. In real life, Christopher Bush while teaching at Wood Green School had attended evening classes at King's College, London, obtaining there an Honors Degree in Modern Languages in 1913, a year before the outbreak of the First World War. He was fluent in French and during the Second World War claimed to have an "intimate knowledge of France over many years."

Like Christopher Bush, Ludo Travers deems himself unsnobbish and non-insular; and on returning from the South of France he made sure, his more than ample means notwithstanding, to book reservations on a second class carriage. As a self-styled "student of humanity," he looks forward to enjoying a night of interesting company:

> He wondered who would be in his compartment. Some English people, he hoped, and some French; and of course there might be an Italian—and better still, an American or two. Delightful people he hoped they would be; not spoilt by money like most of the first-classers; people who would talk interestingly on interesting things; people of whom one could afterwards think with a grateful, appreciative, reminiscent chuckle.

Sadly Travers finds something less than appealing the six individuals, (including the titular three men with strange faces), who in the event share a compartment with him. These are James Hunt, a splenetic and spotted old man ("Small, [the spots] were, but a violent red, and they spattered the old man's jowl like the scanty currents in a homely pudding."); Leslie Hunt, the old man's nephew, a vapid young fellow much addicted to paperback thrillers; Thomas Brown, the old man's much put-upon valet; Pierre Olivet, a florid Frenchman with a club-foot, and his forward French wife, Marie; and Frederick Smith, a heavily-tanned London bank clerk on holiday. Then there is the overbearing French Provencal who plants himself in the corridor and will not depart. But things become yet more vexing when two of Travers' compartment companions expire mysteriously and the French police turn suspicious eyes on Travers himself!

The gentleman amateur sleuth manages to extricate himself from this sticky situation by resorting, yet again, to a bit of strategic name-dropping, specifically the names of his uncle, Police Commissioner Sir George Coburn, and his good friend Superintendent George Wharton, one of the Big Five at Scotland Yard. He even makes a new police friend in France, Inspector Gallois of the Sûreté, who a half dozen years later would make another appearance in a Travers mystery, *The Case of the Flying Ass* (1939), the last Bush detective novel written before the outbreak of the Second World War. However, after Travers learns that James Hunt's home (Marsh View, near Rye, Sussex) was burgled after Hunt's mysterious passing, the inveterate snooper decides, largely on account of his "strain of cussedness and determination," to look into the case himself when he returns to England. (Travers is quite familiar with Sussex, spending most of his weekends at Pulvery Manor, his sister and brother-in-law's Sussex country place, as was the author himself, who resided in that county.) Soon Travers, his Isotta now replaced with a Bentley, is working in tandem with Superintendent Wharton to solve one of the strangest cases which he has yet encountered, in which some of the darkest of human impulses are implicated.

CHAPTER I
A JOURNEY BEGINS

THIS IS the story of the men with the strange faces, as Ludovic Travers told it to the examining magistrate, and later to Superintendent Wharton of Scotland Yard. But that is not strictly true. Many of those happenings of the evening of June the 29th and the morning of June the 30th came back to his mind only as the case progressed, and it is what might be called the grand, ultimate sum-total that is here set out for convenience. To repeat then: this is the story of the three men; one whose face was spotted, one whose face was brown, and one whose face became a most extraordinary red. There is also the fourth man whose face was altered, but he comes into the story much later.

The whole affair, as far as Ludovic Travers was concerned, was fortuitous if not strange. He rarely spent holidays abroad, for instance, and it was influenza that accounted for his presence on the platform at Toulon at a quarter to four on the afternoon of June the 29th. The attack had been as long back as the beginning of May, and it had been that gastric, virulent type that leaves the convalescent with queer depressions. He knew, even when he was on his feet again, that he had lost grip of things. His mind refused to settle, and he was as certain—as he was certain of anything—that he would never be really well again. Sir Charles Lambry listened to all that with patience, knowing there was more in it than deranged digestion. That enormous and ramificatory business of Durangos Limited, of which Travers was an exceedingly live director, had made a lot of demands. Then there was that revised and cheap edition of "The Economics of a Spendthrift," on which its author had spent the time that should have gone in outdoor leisure. Lambry, in short, first nodded gravely at Travers's disclosures, and then prescribed the South of France, and it was only as his patient left that he dug him in the ribs and assured him that he would soon be as active as a mosquito.

It was the quiet resort of Bandol, near Toulon, that Travers chose on the recommendation of a friend. There he tramped about, swam about and lazed about. Inside ten days he was eating ravenously and sleeping abnormally well. At the end of a fortnight he was itching to get back to London, in spite of Lambry's insistence on a month at least. At the end of three weeks he could stand it no longer. He had never felt so fit and mentally alert. Durangos was calling, and his manuscript was calling; and on a sudden resolve he wrote to everybody that he was coming back, and he booked his reservation. Then, having taken those decisive steps, he had leisure to see things in a rather more sane perspective, and he felt the least bit of a fool.

Then there was the matter of that reservation which might seem strange for a man as wealthy as he was. A first-class or a sleeping berth seemed the right and proper thing, and yet it was a corridor, corner, second-class seat which he booked. The expense of anything else seemed to him not only disproportionate, but—considering the times in which one lived—utterly preposterous. As he saw it, it was not a question of thrift being fashionable, but of its being sheer horse-sense. And there was a far more important reason that made him choose that second-class seat. He was a student of humanity. The world was his perpetual theatre, and a railway compartment for the space of one night, a brief and intimate stage. It had in it something of the quality of the gallery at Covent Garden. One came to close quarters with living, interesting, cultured people. For a night they slept in one common bedroom. When they talked they showed new angles and ideas. For fifteen hours one heard the unusual—even in snores—and contributed as the circumstances demanded.

Travers was thinking of something of that as he waited on the platform at a quarter to four that afternoon. He wondered who would be in his compartment. Some English people, he hoped, and some French; and, of course, there might be an Italian—and better still, an American or two. Delightful people he hoped they would be; people not spoilt by money like most of the first-classers; people who would talk interestingly on interesting things; people of whom one could afterwards think with a grateful, appreciative, reminiscent chuckle.

It was a trickle of perspiration that took his mind off that. It had been a sweltering day—the hottest known for years—and what air there was seemed to come straight from the Sahara. Even in the shade where he sat, he was horribly damp and his collar, when he wiped round it with his handkerchief, was sticky and limp. Then the train, dead on time, came rolling in, and he picked up his bag and prepared to find his carriage. The gust of air as the train fussed to a halt had something stifling and steamy about it.

The carriage was found easily enough. It was a hybrid affair of mixed thirds and seconds, and it was with the old, pleasurable anticipation that he looked inside what was certainly his own compartment. To his surprise it was almost empty. When his bag was on the rack and he had taken his own corner seat facing the engine, all four corners—and all four corners only—were occupied. As for the three occupants, a quick glance round could take them in.

Opposite him was a black-haired man of about thirty; his face deeply tanned. He was wearing grey flannel trousers and a grey coat, but no waistcoat, and in spite of the opened windows he was looking uncomfortably hot. The book he held in his hand was that yellow-backed volume of information on the Riviera coast issued by the P. L. M.

In the far, window corner, with back to the engine, was an old man who was ignoring the entry of the newcomer, and staring surlily out at the distant platforms. In spite of the heat he had on a light overcoat, the collar of which was turned up to his ears. Lower, it was open, and Travers could see the black jacket and—incongruity of incongruities—a white waistcoat. His hair was white and his face unhealthily pallid, and as Travers caught him slightly more full-faced, he saw the deep, peevish grooves that ran down from the nose to the sides of the bluish, vicious-looking mouth.

Opposite him, in the remaining corner, was a young man of certainly not more than twenty. He, too, was wearing grey flannels, and his flannel sports shirt was open at the neck. His nose was slightly hooked, his chin fell away, and there was something weak about his face and something of the petulance of the old man who faced him. Travers imagined a family resemblance, and from the way the younger man looked at the older, he was sure of some relationship—son and father, it might be, or nephew and uncle. And one other thing he noticed—that there was little luggage in the rack above either of their heads. From that he deduced they were going straight through to England, and were not staying in Paris.

As he leaned back in his corner after that first survey, there flashed through his mind a small gratification, but behind it was a background of disappointment. True there would be room to stretch one's legs, and Travers—rather like a bifurcated lamp-post—knew the value of space; but on the other hand the pleasant companionship, the good-natured crowding, the merry quip and the inconsequential chatter would none of them be there. The old man in the far corner seemed infuriated with his own company, and uncommonly unlikely to tolerate in any kindly fashion that of others. The youth who faced him looked spineless and vapid; and as for the black-haired man—whose initials on the suit-case above his head seemed to be F.S.—a person who chose a railway guide as reading matter was likely to be neither interesting nor informative.

All that had taken perhaps a matter of three minutes, and then there came the usual tooting of horns and shouts of porters and officials, and the train moved off. Through his blurred hornrims Travers caught sight of the green reservation slips that were pinned above the four vacant places in the compartment, and immediately he cheered up. He hooked off his glasses and began polishing them furiously, and as he did so he wondered again just what sort of people they would be who were to fill the empty seats. Then he craned forward, wondering if written on the slips would be the place of entry.

"They're getting in at Marseilles, sir," came the voice of the man opposite.

Travers blushed at being caught out in so flagrant a piece of inquisitiveness. He cleared his throat gently as if the matter were perhaps excusable.

"Yes—er—quite."

F.S. tucked the yellow-backed book behind him, and wiped his neck with a white handkerchief that looked as if it had done duty before.

"Tremendously hot, isn't it?" he said. His voice lacked quality, and Travers put him down as the representative of some business house. And as soon as he had a good look at him, he began to be fascinated by his face. It was not mahogany, nor walnut, nor ebony, but rather the colour of fumed oak with something of gold in it.

"Tremendously hot," agreed Travers, still exploring the tanned face.

"Yes," supplemented the other; "sort of night it's going to be when you wouldn't mind if nobody else got in at all. What it's going to be like when we're full up, I don't know."

"Let's hope for the best," smiled Travers, and opened his coat to let the breeze play round him. He stretched his long legs to well under the opposite seat. At the other end of the compartment both large windows were fully down, and yet the air that came with the gathering progress of the train was not a cooling wind but a kind of hot, uncomfortable draught. To close the corridor door might make things better, thought Travers, and promptly closed it. The old man's voice came with a snarl.

"Confound you, sir! What do you mean by shutting that door?"

The voice and manner were those of a stage colonel, but nobody looked less military than the sallow, thin-lipped, shaggy-browed man who was glaring from the corner. Travers smiled amiably.

"I beg your pardon. I thought perhaps there might be less of a draught."

"Draught!" He snorted. Then he glared at the door, saw it was opened again, and resumed his scowling at the landscape. Travers, feeling rather flustered and vaguely ashamed, caught the eye of the young man who had no chin. It was a fish-like eye which fell as soon as it met his own, and then regarded solicitously the old man opposite. Travers was even more sure of some relationship, and the old man he put down as a country lawyer.

Just then the train flashed into a tunnel. With a little inward chuckle Travers once more drew to the door to keep out the smoke. F.S. in the same moment turned on the electric light, and there was the supposed nephew hastily putting up the uncle's window and his own. The smoke was already in the compartment and the old man began a fit of coughing. Then the train left the tunnel again. On the right was sheer mountain and the sea on the left. Travers drew back the door.

"Rather unpleasant things, these tunnels," he observed courteously to the old man. There was some sort of grunt. The nephew put down the two windows. Travers, leaning back again, resorted to philosophy. There were, he thought what the Navy calls happy ships. That compartment hardly came under that heading. A pipe might be a good thing, perhaps; a general, sociable pipe, which might create a better atmosphere. The pipe of peace, in fact.

He got his pipe going and then offered F.S. a cigarette, and held the light for him. Hardly had he replaced the case when the train again ran into a tunnel, and it was then that the first really peculiar thing happened. F.S. made no attempt to turn on the light. Without even an "I beg your pardon," as he kicked against Travers's legs, he went out to the corridor, where the window was open and smoke was rushing in. Travers—always ready, and anxious, to find a reason for everything—knew that F.S. was having the sense to shut the offending outside window, and hastily switched on the light so that he might see. What he saw, in that split second, was F.S. hurling from the window that yellow-backed guide-book to the Riviera Coast.

Superintendent George Wharton of Scotland Yard, in the nearest he ever got to an epigram, once said of Ludovic Travers that the fact that there are two sides to every question, was for him merely an incentive to hunt for a third. In any case, long before F.S. resumed his seat, Travers was wondering. Why throw away a perfectly good book? The rack had heaps of room; there was the space between the back and the front cushions; there was himself who might have been glad—for all F.S. knew—of a look at the volume. But he gave F.S. no sign of what he had seen; indeed he swivelled round slightly so that his eyes fell naturally away, and that brought them on the two men at the other end of the compartment.

Again something peculiar was happening; not with the nephew, for he was moodily regarding a magazine which he had brought out while the train was in the tunnel. It was the uncle who now attracted Travers's attention. With a look on his face that was perfectly diabolic, his finger hooked itself between his neck and the stiff, white collar, and he began to rub. Then he wriggled his shoulders into the cushions behind him, and rubbed against them with a viciously steady motion.

Once more Travers smiled somewhere inside. It reminded him of an occasion when he had been packed with some of his men in a horse-box on the way to the Somme, and all of them had unashamedly and whole-heartedly used the wooden sides as scratching posts, with the too optimistic hope of moving unwelcome guests from one part of the body to another. But the reminiscences were shattered with the sudden outburst from the old man.

"Anything I can do, uncle?" the young man had said.

There was half-splutter, half-growl, before the words came. Then he spat them venomously.

"Don't sit there looking like a fool. Fetch that fellow Brown. Why isn't he here?"

The nephew hopped up like a shot, and his face was flushed as he stepped round Travers's legs and out to the corridor. At closer view the face looked weaker than ever, and for two pins it seemed as if he would have burst into tears.

"Irritable old swine!" thought Travers, and met the eye of his neighbour. F.S. gave a quick lift of the eyebrows. The corner of his mouth drooped and before the sign could be acknowledged he was looking idly out of the corridor window. Travers squinted round again at the uncle. He had now turned down the collar of the overcoat, and was wriggling his neck as if the linen collar irritated him. It was then that Travers became aware of the spots. Small, they were, but a violent red, and they spattered the old man's jowl like the scanty currants in a homely pudding. Through Travers's mind flashed thoughts of measles—scarlet-fever—small-pox!—and then, in the same moment, he felt rather ashamed of himself for his reminiscences of de-lousing, and he knew, whatever the spots were, they must be giving the old man hell. Then voices were heard in the corridor, and the nephew reappeared.

With him was a man of about fifty, and his black announced him as a valet or personal servant. His face was clean-cut, professional and impassive, and his voice was the type that marks the butler or superior man. He bowed slightly as he saw the courteous withdrawal of Travers's long shanks.

"I'm sorry to disturb you, sir."

"That's all right," Travers smiled at him, and then the old man's voice came again.

"Damn you, Brown, where've you been? Didn't I tell you to come before we reached Marseilles?"

The man bowed deferentially, and Travers wished he could see his face.

"If you'll pardon me, sir, it's twenty minutes yet before we reach Marseilles."

The old man gave him a look that should have murdered him.

"Damn you, don't bandy words with me!" He glared again. "Where's that lotion?"

"I have it here, sir," said Brown, and produced a small bottle from his breast pocket.

The old man nodded sneeringly. The thin, blue lips slit out to a smile.

"What is it? Poison?"

The valet said nothing, and Travers felt indescribably sorry for him as he stood there with the same deferential pose. He could see only his back, and the old man; it was the nephew who was hidden. And then something malevolent and crafty came over the old man's face, and he turned deliberately to the two at the corridor end.

"You wouldn't care to be poisoned, gentlemen?"

F.S. shuffled uncomfortably. Travers smiled dryly.

"I don't know that I would," he said, "but there are quite a few people I wouldn't mind poisoning."

The old man grinned. It was as if he had met a brother spirit. Travers loathed that grin. Somehow he knew it to be the grin of a man who cuts another to the very raw, and takes onlookers into his confidence with heavy sarcasm, concealing cruelty with the pretence of a joke.

"You hear that, Brown?" he said, and the thin lips closed to another sneer. Even then he could not let the crude pleasantry of it rest. He peered up at the valet again.

"Jail, Brown. A damned unpleasant place. And they hang them by the neck."

He gave a sort of cackle that was part growl, and Travers felt a slow surge of anger. Then the old man got to his feet. He thrust aside the arm of the valet as it went to steady him. The nephew followed them with obvious self-consciousness to the corridor.

"Where's he gone?" asked F.S. "To the lavatory?"

"I imagine so," Travers told him. "That's about the only place where he can dress those spots."

The other nodded. "What are they, do you think?"

Travers pursed his lips. "Nothing virulent, or he wouldn't have been such a fool as to travel. None too charming a person, was he?"

"Charming!" F.S. grunted. "If I'd been that valet—or whatever he was—I'd have swiped him across the mouth."

"You had much of him?"

"Ever since St. Raphael. We both got in there." He peeped round into the corridor, and his voice lowered. "That nephew is waiting outside there. The old man's been treating him like a pig all the way, and he never had the guts to answer back."

Travers nodded. "Makes it unpleasant for the other occupants of a carriage. Let's hope he doesn't keep it up all night."

"His name's Hunt," volunteered the other, and then as a quick afterthought, "My name's Smith, by the way. You see, I know his name because there was a chauffeur who saw him into the carriage here along with Brown. What I gathered was that the chauffeur's taking the car and the big stuff by road to Calais, and the old man and his nephew are going by train."

Travers nodded again. "You been at St. Raphael yourself?"

"Yes," said Smith, rather tentatively. "You know it at all, sir?"

Travers smiled. "Devil a bit. Too fashionable for an old codger like me." The tanned face thrust itself on his notice again. "You've been in for sun-bathing, apparently."

"Rather!" said Smith with a reminiscent appreciation. "I've been at the 'Torino,' you know. The meals are very good, and so on."

"And then you lolled the rest of your time on the sand," Travers suggested obviously.

"That's right," said Smith. "That's the wonderful part of it. I mean, if you were in England and you exposed your navel, there'd be the devil of a row."

"In the case of some navels, I can well believe it," said Travers dryly.

Smith smiled. "Well, you know what I mean, sir. So long as you aren't actually indecent, you can do what you like. Get the rays all over your body," he explained, and rather lamely.

"Exactly," said Travers. "Only I happen to be the tiniest bit too old for the nude. By the way, how do you keep yourself from skinning?"

"Skinning?" Smith stared puzzled. Then a glow of intelligence suffused his face. "Oh, you mean the sun!" He smiled. "You use oil, and rub yourself all over, and then it doesn't matter."

"Rather trying for you, wasn't it?" asked Travers. "Bit of a nuisance every time?"

"I didn't find it so," said Smith. He changed the subject abruptly, and symbolically buttoned his coat. "Pretty near Marseilles by the look of it."

Travers agreed. The train had slowed and was rattling its way over innumerable points. Voices were heard, and people

came out to the corridor and blocked the view. Descending passengers fussed among them with luggage, and then the voice of
old Hunt could be made out as he tried to make his way back to
his seat. Brown's voice superseded it with a volley of "Pardon
me, sir. If you don't mind, sir. Thank you, sir," as he cleared a
way for the old man and the nephew. The two got back to their
corners, and as the train grinded its way along the now visible
platform, Hunt settled into his corner, and watched the door
with cold, malevolent eyes.

Travers had the same anticipation—if more pleasurable—as
he thought of the people who would fill those four vacant seats.
Once more he wondered what they would be like, and then as
the train drew almost to a halt, Smith went out to the corridor
again. He cut through between a couple of descending passengers, and regardless of everybody, leaned out of the window.
And the peculiar thing this time was not the discourtesy of
blocking the corridor with his stern, but that he was wiping his
face and round his neck with a handkerchief that was flamboy-
antly new—and its colour was an emerald green.

But Smith's survey of the platform was over as soon as the
train stopped.

"Pretty crowded out there?" Travers asked.

"Yes," said Smith, with a slight hesitation, and: "I always like
looking at crowds; don't you?"

"I'm afraid it depends," smiled Travers, and then, noticing
the lace as he shifted his position and set his foot on it, "If you'll
pardon me, your shoelace is undone."

"Thanks," said Smith, and stooped down to fasten it. And
then yet another peculiar thing happened. It happened, indeed,
twice; as he stooped and as he rose again. The shirt bulged at
the neck where a button was held only by a thread. That was
when Smith stooped to tie the lace. As he rose, the button had
gone altogether, and the shirt gaped still more. What Travers
had seen was that that superb colouring, that golden brown tan-
ning which Smith had acquired by weeks of sun-bathing at St.
Raphael, had never been acquired that way at all. It was an ar-
tificial colouring out of a box or bottle, and it had been careless-

ly applied. An artist in lying would have coloured as far as the waist; this colouring ended just below the neck. And it did not shade off harmoniously as it would have done if nature and the continual wearing of a shirt had been responsible. It was jagged at its end, and there had been visible the smear where the brush or rag that had applied it had slipped.

Through Travers's mind there flashed a quick interest. Then before he had time to analyse the matter; to wonder, in short, if Smith were anything more than a cheap and boastful liar, there was a movement outside the door, and the light was blocked. The first of the owners of the four vacant seats had arrived.

CHAPTER II
A JOURNEY CONTINUES

IT WAS AT that precise moment in his story that Travers had paused to make an apology or a series of excuses to George Wharton. Not that excuses were necessary. Travers, as Wharton knew only too well, was several degrees removed from a fool. On that train journey he was to show that he had lost neither his grip nor his powers of observation and retention. If deduction had been all wrong, the reasons were obvious. Travers had not been placed in that train with the mission to observe and deduce. He was a casual traveller, with no expectation of mystery. He observed because he was fond of observing, and if he deduced it was merely as a private satisfaction for his own whimsical and disturbing curiosity.

As the corridor windows darkened then, Travers drew into his corner and prepared to be interested. First into the compartment came a porter with a couple of bags. He was a fat man and fussed considerably, so that Travers watched him amusedly, and it was only when he had backed out again that the two newcomers were really visible.

Even if the conversation had not told him so, he now knew that these two with whom he was to spend the night were French. The man entered first. He was tall but slimly made; his face was almost white in its paleness, and yet the pallor was not an unhealthy one, but something due to type. He looked about fifty. His hair was greying, and his buffalo moustache was greying, and greyer still was the old-fashioned imperial snuggling neatly beneath his lower lip. His clothes were a bourgeois black, his wide, felt hat was black, and over his shoulders was a rather patrician black cape. But the most noticeable thing about him was his lameness. Not only had he a club-foot, but he managed it with difficulty, and supported himself heavily with an immensely stout walking-stick.

The woman who followed him was apparently his wife. She was in the comfortable forties; a bold, handsome woman, well-preserved. She ran slightly to fat, but the plumpness was generous and not unsightly. There was a hardness in her face that showed itself in a frown of annoyance at the stare with which Hunt met the advance of her husband, and the churlishness with which he made no attempt to steady him into his seat. Even the nephew merely regarded him with complacent superiority and that rather bored indifference which is the mark of the untravelled.

The musician—that was what Travers at first guess took him to be—sank down into the seat with a nod of satisfaction. His wife consulted the reservation labels, and expressed herself as satisfied too. Travers, interested more in a chance to polish his own French than in the conversation proper—understood her to say that his seat was next to the old gentleman in the corner, and hers next to the young gentleman. The musician made a gesture of acceptance and added the proviso that he had to face the engine. Forthwith the two changed places.

"You'll pardon me, madame," Travers said quietly, "but if monsieur wishes to face the engine, he must remain where he was. The engine is reversed here at Marseilles while we are waiting."

The atmosphere changed as by magic. The musician smiled. His wife beamed. Both began to gabble as if the discovery were a wonderful one, and the English gentleman the most courteous and charming of new acquaintances. The positions were changed while Hunt scowled round irritably in case the small-est inch of his own seat should be encroached upon or himself disturbed. But in a minute the compartment was at ease again. Madame gave Travers a delightful smile; monsieur said it was hot, and—except for the Hunts—there looked like being a har-monious party for the night. Even Smith, who—as he confided to Travers—was bad at the lingo, was included in the general atmosphere of ease. Travers leaned back once more in his seat to await the arrival of the two who should complete the party.

The minutes went by and nothing happened. At every mo-ment Travers expected to hear the approach of a pair of seatless travellers, headed as ever by a fussy official. There was a slight jolt as the new engine was backed on, and still nothing hap-pened. There was the usual clamour from the platform; friends said yet another good-bye; travellers climbed aboard; the horns tooted; the engine shrieked prodigiously and the express jerked off. Except for a short, purple-jowled man who had some time before taken up his position in the corridor and was using a stout suit-case as a seat, there seemed no claimants for the two vacant places.

"Looks as if we've struck it lucky," said Smith.

"Yes," said Travers, who also found the situation to his lik-ing. "But where's the next stop?"

"Avignon," Smith told him. "I took the trouble to inquire be-fore I started. Then we stop at Lyons, and that's the lot till we get to Dijon."

Travers had been thinking. "When you come to work it out," he said, "it doesn't matter where we stop. Those two reservation slips say the seats were booked from Marseilles; therefore no-body can claim them now. I don't mean to say that somebody mayn't be short of a seat and get the guard to dump him in here."

"What about the chap outside?" asked Smith with a squint round the door.

"Looks to me like a third-class," was Travers's opinion. "Fun-ny thing, you know, but I've noticed it before, how quite a lot of people rather like spending a night in the corridor."

Smith turned out to be a chatty sort of person, and as the train pulled steadily up the slope, he reverted—to Travers's amusement—to St. Raphael and the life there. It was his first experience of the Riviera, he said, and Travers—now abnormally alert for peculiarities of speech or conduct—fancied somehow that there was more in his chatter than met the ear. Preposterous though it might appear, it seemed that he directed his confessions as much to the Frenchman and his wife as to Travers himself. The name of St. Raphael was repeated till it must have reverberated through the compartment and been carried by the stifling breeze to the ends of the corridor. Then came a brief interlude. Travers became aware that the musician had been talking to his wife, and the words he caught were an injunction to remove her hat.

Travers stole a look. Her face, in spite of the opened door and windows, was a moist red, the perspiration stood in pinkish pearls on her forehead, and she was giving little puffs to cool herself, and fanning with a slip of a handkerchief. Her husband sat motionless, and whitish pearls showed on the ivory skin of his temples and forehead.

"It is very hot, madame," said Travers consolingly.

She smiled. "Very hot, m'sieur, as you say."

"Take off your hat," persisted her husband. "It will be cooler like that."

She gave a shrug, and then began to remove the hat. It had a narrow veil all round it, and it was a largish hat that had hidden her hair. As soon as he saw that coiled mass of black hair, Travers wondered what was strange about it, and he smiled to himself as he answered his own question. What was strange in those bobbed and shingled times was that it was hair at all. Beautiful hair it was, of a silky jet, and rarer still, there were two long hat-pins that held the hat to the head. Travers, ready to be interested in anything, admired the quick movement as she looked round for a safe depository, and the neat stab with which she pinned the hat to the back cushions above the vacant seat on her left.

The train was now rushing through the countryside; past olive groves and stretches of vineyard and white roads where the plane trees were covered with grey dust. In the far corner old Hunt was lying back in his corner as if asleep. The nephew got up and reached almost furtively for the small case above his head. He took out what was almost certainly a thriller, with a gaudy cover streaked with pink like the rising sun of Japan. Travers could even catch two words of the four or five that composed the title—the not unexpected words "Mystery" and "Murder."

Travers rolled back into his corner. Smith began yet another conversation, but Smith was a boring person by now, and after a few strained smiles and a nod or two his listener discovered that his hands were filthy from the dust of the train, and rose to find the lavatory. The third-classes as he passed them, were far from full. In the end one of all Brown was sitting by the corridor window reading a newspaper.

Travers took off his coat, rolled up his sleeves, and prepared to make a good job of his toilet. Half-way through it he heard in the corridor the ringing of the steward's bell and the announcement of first dinner. The bell neared, passed the door and went on. Travers got his hair into shape, polished his horn-rims, put on his coat, and stepped outside again.

Two things happened then. Waiting by the door was an oldish man, grey-haired, somewhat bald, clean-shaved and wearing yellow-tinted glasses, and with him Travers made a perfectly gorgeous collision. He was English, and he failed to see the humorous side of it. Travers's apologies were, in fact, curtly and coldly received. Then as he disappeared inside and Travers turned into the corridor, who should be seen but Smith emerging from his compartment. There seemed to be a flash of white and a something which fell by the purple-jowled Frenchman of the corridor, whose foot at once shifted. Travers blinked. Imagination probably—and yet there had been a flutter of white, like the twirl of a tiny butterfly. And the Frenchman's foot had certainly moved.

Smith came breezing along.

"You coming to the first dinner, sir?" he asked as he drew up.

Travers smiled. "The second's more in my line. It passes the evening away better, so to speak."

"I suppose it does." He stopped irresolutely for a moment. "Well, see you later." He hurried away to his meal.

Travers stood for a minute or two looking at the landscape as it flashed by. As far as he could judge, one foot of the purple-jowled Frenchman was still thrust out slightly beyond the other. A typical Provençal, he looked, as he sat over his meal, back to the landscape. On his lap was a pile of food which he was eating with a complete absence of reticence, and on the floor at his left hand was a wine bottle. Travers had a sudden scheme.

"Pardon, m'sieur," he said, pointing to the cluster of houses on the distant hill, "but what is the name of that town there?"

The Provençal went on chewing for a moment. When he looked up it was with a shrug of the shoulders.

"Sais pas, m'sieur."

Travers said nothing. There was nothing he could say. By rights the man should have turned towards the window and moved the foot beneath which was possibly a piece of paper. But Travers was not yet beaten. He waited for the precise moment.

"Pardon, m'sieur, but you are third-class?"

Another shrug, a *"Oui, m'sieur"* and the meal went on.

"What I meant to say," went on Travers, "was that there are some vacant places just along there."

"Bien, m'sieur" said the Provençal, and went on gnawing his cold leg of chicken.

Travers knew when he was beaten. He smiled at him cheerfully, and resumed his seat. The whole thing might have been imagination, and yet he was sure he had seen a backward flick of something white as Smith left the compartment, and it was an indisputable fact that the foot of the man in the corridor had covered that something, and—what was more—was pressed to the floor in as awkward a position as one could choose. And it was a fact that Smith was a liar, either from vanity or deliberate design.

Ordinarily Travers could find reasons for everything. It was said of him that given merely a minute for the assembling of ideas he could account for the gullet of Jonah's whale or the larynx of the ass that spoke to Balaam. But now he was gravelled. He was finding mystery where he had expected none. Of one thing only was he sure as his thoughts hurried nimbly on. The train thieves of the Continent had lurid reputations. If Smith and his purple-jowled friend outside were two of that kidney, there would be one piece of luggage they would not steal—and that was the suit-case that rested above his head.

Madame's voice now broke in on his speculations. "You are going to England, m'sieur?"

"That's right," Travers smiled at her. "Straight to Dover. And you too, madame?"

The husband stepped in there. His nephew had a restaurant near Leicester Square, and he gave the name, which Travers did not recognize. Three or four times a year he went over to England to see the business, in which he had some financial interest. His wife went with him because—as m'sieur would understand—walking was none too easy with a shortened leg. Travers duly sympathized. His own business being hinted at, he told about his 'flu, and duly received sympathy in return. The entry of Brown cut short further revelations on both sides.

The valet brought with him this time a large luncheon case. The adjustable table beneath the windows was let down, and he set out the evening meal—the eternal cold chicken and ham, by the look of it, and some biscuits and cheese. Hunt watched morosely. It was when the valet stepped back that he spoke.

"What's in that bottle?"

"White wine, sir. A very light one, sir."

"Take it away," snapped Hunt. "Get me some Vichy. And Mr. Leslie too."

There was no word spoken in the compartment till Brown reappeared with the Vichy.

"Anything further, sir?" he inquired.

"No," said Hunt curtly. "Be back in twenty minutes."

"And the lotion, sir?"

The old man peered up at him with a look of the most deadly malevolence.

"Damn you, no!"

Brown bowed and backed out. Travers looked away with a resentment that was becoming intolerable. More than once before he had heard servants spoken to like pigs, but anything so flagrant as the conduct of that damnable old swine Hunt had never come within his experience. And when he glanced at Hunt again, there he was piling up his plate and surveying the prospective meal with the nearest thing he had shown to geniality. Then madame said something to her husband, who nodded, and before Travers could lend a hand, she was getting down one of the cases, and in a couple of minutes another meal was in progress.

"You dine on the train?" asked m'sieur courteously.

"Thanks, yes," said Travers. "In a very short time now, I expect." And with a sudden brain wave: "You will keep an eye on my bag?"

"But certainly!" they both assured him.

"You never know when thieves are about," said Travers, half out of the door, and for the benefit of the stout Provençal, who had now finished his dinner and was smoking a cigarette. The express was slowing for Avignon, and in the distance Travers was sure he could hear the sound of the steward's bell announcing the second sitting. Thinking of that somewhat abstractedly as he turned the bend towards the toilet place, what should he do but run once more into the ill-tempered gentleman with the yellow-tinted spectacles.

That, as Travers recognized, was beyond a joke. He apologized profusely and servilely.

"I'm awfully sorry, sir," he said. "Most unfortunate. I think something must be wrong with my spectacles. I'm dreadfully sorry."

The old gentleman growled out something, but whether an acceptance or a reprimand Travers could not interpret. But he did do the decent thing in hurrying away from Travers's objective, and inside Travers popped.

As he sluiced his face in the bowl he heard the sound of the returning diners and the bell hard on their heels. At dinner nothing whatever happened. There was heaps of room, and the meal was filling enough, and he dragged it out with coffee and liqueur to shorten the time before sleep. It was a Travers comfortable in mind and body who made a slow progress back along the long corridors of the rocking train. And then, to disturb his complacency, there at the end of the very last corridor stood his old acquaintance of the yellow-tinted glasses. Travers almost shied. Somehow he knew he would do something awkward as he passed. The wretched train would rock still more so that he kicked the old gentleman's shins, or they would meet with a crash as the train careered round an unexpected bend.

He went forward cautiously, and yet again the unusual happened. The old gentleman seemed to have been waiting for him, and he hailed his approach mysteriously.

"You'll pardon me, sir, but might I ask you a question?"

"Most certainly," smiled Travers, with the sheepishness of relief.

"Most confidential," whispered the other. "Most confidential."

"That's all right," Travers assured him cheerfully. "I can keep a secret."

"It's the man in your carriage," went on the other. "The man with those spots. I happened to see him. Between ourselves, you don't think they're anything catching? I mean it's so—so dangerous, that sort of thing."

Travers gave a reassuring opinion, and added that lotion had been applied. The old gentleman nodded.

"Well, so long as it isn't dangerous. But you can't be too sure. Small-pox, you know." He said that last with an air of tremendous earnestness.

Travers nodded gravely, though inwardly highly amused. The old gentleman craned up his neck again, and Travers stooped to meet him half-way.

"You won't mention what I've said? You know what people are." And before Travers could do more than nod once more: "May I offer you a cigar? I have some excellent ones in my bag." He jerked his bald head back to the second-class compartment that was nearest.

"Thanks, no," said Travers hastily. "Very kind of you, but I rarely smoke them." He smiled genially, nodded again and moved along towards his own compartment.

A most amusing and dramatic encounter, he thought as he went round the bend. In fact, he had hardly ever felt on better terms with himself. That short interview with the fussy old fool in the yellow glasses had been most ridiculous. Then suddenly he wondered if any more travellers had invaded the compartment at Avignon, and he wondered, too, about the purple-jowled Provençal whom he had left stolidly smoking in the corridor. But a casual glance into the second of the two third-classes showed him that gentleman sitting on a middle seat, though his case was still outside by the door. That came to Travers rather as a shock. Was the gentleman no luggage thief at all, but merely a good bourgeois who had wished to enjoy his dinner in the comparatively fresh air of the corridor? And had that business of the flicked note and the foot that had moved out to cover it definitely been imagination too? Travers smiled to himself. A good dinner had lulled his suspicious faculties, and at the moment he was not only on the best of terms with himself but with all the world—even the rogues.

He was still smiling as he settled again to his seat. No more places were occupied, and everybody looked like having a comfortable night. But it was still hot. The Frenchman had removed his broad hat, which now rested in the rack, and though the wind blew his greying hair, he was making no complaints. He looked indeed rather venerable as he sat there, leaning both hands on the knob of that stout walking-stick of his.

Old Hunt lay back in his corner, eyes half-closed, the collar of his overcoat still turned up to conceal the disfiguring spots. The electric light was now on, and the shadows set in such clean outline the wicked grooves that ran from nose to chin that—given two horns—he might have been a gargoyle of the devil. Young Hunt lounged moodily, and there was no sign of the thriller which he had taken from his bag. Smith's voice broke in.

"Enjoy your meal, sir?"

Travers smiled. "Yes, I think perhaps I did."

But he was not in the mood for gossip, and Smith was unusually quiet, too. Travers leaned back luxuriously over his pipe, his legs well under the opposite seat in the position he had designed for them during the night. In a couple of minutes he was disturbed. Brown appeared at the door.

"Pardon me, sir," he said to Travers as he looked in, and then: "At your service, sir, if it's convenient."

Hunt shuffled up in his seat. He decided apparently that he was being too gracious, for he suddenly glared at the man from under his eyebrows.

"Go and wait outside."

"Very good, sir," said Brown imperturbably. Old Hunt felt his breast pocket to see if something were there; then young Hunt got up, and the old man snarled at him and asked what good he thought he could do. Travers regarded the old man with a look of whimsical affection as he went out at the door, and received neither glance nor sound for his pains.

The first evening cool is a mysterious thing. It comes at odd times, and sometimes there is no cool at all, and the night is stifling and sleep hard to find. The cool came suddenly that night, and all at once Travers felt a little shiver in the air. The Frenchman felt it, too, and gave a shake of the shoulders. Travers drew the door across. Madame asked her husband the time. Travers, glancing at the luminous dial of his brand-new wrist-watch, saw to his surprise that it was almost ten o'clock. Madame glanced at the light, looked all round the compartment, and then at her husband, and Travers gathered that she was thinking about turning in.

"As soon as the gentleman returns we will think about sleep," said m'sieur. He looked at the window by which old Hunt had sat, and then moved over, half-shuffle, half-roll, and made as if to lower it.

"I say, I shouldn't do that if I were you," burst out young Hunt.

The Frenchman had apparently no English. He gave a puzzled look, and then resumed his tugging at the window. Young Hunt appealed plaintively to Travers.

"I say, tell him to stop, will you? We must have the window open."

"Why *must*?" Travers smiled at him. The young man's voice was most unpleasant—a kind of throaty squawk.

"Well, my uncle always sleeps against an open window. He likes it." Rather lame that last, but it was easy to gather what he meant.

"I see." He looked round. "Perhaps we'd better put it to the vote."

"As far as I'm concerned," began Smith, but what he was about to concede nobody knew, for old Hunt's voice was heard growling by the door. He exuded a faint odour of ointment, and on his jowl Travers—looking up almost startled—saw a film of white that now concealed the spots.

"Do you mind moving your feet?" Hunt was saying. Travers's self-appointment as chairman of the window and door committee came to an abrupt end. Young Hunt plunged into an immediate explanation, and the Frenchman shuffled back to his seat—or rather to that midway position which he had occupied between Hunt and Smith. The old man glared round at the compartment generally, then felt the window as if to see that it had suffered no unhallowed handling. He nodded over at his nephew.

"Time to go to sleep."

"Do you mind if I shut this window?" asked his nephew, with a humility that was almost ingratiation.

"Do what you like," growled Hunt curtly. He peered round at the rest of the compartment. "This one of mine remains open, and other people do what they like with their own windows."

"You'll pardon me," cut in Travers, "but there are no more windows. If you refer to the door, that must be kept shut if we don't want the light in from the corridor."

"Well?" said Hunt challengingly.

"Moreover, the window you are sitting against is most decidedly not your own. The draught affects everybody—if there is one."

He was looking old Hunt clean in the eye. The old man seemed to be really aware for the first time that he was up against somebody different. There was an authority and stamp of dignity about Travers when he cared to assume them, that would have pulled up stronger characters than Hunt. Besides, as Travers could see beneath the heavy veneer of rudeness, Hunt was a man of some birth and breeding. At any rate, the challenge was declined. Hunt's eye fell first.

The Frenchman meanwhile had been looking from one to the other. The precise import of the conversation he had certainly not gathered, but he knew it was something about the window, and he knew instinctively that Travers was on his side. But when his champion settled again to his corner as if the affair were over, he was at a loss. He spread out his hands with a gesture of incomprehension, and said something to his wife. What it was, Travers could not follow, but it must have been something about getting ready for the night, because she immediately arose. Then everybody got up, and there was a rummaging in cases and bags, and the compartment was all at sixes and sevens. It was then that something really happened.

CHAPTER III
JOURNEY'S END

IT WAS THE Frenchman who blocked up the centre of the compartment, and it was that stout walking-stick of his that caused it, for he stood there holding it irresolutely in the air as if wondering whether or not to place it in the rack. And that, of course, left no support for his clubfoot, and his left hand clutched the rail of the rack till his wife should help him to some sort of settled condition. He had his back to her when Travers first saw what was happening. She was between her husband and the two Hunts, of whom the old man was sitting and the younger standing. In madame's hand was her hat which she had taken from the cushion, and that, too, was apparently being placed on the rack for the night. All at once she turned to face old Hunt, and to Travers's surprise she spoke in English—a halting, ragged English, but easily understandable. When he came to think it out, he knew that she had been getting the words ready for some moments before.

"The window. You must shut it." She pointed at it with the two hatpins which she had in her right hand.

Hunt looked at her. He was surprised, too, to hear the English. But he said nothing. He merely shook his head. Madame let the hat fall on the seat behind her and pointed again. Her face flushed, and her expression was a nasty one.

"You shut it. You shut it now!"

Her husband began to speak. Then the train lurched slightly, and there was a mix-up. Travers lost his balance, and all he knew was that with a startling suddenness a clamour had arisen that must have been heard the length of the carriage. There was the Frenchman's raucous baritone; the squawking of young Hunt; the furious growling of old Hunt, and madame's mad spit and spatter of unintelligible words. There seemed to be some sort of fight going on. Smith clutched Travers's arm.

"I say, what's happening?" His eyes were bulging.

The clamour became louder. Then, amazingly it quietened; and as if everybody had become aware of the presence of Travers, they all appealed to him at once as witness and interpreter. What madame was spitting out he didn't know—she spoke far too quickly—but her bosom was heaving, her eyes flashing, and she held the hatpin as if at any moment she would thrust it into old Hunt's ribs. Her husband was gesturing with his free hand, till the train lurched again, and he swung round and sat, rather grotesquely, on the seat.

"I tell you she tried to stab me!" shouted old Hunt, and he was ridiculous, too; trying to keep Travers in one eye and the hatpin in the other.

"She was! She was! I saw her!" young Hunt was shrilling that at the top of his squawky voice. Madame was gibbering at the same time, and her husband had Travers by the coat and was explaining something, and altogether it was a perfectly absurd pandemonium. Voices were heard in the corridor as the curious came up to see what the matter was, and the purple-jowled Provençal from the third-class actually thrust his head inside, with mouth half opened. Brown was there, too, and half a dozen people were between him and the door.

Travers let out a holler. Perhaps it was the unusualness of that, or the sight of the inquisitive and frightened crowd at the door, that brought the brawlers to their senses, for the noise stopped miraculously.

"What's the matter, m'sieur?" began the Provençal.

"Nothing at all," Travers told him, pushing him good-humouredly outside the door. He stuck his own head out, and explained that it was merely an argument—a matter of politics— and the inquisitive began moving slowly away again. Then he spoke to madame, and the hubbub recommenced. By the time it was quietened, the Frenchman was talking to her with the most complicated gestures, and telling her to sit down, and the whole thing was nothing. Then Travers began to get some idea of what the trouble was.

Madame said she had fallen accidentally against the old man, and he had struck her and thrown her back by force. Hunt said the woman had tried to stab him because he wouldn't shut the window. Young Hunt corroborated. Smith said he hadn't seen anything. The Frenchman shrugged his shoulders, and hinted that Hunt was a liar. His wife would never touch a fly; besides he had seen it all, and it was as his wife had said—purely an accident, due to the lurch of the train. Travers explained to Hunt.

"He's a liar, too," said Hunt curtly, and gave him a look that ought to have annihilated him. "He raised that stick of his to me, too. My nephew saw him."

The nephew promptly corroborated.

Travers worked desperately in the cause of peace. Though the affair had had its ridiculous side, it had been unpleasant and decidedly embarrassing. But he got old Hunt into some sort of reasonableness by the concession of the opened window; then he flagrantly explained in French that the gentleman had apologized handsomely, and the affair was at an end. Madame nodded darkly at the old man as if she heard what was said, but had her own ideas. The Frenchman actually smiled—a gesture which Hunt ignored. For five minutes the compartment simmered. It simmered more slowly. Blinds were lowered till there was darkness. Five minutes more, and there came the first snore. Another followed it. The compartment was at peace.

Travers lay back in his corner, feet well under the opposite seat, the calf of his left leg resting lightly against the leg of Smith. He had thought that out long before. If there was, after all, any question of the theft of luggage, he would be awake as soon as Smith stirred. Not that Travers was anticipating much sleep. The clickety-click of the coaches, soothing as it was to some people, always kept him awake; and there was the unusualness of it all, and the lack of real comfort. But he hoped for the best.

All at once the brakes grinded, and the express began to slow. A glance at the wrist-watch showed him it was ten-thirty, and he smiled to himself as he realized how suddenly that scene had arrived, and how suddenly—taking everything into consideration—it had subsided. A squint through the slit of his own curtain revealed the lights of a distant town, and he knew they were approaching Lyons. Before he was really aware of it, the train was in at the station. Everything there was funereal. Lights were dim, and there seemed to be few of them. Scarcely a sound came from the platforms, and it was as if something furtive was going on—that people were getting off the train and others getting on as though they were ashamed of it, and the porters were ashamed too.

In the compartment itself there was just enough light to make out individual blacknesses in the general dark. But there was one patch of lighter blackness, and that was the white waistcoat of old Hunt. With the quick aptitude of the old for sleep he seemed to have dropped off at once, and his breathing was heavy as if the lowering of his chin impeded his air passages. He seemed settled to fill his corner so that the white waistcoat was seen in full, and his hands were in his coat pockets. His head rested against the blind which, but for that, would have flapped when the train was in motion, for the window was down to its lowest.

The nephew was either not asleep or sleeping quietly. There was no sound from his corner, and with window shut and blind down, he was practically invisible. Madame lay back snoring gently, her mouth half-opened. Her husband was snoring more raucously, and his white face was turned sideways to the cushion in the direction of Hunt. Smith was lying back, breathing steadily, head cupped in his hand. The door was shut, and already there was a slight smell of humanity and too much breath.

The train jerked and moved off. Travers saw it was ten-thirty-five. Then he remembered. They should have left at ten-thirty, and the train was therefore running slightly late. There was the usual rattling over points till at last the train gathered speed and the rails were giving their clickety-click. He glanced at the watch again. Ten-forty-five.

_10.45._ Smith, it struck him at that moment, was definitely asleep. His breathing was regular, and every now and again there was a little gurgle. His head moved down. He half-woke. His hand went into his coat pocket, and the head rested of itself back in the corner. Curious, thought Travers, who was no nearer sleep than he had been an hour before. If Smith were a train thief—and he found it hard somehow to relinquish so fascinating a theory—then it was strange that he should sleep at all. If anything, he should have been making a pretence of it, and he was certainly not doing that. And what about the supposed confederate? With a smile to himself, Travers drew back the blind to the merest slit. To his amazement, there was the Provençal seated on the suit-case where it had been at first. And he was definitely not asleep, for there was the glow of a cigarette.

Travers leaned back again with a little frown. Very strange. One might almost say that while Smith slept, the other watched. And if that were true, there would be one way of proving it. Later on in the night Smith would watch while the other slept. And what were they watching? The opportunity for wakefulness, to go through handy compartments, and then slip off the train?

And then Travers thought again. If they were to slip off the train it would be when the train was coming to a stop. And, if his memory were correct, that could not be till Dijon, and Dijon would not be reached till best part of another three hours—

at one-thirty. He nodded to himself. Whatever happened, he would be awake himself before then. Indeed, but for disturbing his fellow-passengers, he would have smoked, and drawn back the blind sufficiently to read by the percolation of the corridor light.

But Travers had forgotten one thing. He himself was not the man who had been unable to sleep the last time he had travelled in an English train by night. That very morning he had swum for half an hour, and he had sat on the beach, and had taken a walk. The very heat of the day had weakened somehow and disposed him to sleep. There was the smooth swing of the express through the velvety night. And so the clickety-click gradually became less insistent. It soothed. It smothered. Travers fell asleep.

11.35. He woke. By some instinct he woke without movement, though immediately aware of the crampedness of his legs. His eyes closed to a slit. It was not a chance movement of Smith that had wakened him, and at once he began breathing as if in sleep. The time he had seen, and he knew they were far off Dijon, and yet there was Smith moving open the door with infinite care. But he opened it no more than an inch, and his toe went into the aperture to keep it from closing. He stopped and listened. Then with the same infinite caution he began to get to his feet. His face was still towards Travers—the position of the foot in the door ensured that—and it was his left hand that fumbled behind him on the rack.

Travers was so interested that he forgot his regular breathing, and found himself holding his breath. So he simulated a kind of sleepy moan and shifted his head. Smith held motionless for a moment till the regular breathing was resumed. Then, before Travers was ready for him, he was passing something out of the crack in the door. Who took it could not be seen, but it was the stout walking-stick of the Frenchman!

Smith sank down again into his seat. In a moment his breathing was what it had been before. Travers stared across and wondered what was in the wind. The other occupants of the compartment still slept normally. A minute went by—five minutes—and then with uncanny silence the walking-stick re-appeared as if magically through the door. Smith rose again. There was the same cautious movement. When he sat down the stick was evidently in its former place on the rack. The door was drawn gently to. Smith went to sleep again.

Before Travers's reasoning powers could get to work on that, there was a faint sound from the corner, and the form of young Hunt detached itself from the gloom. He picked his way with tremendous precaution across the stretched-out legs, and as he leaned over Smith, Smith stirred. It was a natural and an artistic stirring of a sleepy man disturbed. Hunt whispered a "Sorry!", drew back the door and went through. As he did so there was a slight clatter. Travers—now too excited to keep control—drew back his blind. What had fallen to the corridor floor—and apparently from beneath young Hunt's coat—was that thriller he had been reading. In a moment he had picked it up again, and had gone in the direction of the lavatory.

"Bit stuffy in here," Travers said to Smith, as if to announce that he had just woke up. But Smith gave no reply. All he did was to roll slightly and curl into his corner, and then he was pretending to be sound asleep again. With a sudden impulse Travers got up and went out to the corridor. The Provençal was now lying on the floor with the case for a pillow—and apparently he had been asleep for hours, for he snored as well as a man on his back might. And of one thing Travers at that moment felt pretty sure—that whoever had been in the corridor to receive the Frenchman's stick, it had not been the Provençal.

He lighted a cigarette and leaned for a bit against the corridor rail. The more he thought, the more fuddled he became. That cigarette finished, he lighted another, and there was still no sign of young Hunt. Then—ridiculous thought—he remembered the old gentleman in the yellow sun-glasses, and by some queer connection of ideas, found himself moving along towards the scene of those two amusing collisions. He went round the bend, and into the other carriage. Blinds were all drawn, and there was no sound except here and there a muffled snore. Travers turned back. Just short of the connecting platform there was a noise, and the lavatory door opened. Young Hunt came out. Travers stood still. Hunt stood still, too. In the faint light of the corridor—from where he himself stood motionless in comparative darkness—he could see young Hunt moisten his lips. Then he began to do something peculiar. His hands went to his left ribs, and he began to rub. A moment of that, and he moved off again.

Travers hardly kept back a smile as he guessed why young Hunt had scratched. It was those spots he had caught! And he'd caught them from his uncle. Perhaps he'd been applying lotion to himself. And if so the lavatory would show signs of it. In a second Travers—enormously anxious to confirm yet another theory—was inside with the door locked.

But no sooner had he locked the door than he recognized he was being somewhat foolish. Travers was like that. What some would call curiosity and he himself regarded merely as interest in his fellow men, was always leading him into situations where cool reflection made him blush. As a sop to his conscience he turned to the wash-basin, but it was half-filled with dirty water; there were soot marks everywhere, and the floor was splashed and filthy. Then he stooped and picked something up from the same filthy floor. He hooked off his glasses and polished them, then looked again. There seemed to be no doubt about it. And by a fortunate chance, the piece of torn paper he was holding contained the top of a page and part of the title, "Murder at the Sal—."

Travers looked a bit startled, then he began to search the floor again. In five minutes he had four more pieces of that detective novel that young Hunt had torn up, but none with the full title. What "Sal—" was he could not precisely determine; "Salon" was the nearest he could come at it. And the book that young Hunt had read had had as its title "Mystery and Murder" and a word or two more. Where, then, was that book? And why had this one been torn up and washed out to the permanent way? But certain it was that it had been torn up, for there was other evidence that proved it, and when Hunt a minute or two before had left the lavatory he had carried no book with him—unless he had had it in his pocket.

In a couple of minutes Travers was again in his seat. The compartment was still and every soul seemed asleep, and out in the corridor the Provençal was still sleeping soundly too. He drew the door to, and everything was dark again. But old Hunt's waistcoat still made a patch of dull white, and there was the whiteness of the Frenchman's face now turned his way. Travers began to think. Thoughts led him into a groove, and the groove led to sleep.

_1.25._ Something was happening in the compartment, and yet nothing could be happening. There was the same slow breathing around him, and then the movement came again. Travers blinked. Something was different in the surroundings. The white patch which represented old Hunt had shifted. The Frenchman was moving restlessly, and Travers saw why. Hunt had moved during sleep from his corner, and now he reclined with his back against the Frenchman, who was trying to dislodge him. The Frenchman gave a grunt. He leaned forward so that Hunt slipped imperceptibly behind his back. He got to his feet, and Travers was too surprised to wonder why he stood so upright. Then he moved, and the movements were so still and indistinct that it was only when they were completed that Travers saw what had been done. And as he realized it, he gave that same old, whimsical chuckle inside as his mind ran back to his young days; how a friend of his had stayed the night and both boys had slept in the same bed, and how, in the middle of the night, he had been crowded almost out by his companion, and had, therefore, got out of bed and in again the other side. That was what the Frenchman had done. Old Hunt lay sleeping somewhere on the seat, and the Frenchman had his place by the window.

In a moment or two there were other movements. The Frenchman felt the window blind, as if not knowing how to manage its fluttering. A minute of that, and Travers judged that he settled himself. Two minutes, and he heard his quiet breathing. He snored gently. And just then the brakes began to grind, and Travers knew the train was running into Dijon.

<u>1.30.</u> It was strange that Travers should have had that overwhelming itch to get up and stroll for a time on the cool of the platform. The compartment was unbearably stuffy and his collar was saturated with perspiration, and yet he knew that he must keep an eye on Smith and his friend outside. So he gave a little roll in his corner and grunted; then settled to pretended sleep again. But his hand had moved the blind so that he could see through. The Provençal was out of sight—except for his boots— and Smith, unless he were the world's best actor, was sleeping sound enough too. Outside on the platforms there seemed the same furtive darkness, the same scarcely audible movement of people in the gloom, and the same faint smell of engine smoke. Travers lay motionless and watched a pair of boots. Five minutes passed. The engine whistled into the night, and the sound echoed to wake the dead. Another engine somewhere seemed to answer it. It was one-thirty-seven, and the train moved off dead on time.

<u>1.38.</u> There was again a rattling over the points, and then a movement in the corner where the Frenchman sat. A moment or two, and he began to fiddle with the blind. He seemed to be holding it with one hand, and with the other he tugged at the window. He got it up so far, and it stuck. He tugged again with little grunts. The window still stuck. Then it shot up with a click that seemed as if it would wake everybody. But nobody stirred. The Frenchman settled to sleep again. Travers wondered just what would happen when Hunt woke and found seat gone and window shut. The thought amused him, and his mind went back again to that memory of youth and how he had got into the bed on the other side. Two minutes after that he was asleep.

<u>2.15.</u> Travers stirred once more and looked sleepily at the time. His eyes went round into the darkness. Before he fell asleep again, he seemed to be aware with any certainty, of only two things: that, but for the noises of sleep, the compartment was

deathly still—and that in some curious way the white waistcoat of old Hunt had shifted back to its corner.

5.35. Travers woke. There was no sleepy stirring this time, for he was suddenly wide awake. He moved the blind and there, outside the corridor window, the sun was shining full, and it was as if he were inside a black tunnel that hurled itself along in the middle of broad day. Then he remembered that appalling lavatory—and all train lavatories—where the water would soon be exhausted and late-comers find none for their toilet. A quarter of an hour later he had shaved perilously, had a semblance of a cold rub down, and was feeling his old bright self. In the corridor he lighted a cigarette before going back to his seat. The Provençal, too, was by that time blearily awake. With a sudden gesture Travers offered his case.

"Vous fumez, m'sieur?"

The other's face lit up. He helped himself to a cigarette, and said that Travers was very kind. Travers held him a light.

"You are going to Paris?" he asked, and knew as soon as the words were uttered, how fatuous the question was.

"Oui, m'sieur," said the other. "And then to Calais. I have business there."

"I am going to Calais, too," Travers told him. "Then on to London. You know London, m'sieur?"

The other said he didn't. The short conversation petered out, and Travers realized that he was still holding his toilet things. Inside the compartment Smith was stirring, and he gave Travers a bleary-eyed good morning. Then young Hunt was seen suddenly to be standing up—and while he came towards them, something happened. The express gave a violent lurch as it took a bend. The carriage swayed, and Travers fell backwards into Smith's lap. And as he fell he saw somebody else fall. Not madame, for she merely rolled towards them, but old Hunt who slithered in the most amazing way and then fell to the floor. He lay between the seats, face upwards.

"Sorry," began Travers to Smith, and broke off foolishly. Smith was staring, too, for Hunt made no movement. The nephew scrambled between them to the corridor and was gone, for his face had always been towards the corridor, and he had seen nothing.

Smith still stared, and somehow Travers felt his stare. He moved over towards the old man, while the Frenchman—stirred by the same lurch that had capsized old Hunt—blinked his eyes and yawned. It was more of a gurgle than a yawn, and the face—had Travers noticed it—had no longer the chill pallor of night, but was a salmon-pink.

But Travers was looking down at the motionless man. He moistened his lips and stooped. Smith saw his hand go to the breast, and his mouth go suddenly agape.

"What is it? Hurt himself?"

Travers shook his head and moistened his lips again.

"He's dead."

"Dead?" He stared. "What do you mean—*dead?*"

Travers found no answer. He shook his head, and his eyes fell aimlessly on the face of the watch which glowed faintly in the comparative dark of the floor. The time was precisely six o'clock.

CHAPTER IV
A MIRACLE HAPPENS

TRAVERS GOT to his feet. What he had expected to see was a red mark on the dead man's waistcoat—the mark of the blood that had followed the withdrawal of the pin with which madame had stabbed him. But the waistcoat was immaculate, and he realized somewhat sheepishly why the thought of murder had entered his head. He had dreamed about that murder; it had been the thought with which he had woken up, and it was the beauty of the morning, as he had viewed it, that had put the dream immediately from his mind.

"Shall we get him off the floor?" came Smith's voice—very matter-of-fact—at his elbow.

They lifted him to the seat and, when the Frenchman had moved up, laid him at full length. Travers spread the overcoat to cover the face and the folded arms. The Frenchwoman grew suddenly suspicious, though she was hardly more than just awake. She grasped Travers's arm from behind.

"What is it? Is he ill?"

Travers thought it best not to beat about the bush. "He's dead, madame. His heart probably. He was an old man."

Her eyes opened in horror. Then there came a gurgling sound from behind, and Travers whipped round. The Frenchman was leaning across the suit-case which, at some time in the night, he had placed at his side as a rest for his arm. It was he who was making the gurgling noises, and his face was a scarlet red. His eyes were goggling, and he was holding his throat. He seemed to be asking for something to drink.

Travers and Smith looked at each other with a quick surprise. Madame was on her knees trying to make the sick man speak.

"My God!" thought Travers, "what in blazes is happening now?" He turned to Smith. "You stay here, and I'll find the *chef de train.*"

He went out to the corridor, undecided for a moment which way to turn. Brown stepped out from the door of his compartment. Travers hailed him at once.

"Just a moment," he said, and drew him along to the connecting platform. The valet showed no more than a grave uneasiness when he heard the amazing news. He shook his head.

"In a way I'm not surprised, sir. He's been none too well lately. Irritable, sir; most irritable—as you perhaps noticed."

Travers nodded. "You'd better break the news to his nephew. He's in there. Then wait outside the compartment till I get back."

He found his man by the restaurant car, talking to a fellow official in peaked cap. Travers expected excitement, but the *chef de train* was perfectly calm.

"We will see this dead man, m'sieur," he said at the end of Travers's recital, and beckoned to his subordinate. Travers gave yet more details as they made their way along the corridors. The *chef de train* suddenly stopped.

"Spots?" He raised his eyebrows. "What sort of spots?"

Travers did an artistic shrug. "Nothing dangerous, I imagine," he said. "But we can ask his valet."

As they came down the last corridor, who should be peeping out of his door but the old gentleman in the yellow-tinted glasses. He drew in his head when he saw the coming procession, but Travers, casting a quick look back from the connecting platform, saw the inquisitive head again well out. The Provencal sat just clear of the door of the compartment where the dead man lay, and was imperturbably smoking a cigarette. Brown and young Hunt stood by the door. Brown whispered to Travers.

"I think that man in there has had a sudden attack of some sort of fever, sir—or tonsilitis."

The two officials went inside. Madame seized Travers at the door. "A doctor, m'sieur. Will you find if there is a doctor on the train?"

She seemed to have been crying. Her face was pale, and there were purple bags under the eyes. In the morning light she looked cheap and somewhat bedraggled, and for all its appeal there was something common about her face; some coarseness and hardness that he sensed rather than saw. He looked at her husband. She explained volubly.

"You will pardon us, m'sieur, taking your seat, but we thought it best that he should have the corner. He is better now. It was the wine that he was wanting."

Travers looked at him as he lay back in the corner. His face now was the most violent red, and he seemed to be having difficulty with his breathing, and all at once he gurgled and raised his hand to his throat. Madame hovered over him at once. Then the official voice called to Travers.

"You saw him die, m'sieur?"

Travers explained again. The junior official was despatched to find a doctor. There was a brief consultation about what to do with the body.

"Why not leave him where he is?" suggested Smith. "There's that other poor devil in the corner there who seems to be pretty ill too. His wife can have my seat and look after him, and the rest of us can go to the corridor—till we get to Paris. What's the time?"

"Half-past six," said Travers, and interpreted what Smith had said. The *chef de train* agreed. The train was two minutes late, but in twenty minutes there would be a stop at Marignac. From there he would phone to Paris, where they would be in just an hour. In the meanwhile he would like to ask a question or two. He produced a note-book.

Travers gave his own particulars. Madame he thought, for all her attention to her husband, had an ear for what he was saying, but he made no mention of the previous night's quarrel. Then madame herself was called over. There were the usual courteous apologies, and then the questions direct.

Her name, she said, was Olivet—Marie Olivet—and her husband was Pierre Olivet, restaurant-proprietor—retired, of the Rue Naucelles 26, Marseilles. They were going to London where M. Olivet had business. Madame Olivet returned to her husband, and the *chef de train* was suddenly aware that Smith was standing at his elbow ready to be questioned. Travers pricked his ears.

Smith said his name was Frederick. He was a London bank clerk on holiday. He had just spent three weeks at the Torino Hotel, St. Raphael, and was on his way to England. Brown was called in.

His name was Thomas Brown, and he showed his passport. He had been personal servant to the dead man for the last ten years. The party had been staying at the Villa Marguerite, Rue Ginette, St. Raphael, for three months. The spots, in his opinion, were indigestion spots, due to something that had disagreed with the dead man. Once they had been soothed with lotion, there was nothing alarming about them.

"What lotion were you using?" asked Travers, who, as interpreter, was able to satisfy some small curiosities of his own.

"An ordinary lotion, sir," said Brown. "I got it at the chemist's just at the end of the road as you go to the station."

"You mean the end of the Rue Ginette?"

"That's right, sir," Brown told him.

"And where was the party bound for—if things had been normal?"

"To Peddleby, sir. That is the master's place, sir. Near Rye, sir, if I may say so."

So much for Brown. Young Hunt, who kept licking his lips and stammering, bore out what the valet had said. He lived with his uncle at "Marsh View," Peddleby. Questioned by Travers he added that he had done so since his father died, which was when he was quite a boy.

"You heard or saw nothing in the night?" asked Travers, anxious to settle some small inquiries of his own. "I mean, you had no idea your uncle was ill?"

Hunt shook his head vigorously. "Oh, no; I didn't see anything. I slept all the time—except when I got up once, and I don't quite know what time that was. But I think it was early. I mean, not long after we turned in."

"Your uncle was pretty ill, wasn't he?"

Hunt seemed surprised at the question. He glanced back, and Travers could have sworn that it was at Brown he was looking. And then almost at once he answered brightly: "Oh yes. He hadn't been at all well."

The *chef de train* finished his notes. Then he wrote a message and tore out the leaf. His assistant appeared at the door.

"I asked everywhere. There is no doctor on the train."

The *chef de train* gave a prodigious shrug of the shoulders. "It doesn't matter. See this is sent through as soon as we get to Marignac. We'll hold the train."

He looked round the compartment. "You understand, madame and m'sieurs, that you may be detained in Paris. There will have to be an inquiry. A minute or two, perhaps," and he shrugged again. Then Travers had to translate. The faces of Brown and Hunt showed signs of perturbation, but it was no more than that. Smith looked indignant, and it was he who but-

tonholed the *chef de train* as soon as he stepped into the corridor. Travers, peeping out too, saw the pair disappear round
the bend, and he smiled to himself at Smith's gestures and his
attempts to make himself understood.

Brown and his young master began a whispered conference outside. Travers entered the compartment again and drew
the door to after him. Madame Olivet had drawn the blinds by
the corridor, and now Travers drew the blind of the door. She
looked up as he entered.

"The patient, madame? He is better?"

She looked pretty helpless, and he was afraid she was going
to cry. As for Olivet, he lay back in the corner, face a fiery red,
and but for his stertorous breathing, Travers would have said
he had gone into a coma. And he certainly didn't like the look of
him. If ever a man was in a bad way, it was Olivet, but he said
nothing of that to madame.

"He sleeps, madame. That is a good sign. By the time we get
to Paris he will be better."

She had a tiny flask of eau de Cologne in her hand, and she
went on dabbing at the sick man's forehead with her wispy
handkerchief. Travers sat in the corner where young Hunt had
sat, and began to make notes on the back of an envelope. If
there was to be an inquiry, he meant to be ready for it. Memory for figures was a queer gift with him, mathematician though
he was. He could run his eye down a column of quotations and
remember them a day later, and now he remembered each of
those times when he had woken up in the night. He had even
added a shorthand note to one or two of them when there was a
noise from the corner. Olivet was struggling to get up, while his
wife held him. He was trying to speak, but the words would not
come. Nothing came but that horrible, strangled gurgle.

Travers was over in a flash. Madame said something which
he did not understand, but it meant evidently that he was to
hold him down. She reached up in the rack for the bottle of white
wine, some of which he had drunk before. While Travers held
him, she put the papier-mâché mug to his lips. Travers tilted the
head. Olivet gulped eagerly, with the same horrible spluttering.

Most of the wine must have gone down his clothes, but some reached his throat and eased him, for he sank back in the corner with a sort of strangled moan. Madame wiped his lips and chin. Travers saw that he was quiet again, and got to his feet.

Somehow he began to feel extraordinarily frightened. Those moans and convulsive rackings scared him, and there was the redness of the sick man's face and the perspiration that ran from it. And then all at once he thought he knew what was the matter with Olivet. Though he had never had experience of the disease, he put it down as diphtheria. There was the same contraction of the throat; the same strangled and restricted breathing. Madame spoke:

"You will stay with him a minute, m'sieur? Only one minute?"

"Certainly," Travers assured her, and took the corner seat while she rummaged for her toilet things, one eye still on the sick man. Then she put the wine bottle handy, and gave him the eau de Cologne. As the door opened to let her through, Travers saw Smith outside the door, smoking a cigarette and surveying the railway cutting through which the train was roaring. The Provençal sat on his upturned case within a yard of him, and the two looked the completest strangers. And yet, no sooner did Madame Olivet appear, than Smith switched round and Travers—peeping unashamedly—saw him follow in her tracks.

Then with the grinding of the brakes as the express slowed well on the outskirts of Marignac, so many things happened at once that when Travers began to write them down in some sort of logical sequence, he knew some of the steps were wrong. But certainly the first thing was the awakening of Olivet, and his eyes stared and started from his head like those of an angry pekinese. They bulged; they almost left their sockets; and what was more horrible, he began to make those strangling noises again, and his hand commenced to weave the air with strange passes as if at something invisible to the world, but to himself something only too visible and startling. What Travers did he never knew. He remembered that he tried to soothe the struggling man, and that no French words came, and he had to make mere noises.

And what Olivet was saying he had no idea, for now the sounds that came from his throat could be interpreted as nothing on earth. They were the beginnings of words, forced through the throat, compressed and tortured out of comprehension.

Something else that Travers had feared now happened. The sounds had reached outside in spite of the fastened door, and the door opened and who should put his head inside but the Provençal. His mouth was half opened with that look of startled surprise, and his plump, purple jowl made the look naïve and even amusing. If he had been the devil, Travers would have hailed him gladly, for Olivet was struggling in the seat again, and making wild passes like a madman. There was something he wanted to say, something he wanted—and wanted with all his feverish helplessness—to do, and Travers had no idea what it was. The Provençal watched like a man fascinated.

"Qu'est-ce qu'il y a?" he grunted to Travers, and made his way inside, the door half opened behind him.

Once more Travers's vocabulary failed him. All he could do was to wave his hand feebly at Olivet and stammer something about fever and delirium. And while he was doing that Olivet got to his feet. It was a sudden rise—not the hoisting up that one would have expected from a man so lame that in walking he dragged one foot after him. He shot to his feet as if he had been pricked from behind, and his mouth was still letting out those ghastly noises, and his hands began to weave the air, and he stared at something through the windows above where the dead man's head lay.

The train jerked to a sudden stop, and Travers jerked with it. He almost lost his balance, and he clutched at the rack. The Provençal swung round with him. At that very moment Olivet made a pace forward and, hampered by the enormous club-boot, stumbled too. He turned for the door, and his hand grasped it. Travers, in the act of tottering, reached to hold him back. Olivet thrust him aside as if he had been a child, and disappeared through the door. Travers spun round and crashed against the Provençal. There was a mix-up for a moment, and both rolled on the dead man, and then to the floor. And it was Travers who was undermost.

It was a good minute later before he could make for the door, and as he afterwards recalled things, the Provençal had made for the door, too. But it was not about him that Travers was troubling. Olivet had gone to the left—that much he had seen as he fell—and there was no sign of him in the corridor. At the end of the corridor there was a choice of more corridor or platform, and Travers chose platform. And what should he see, not twenty yards away, but Olivet stumping along at full speed, knee raised high at each step to allow for the club-boot, and hands weaving the air madly in front of him as if he were drunk.

For a moment Travers stood like a gawk, mouth agape. The age of miracles was over, and there was a man—a man who the night before had dragged a lame leg behind him and made a painful progress along the corridor and into the carriage—now moving along the platform at a pace that was veritably incredible. But for that hampering club-boot, one had the idea that he would have galloped. And people were staring at him, and no wonder. One thing only made his movements less incongruous, and that was the fact that quite a lot of people were running from the carriages. But they were running to that long trestle table that is always erected on the platform of Marignac in the early morning and laid out for the sale of *brioches* and hot coffee. That was why the passengers were running, thought Travers—still stock still foolishly-—to get some hot breakfast before the train set off again. But Olivet was hustling along the platform *away from* breakfast, and towards the station buildings.

Travers came out of that surprised stupor as quickly as he fell into it, and made a bolt for the madman who was blindly hurrying along and making grotesque patterns in the air before him, like a wailing Egyptian woman at a procession of the dead who keeps away the spirits of evil with her waving hands. And even if he had not had an interest of other sorts in the mad chase of M. Olivet—the interest of guardianship and the promise made to his wife—the sight of the red-raced, frantically gesticulating man would have been too much for him in any case. Curiosity would have made him turn in his tracks and follow even if the scene had been witnessed from his own room on the fifth floor of Durango House itself.

At first Travers walked, then he shuffled, then he ran. It was a long platform, and he had forty yards to make up. As he hurtled along that platform, hatless and tails flying, he noticed the roofs of the town in the valley below him and a tall factory chimney, and he knew the sun was shining out of a clear sky, and the air was crisp and sparkling. Then he became aware that he was getting out of breath, and suddenly, only ten yards ahead of him, the grotesque figure of Olivet began to stagger. It seemed to stumble and by the time he reached it, it was lying face downwards on the stone-flagged platform.

Travers knew he was dead. Even when his hand was over the heart and he felt the slight movement, it seemed all wrong. Again he knelt there rather foolishly, wondering what to do; his mind adrift in the mad happenings of that amazing morning. Then he got his arms under Olivet's legs and round his waist, and staggered to his feet. Just ahead of him was a bare, uncomfortable-looking barn of a waiting-room. He pushed at the door with his knee and it opened. Just inside was a wooden bench, and he laid the unconscious man gently on it, panting as he did so, and feeling the trickle of perspiration that ran down his cheek. Outside he heard the sounds of steps and voices, and he heard someone say something about a doctor. He gave a little jump as a voice came at his very elbow.

"He is dead, m'sieur?"

It was the stout, purple-jowled man whom he called "the Provençal." In his hand was Travers's hat which he was holding out to its owner.

CHAPTER V
NIGHTMARE

"WHEN ONE IS accustomed to wearing a hat, it is easy to catch cold." The Provençal uttered that great thought as a kind of apology for his own thoughtfulness. Then he repeated his question with a subtle variation. "He is not dead yet?"

Travers, for lack of words, pointed down at the sick man. He seemed now to be alive and no more, and the breathing was slow and irregular. The Provençal nodded, then shrugged his shoulders. He gave his opinion with a complacent indifference.

"It's all over with him. That's what comes from tipping the bottle too much."

"You think that?" said Travers, and immediately wondered. If Olivet was a confirmed drunkard, how did the other know it? And if Olivet had been drinking during the night, why had he not known it himself? And if the attack were delirium tremens pure and simple, it was the strangest attack he had ever imagined. And then, looking down at the fiery red face of the scarcely breathing man, Travers saw something that made him hardly believe his eyes. He hooked off his glasses and polished them rapidly. Then he looked down again. There was no doubt of it. Over the face of the sick man, red spots were appearing; not spots so virulent as those on the face of the dead man back there in the train, but rather a rash that was beginning to fester. The Provençal looked, too—and saw nothing remarkable.

"The dead man in the train," Travers said to him, with idiotic gestures meant to bring the mind of his listener back. "You remember, m'sieur?"

He seemed to remember something, but the application was beyond him. He took refuge in yet another shrug. Travers looked down again at what was certainly a dying man. That bench was damnably hard, even for an ordinary person to sit on, and he looked round for a pillow. In the corner was lying what turned out to be a sack, and he rolled it into shape and placed it gently beneath the sick man's head. That black, voluminous cape which had flapped so incongruously when the delirious man had scurried along the platform, had now slipped half down to the floor, and he drew it out and lay it as a rug over the body. And at that very moment from the engine of the train there was a whistle that brought Travers back to his senses. He stared at the Provençal, then made a bolt for the doorway.

Again a curious thing happened. The Provençal had moved at the same time, and his bulk filled the door. His eyes suddenly turned hard and unfriendly.

"Where are you going, m'sieur?"

Travers stared at him, and as he stared the other drew back. As he saw, there was no need to keep the Englishman from the train, for it was just clearing the far platform. And he realized, too, that he had shown his hand too early. He waved with a fresh access of courtesy.

"Regard, m'sieur," he said, "there is no need to disturb oneself about the train."

Travers saw that as soon as he stepped outside the door. He smiled philosophically, and in the act of smiling, remembered the strange conduct of the man who stood at his side. If he had been English he might have asked him what the hell he had thought he was doing. As it was he scowled.

"Who are you, m'sieur? Why did you try to stop me catching my train?"

The other looked surprised. He spread his hands with a gesture that apparently included half a dozen emotions, and all of them innocent.

"You are English, m'sieur," he said, "and I am an ordinary French citizen. There is a dying man in there, and you were with him from the beginning. I do not know what happens in your country, but here there will be questions asked. If you had joined your train, that might have looked suspicious."

"Yes, but—" and Travers tried his own hand at a gesture while he hunted for the words, "in that train is another dead man about whom I am also to answer questions."

The Provençal nodded. "It is as you say, m'sieur. But that is a problem which will adjust itself."

Half a dozen people were now approaching the station from the platform end. Among them was a man who seemed to be the *chef de gare*, and the Provençal went to meet him. Madame Olivet was there, too, handkerchief to her eyes, and stumbling along just in front of Smith, who seemed loaded with suit-cases. As he came nearer, Travers saw that the two he held in one hand were the property of the Olivets, and in the other hand was his own, with those prominent F.S. initials. The Provençal stopped Madame Olivet, and he and the station master began speaking to her. Smith came straight on. He grinned at Travers.

"Both in the same boat," he said.

Travers smiled dryly. "I missed the train by accident. It looks as though you missed it by design."

Smith put the three cases down by the seat outside the waiting-room door, and began mopping his brow.

"I don't know about that, sir," he said. "I couldn't very well stand by and see that poor woman without lending a hand. As a matter of fact"—and he looked almost challenging—"the train was just moving off when I saw she was going without her luggage; so I grabbed hers and my own, too, and got out."

"Very good of you," said Travers. "And when's the next train?"

"There's an express in exactly two hours," said Smith. He was on the point of adding something else, but the Provençal and the *chef de gare* and Madame Olivet were almost on them. Travers suddenly thought of his own luggage.

"It's all right," said Smith. "I told the porter about it. He's bringing it along here. I'd have brought it myself if I hadn't been too loaded."

"Thanks," said Travers, and then found himself in the thick of things. The Provençal took him affectionately by the arm.

"Let us view the invalid again," he remarked jocularly.

"Remain here a moment, madame, I beg of you," the station master was saying. Smith took her arm, and as Travers passed into the waiting-room, he saw the flutter of her handkerchief again. The *chef de gare* entered, and he and the Provençal stood for some moments by the sick man. Outside the door the voice of Madame Olivet could be heard, and speaking with her in fluent French—so fluent that Travers could make out no word— was Smith, the man who had confessed that he knew nothing of the lingo. Travers snapped his eyes, closed them and opened them again. He had expected to find himself waking from sleep in the corner seat of that second-class compartment. But he was not there. He was in that same waiting-room where he had been when his eyes closed, and he was in the middle—up to the ears, in fact—of some madly impossible harlequinade; some chaotic nightmare that persisted and would ultimately be merely the nightmare that it really was.

The backs of the other two were towards him, and he heard their subdued voices. He caught the words: "He will stay. He will certainly be useful," and wondered if they were applied to himself. He looked across to the far wall of that dingy room, with its distemper of an atrocious pink, its door in the corner, and its window enclosed by the green shutters from which the paint was peeling. Then the two turned towards him, and it was the *chef de gare* who spoke.

"*Alors, m'sieur*; he is dead—your friend."

"Dead?" said Travers, and blinked. It was no surprise, and yet in some strange way the news was unexpected, if only for the manner and suddenness of the telling. And there was something else that was odd.

"My *friend*," he said. "Why do you call him that?"

The other shrugged as if the question were absurd, and the answer obvious. He turned to the Provençal.

"*Eh bien, M'sieur Gallois, vous restez?*"

"Yes," said the Provençal, "I rest here. Let the doctor come when he arrives."

The door was opened and shut again quickly. Outside was heard the voice of Madame Olivet making an appeal. Gallois—if that were really the Provençales name—descended on the body of the dead man like a vulture, and began rummaging in his pockets. There seemed to be little. Some loose money, a handkerchief, a passport and a folded paper or two were the lot. He thrust them into his own jacket pocket. Then, as if he had been alone in the room, he came over to the door and opened it.

"*Entrez, madame,*" he said, and to Smith: "You, m'sieur, remain outside."

Madame Olivet came in. Her face was puffed and swollen with weeping. She looked at Gallois suspiciously, then flashed a look at Travers. Her eyes shifted to the figure on the bench, and in a moment she was on her knees. Travers glanced at the dead man, too, then turned his eyes away. The bulging eyes, the red face and the gaping mouth seemed somehow to horrify him, and at every moment he expected to hear again that terrifying gurgle from the dead man's throat. There was something naïve and yet tremendously tragic in the question when it came.

"He is really dead, messieurs?"

Travers gave a quick, consoling shake of the head.

"Yes, madame; he is dead."

Her hands fell across the black cape, and her head on them, and all at once she began sobbing convulsively. Travers caught the eye of Gallois. He shrugged his shoulders—and opened the door. Travers went out first, and Gallois closed the door behind him. Inside the room the sobs of Madame Olivet could be plainly heard. But what struck Travers was not the frantic sobbing of the widow, but the fact that Smith had disappeared—and with him had gone the Olivets' luggage and his own.

"It is good not to intrude on the sorrows of the bereaved," began Gallois sententiously, and then caught Travers's look. He seemed puzzled.

"He is gone," said Travers, and waved his hand around. "Monsieur Smith, the Englishman, who had the luggage of Madame Olivet and her husband."

"Monsieur Smeet," said Gallois, with a raising of eyebrows. He gave a little pursing of the lips. "I do not know him."

"But you must," explained Travers patiently. "He was the Englishman who was here with madame."

Yet another shrug of the shoulders. "That is not my affair. One comes—one goes. It is a free country."

"Yes, but won't he be also wanted to give evidence?" went on Travers, still very patiently. "He, too, was present all the time, like myself. And the *chef de train* distinctly told him that he would be wanted to give evidence about that other dead man."

"*Asseyons-nous, m'sieur,*" said Gallois philosophically, and promptly sat down on the wooden seat. "If you and I do our duty according to the law, why disturb ourselves about this Monsieur Smeet?"

His manner was so convincing that Travers began to wonder if he himself had suffered from strange hallucinations. That matter of a note flicked by Smith into the corridor the previous evening—the note upon which Gallois had set his foot—that then had really been imagination? And as he passed over his cigarette case and held a light for M. Gallois, he knew that there was about his purple-jowled acquaintance something of dignity and authority; something, in fact, that was vastly different from the air of naïveness and homely ingenuousness that had hitherto distinguished him. And Travers, lighting his own cigarette, was seized with a sudden desire to ask a few questions.

"You, too, have missed the train?" he began.

Gallois nodded. "It is sometimes necessary to change one's arrangements." A smile of something remarkably like irony drooped his lips. "You and I are both Good Samaritans, m'sieur, and that involves many things. Besides, there is another train in an hour and a half."

Travers smiled grimly at the anti-climax. Gallois must be at heart an entertaining fellow.

"And your luggage?" he said.

"As I remarked," said Gallois imperturbably, "the world is full of Good Samaritans. My luggage, with your own, m'sieur, is now in the office of the *chef de gare*, where we shall find it when our train arrives."

He said that last with a retaining hand on Travers's knee, for Travers had started in his seat as if to reclaim the errant bag at once. Travers sank back on the bench again. Why the station master's office he had no idea, unless it were that in breaking his journey—even as a Good Samaritan—he had committed some offence, and the luggage might have to be paid for, or he might be charged for a new ticket from Marignac onwards. So he sat on over his cigarette.

For the moment there was no more conversation. Gallois had resumed his character of amiable bourgeois, and sat with legs extended, puffing into the morning air. Behind in the waiting-room, the muffled crying of Madame Olivet could still be heard. Travers sat thinking and little frowns chased each other across his forehead. If Smith were, after all, a luggage thief, he was a highly artistic one. And there was that matter of the false sunburn, and the handing out of Olivet's walking stick to someone in the dead of night. And to whom had he handed it? Gallois seemed impossible; then who had been the confederate? And why had the stick been handed out? And then Travers, with a sudden grunt, thought of something else. Smith had hurled a book into the blackness of a tunnel; young Hunt had torn up a book and scattered it on the permanent way. And with a connection even more subtle, two men had spotted faces—and both had died. A little shiver went through his bones. Of what had they died? Was it the Black Death, when the plague spotted men one hour and claimed them the next?

Voices were heard, and Gallois started up. Coming towards them were three men; the *chef de gare*, a well-dressed civilian and a short, black-bearded man carrying a bag. Travers stood back during the introductions, but he knew that the man with the bag was the doctor. Then hats were put on again, and the four moved off towards the waiting-room. Travers felt himself shepherded with them rather than invited.

Gallois opened the door and walked in jauntily. A yard inside, he stopped. He looked round the room with a puzzled gaze. He looked back at the four men, and he looked at Travers especially. Then he snapped out something, and was across the room like a streak. He tugged at the handle of the far door. He put his strength into a heave, but the door held firm. Travers, stepping well inside, saw that—but for the dead man—the room was empty. Madame Olivet had gone!

"There was a key," said Travers amiably. "Someone has taken it."

"You saw the key?" Gallois whipped round on him.

"Certainly," said Travers, with a large gesture. "When we left the room—you and I—it was there."

Gallois began to gabble to the *chef de gare*. He gabbled, too, and the speed was beyond Travers's ear. Then something was shouted to the civilian, and Gallois disappeared running. The doctor, who had stared open-mouthed, added as his contribution a shrug of profound mystification. Then he set his bag on the floor beside the bench and leaned over the dead man.

His back was towards them, and he bent down to inspect the dead face. Then he knelt. A minute went by. Travers profited by the proximity of the station master to recall the matter of his suit-case.

"In good time, m'sieur; in good time," repeated the station master coldly. He resumed his frigid viewing of the doctor. Travers peered over, too, but the doctor had now finished, and rose to his feet.

He waved at the dead man. "You are a relative, m'sieur?"

"Lord, no!" said Travers, startled into English. He hooked off his glasses and tried French; talking deliberately and choosing his words, he told what he knew about Olivet and mentioned the other dead man, and he mentioned the spots. The doctor's eyes popped open, and he blew out his fat cheeks with a pursing of the lips. Then he turned on the corpse and began taking off the collar and opening out the shirt. Travers winced at what seemed a desecration, but the other made no bones about it. He grunted something excitedly. Travers, with an excusable curiosity, pushed the *chef de gare* gently aside, and looked, too. On the hairy chest of the dead man was a fester of spots, red and feverish like his face.

The doctor rubbed his hands and frowned. He stood in thought for a good couple of minutes. Outside the far window the shutters suddenly moved, and the face of Gallois appeared. He stared at them all, and then there was a tugging at the outside handle of the door. It still held firm. If Madame Olivet had gone that way she had locked the door behind her and taken the key. The face of Gallois appeared again at the window—then disappeared.

"That other dead man is on the way to Paris?" asked the doctor, eyes going from Travers to the *chef de gare*. The latter spoke, and he pulled out his watch.

"He is almost there."

There was a sound of feet and voices outside on the platform. It was only a slow train for Paris, the station master said, and slow train or not, Travers wondered why he should not have been allowed to take it. The doctor waited till the noise of the incoming train had subsided, then resumed.

"Then this one must go to Paris, too. If there are two men with spots, the inquiry should be on both. I will telephone."

"But why did he die?" burst in Travers. He spoke with tremendous earnestness. "M'sieur, let me assure you that it was terrible. He choked, like this. He made noises in his throat, like this. When he walked, he made gestures with his hands, like this."

Incongruous as Travers's illustrations were, the doctor seemed startled. He shook his head. He frowned. Then he nodded.

"*Eh bien, m'sieur*, they are going to unravel all that in Paris." He turned jocularly to the *chef de gare*, who seemed to be some sort of a crony. "In Paris they know everything; that is so, my friend, is it not?"

The station master let out a stream of words. The two went out to the platform from which the slow train had just puffed. Travers turned that way, too.

"Pardon, m'sieur, but we must remain here," said the civilian. His look was not unfriendly, but it was decisive enough.

Travers shrugged his shoulders. "But why?"

The other gestured indifference and resignation. Then he smiled. "We have already lost one witness. We must not lose you also, m'sieur."

Travers returned the smile. "Stout fellow!" He almost translated into *brave homme*, and hesitated with the words on the tip of his tongue. He lighted a cigarette instead. Then the unshuttered window caught his eye, and he moved across to see what lay outside. The civilian came with him.

"You go to admire the view?"

"Precisely, m'sieur," Travers told him, and stood there contemplatively. Outside the window he could now see the steep slope covered with grass and weeds through which a path led to a street of the town. His eye ran along it, to the iron railings that bounded the road, and beyond them to the garage whose tin-roofed buildings stretched for fifty yards in the direction of Marignac itself. He smiled to himself for one mad moment. For some reason or other he was under surveillance. That efficient-looking civilian was in the room for one purpose only—to keep an eye on himself. One flick of that fastener and he could be out of the window and down the slope. And to do what? Travers gave a little shrug. To do nothing, except miss what would probably be the explanation or the mad nightmare that had gradually got hold of him ever since he had set foot in that damnable train. And besides, wasn't that Gallois down there, talking excitedly to a mechanic at the garage?

Gallois it was. A closed car was drawn up before the main garage door, and now a driver in peaked cap came hurrying out of the building. A man in a tightly buttoned blue overcoat appeared from nowhere and joined him. Gallois leaned inside as if for a final word of advice. He withdrew again, and the car moved off. Gallois watched it till long after it had disappeared from Travers's view. He turned with profuse gestures to the mechanic, then pulled out his watch, and finally raised his hat and began walking rapidly towards the station.

Travers grunted to himself. If what he had seen meant anything, it was that madame had made a perfectly good getaway by an earlier car from the same garage. Gallois, either on his own authority or—far more probably—on that of the *chef de gare*, had dispatched a second car in pursuit. He turned away from the window with a smile as his mind alertly summoned visions of the chase. His eye fell on the dead man whom he had for a moment or two forgotten—and the smile went. No one could smile in the presence of that face with its eyes that bulged almost from their sockets, and its mouth that gaped as if to let out the last breath of choking air. Travers moistened his lips, and at the same moment by some absurd incongruity, knew that he was feeling amazingly hungry.

There was a patter of feet outside. The door opened and Gallois appeared. He had a look round the room as if hoping that madame might be there after all.

"She has disappeared," he said to the civilian. He expected no answer, for his eyes switched straight to Travers.

"Your name, m'sieur. I do not know your name. You have perhaps a passport?"

Travers found it in his breast pocket and handed it over. Gallois and the civilian examined it. The name was pronounced with a questioning look. Travers pronounced it his own way, and the three of them smiled. It was suddenly all very friendly. Gallois pocketed the passport.

"Pardon, m'sieur, but it is official. You will understand."

Travers understood nothing, but he took it smiling. Then he broached the question of breakfast. Gallois appeared desolated that Travers should be hungry. He would see to it himself. Coffee and rolls would be agreeable to M'sieur Travers? But first of all, it was realized, was it not, that M. Travers must accompany them to Paris where there might be a short inquiry into the affair of the dead man there on the bench?

Travers said it was understood perfectly. He added maliciously that if M. Gallois feared an escape like that of Madame Olivet, he might reassure himself. There was no question of escape—or, to put it more politely—of avoiding a duty. Besides, the main question was one of breakfast.

Gallois smiled and shrugged—this time with an elephantine grace. Then his eyes fell on the face or the dead man, and he, too, appeared somewhat startled as Travers had been. The bulging eyes disturbed him, and with a quick movement he took the collar of the cape and drew the garment over the dead man's face.

Travers made a sudden exclamation. Gallois looked at him. He followed Travers's eyes—and then he stared. On the lame foot, which the drawing up of the cape had now exposed, was nothing but a grey sock. The club boot had gone!

CHAPTER VI
TURNED LOOSE

GALLOIS RAISED his hands to heaven. He raised them so high that Travers thought he would reach the ceiling, and when they were slowly lowered, it looked as if he were about to tear his hair. But the hands fell, and he merely nodded once or twice, and clicked gently with his tongue. It was as if a lion had commenced the roar of a lifetime, and had let it dwindle to the twitter of a dying canary.

And then all at once he swooped down on the feet of the dead man. He clutched each leg by the ankle and pulled. Holding them in his hands, he turned to the other two men to invite their inspection. Travers spotted the point. The legs were the same length—or nearly so—though the foot on which the club-boot had been was slightly shrivelled. Whether Olivet had been lame or not was questionable; that he had had no need for a club-boot was absolutely certain.

Gallois let the two ankles fall. He pulled himself up like a man who has a plain duty.

"I go to telephone," he announced, and made for the door.

"One moment, m'sieur!" Travers stopped him.

"The breakfast?" said Gallois. "I have remembered it." And he started off again.

"Not the breakfast," said Travers quickly. "There is something I would like to mention about all this. Something important."

Gallois stopped. He looked knowingly at the civilian. "The gentleman has something important."

Travers ignored the irony. He cleared his throat. "What I would like to say is this, and I say it seriously. Curious things have happened, M'sieur Gallois; things I do not pretend to understand. Two men have died—and died suddenly. The widow of one has disappeared. And somebody else has disappeared."

"And who is that?" asked Gallois quickly.

"The English gentleman—Smith."

"Ah!" said Gallois. "M'sieur Smeet. And what of him, m'sieur?"

"He was not a friend of yours?"

"A friend of mine?" Gallois appealed with spreading hands for confirmation of the absurdity of the question. "I know nothing of this Smeet. I see him in the train as I see yourself—that is all."

"It was not to you that he handed out the stick of this dead man through a crack of the door last night?"

The eyes of Gallois narrowed. This was something disturbing—something important which he ought to know, and should, perhaps, have known. "What is this about a stick and a crack in the door?"

Travers told him what he had seen. Gallois turned to the civilian. "This becomes interesting. Continue, M'sieur Travers."

"This morning, just before we reached here," Travers duly continued, "Madame Olivet left the compartment to go elsewhere. As she entered the corridor, Smith followed her. It was he who told her that her husband had rushed madly along the platform. It was he who followed her with her luggage. It was he who disappeared with that luggage while we were inside here. Then madame disappeared while we were outside there. You seek madame. Then why not seek Smith? Where he is, madame is."

He stopped with an air of, "I have spoken." And if he was convinced of one thing, it was that he had suffered from some trick of sight when he had imagined the flicking of a note and the falling of Gallois's foot. The Frenchman was now looking at him with quick nods of the head.

"Where madame is, there Smeet is. M'sieur Travers, I hope that you have spoken the truth." He shrugged his shoulders again. "I go to telephone." And off he went.

Travers asked the other his name. M. Valent gave it at once, and spelt the word out. He wondered if breakfast would not be better in the open air. Travers, watching yet another suburban train come in, preferred privacy with the corpse. Ten minutes later the breakfast arrived, borne by Gallois on a tray.

"It is permitted to have my luggage now?" Travers asked him. "I left my pipe in the train, but there are spare ones in the case."

Gallois said he would fetch the case himself. He did so, and he must have entered the office and come straight out again. Nevertheless, when Travers—his meal over—hunted up a pipe, he saw that the clothes that he had folded were now folded less meticulously. But the lock was untampered with—except for a scratch or two—and there appeared to be nothing missing.

He sat for half an hour on the seat outside enjoying his pipe. Valent left him to his own devices, and there was never a sign of Gallois, who apparently was doing the devil of a lot of telephoning. Out of that gloomy waiting-room and the company of the dead man, Travers's spirits were beginning to rise. He was looking forward with considerable interest to his interview—wherever it was and with whom. Through his mind there began to run the things he would say and the points he would make. And when he got in the train for Paris he would write down all he remembered of the affair; everything, in fact, since he first set foot in the train at Toulon all those infinite ages ago.

A stretcher arrived and two men with it. The body of Olivet was decently covered and transported ready for entraining. Valent appeared on the platform again; a passenger or two arrived; porters woke up and Gallois—now shaved and sartorially a new man—seemed to announce that the express was due. It came in on time. Valent apparently supervised the loading of the corpse. Gallois attached himself to Travers. The station master and the *chef de train* interviewed each other, and finally, when the train moved off again, Travers found himself alone with Gallois in a first-class compartment.

The train gathered speed. Gallois rolled himself a cigarette. Travers got paper from his case and wrote furiously. His companion regarded him with a respectful interest. Ten minutes passed, and he could keep back the question no longer.

"You are writing, m'sieur?"

"That is so," said Travers gravely. He regarded Gallois with a look of whimsical confidence. "I am a poet."

Gallois raised his eyebrows. "A poet, m'sieur. Then you compose a poem. Is it permitted to ask about what?"

"I write an ode," said Travers. "An ode to the League of Nations."

Gallois raised his shoulders the merest half-inch. *"Vive le sport, m'sieur!"* He concentrated on the flying landscape. Travers scribbled on.

The suburbs appeared. The train slowed and then crawled. Before he was ready for it, the Purlieus of the station appeared. Gallois got down his bag, and Travers did the same. Five minutes' crawl and the train drew in. The two descended to the platform. Gallois looked round him, and an official-looking gentleman came up. There was some conversation at a little distance, then Travers was nodded at, and the three went across to where a closed car was waiting.

Travers had a bad view, and he knew little of Paris. There seemed to be a lot of twists and tooting of the horn and sudden application of brakes, and when the car did draw up to the kerb, all he saw of his surroundings was a stretch of pavement and the pedestrians between whom he dodged. But it was an immense building that he entered. There was a wicket door at which Gallois signed a book. Travers's suit-case was taken, and a numbered slip was given in return. The two passed through to a waiting-room. In a couple of minutes Gallois was called away, and what Travers took to be a plain-clothes man took his place. Travers, told that he might smoke, got his pipe going and read the newspapers diligently.

An hour passed. At midday another caller put his head through the door and said something about lunch. It came on his heels—a perfectly good meal with a half-bottle. Travers thought of something. Would it be allowed to send some telegrams? The gist of the answer was that there would be no harm in trying. Travers wrote out three—to say that he was delayed and might not be back, after all, for a day or two—and then set about his lunch.

At one o'clock the attendant was relieved. Travers, who had more than a shrewd idea that he was in the Sûreté—the gendarme on duty outside, for instance, and the glimpse of a couple more—asked the new-comer point-blank.

"Oui, m'sieur" he was told.

"And how long am I likely to be here?"

"It is forbidden for me to talk," was the answer, and so much for that attempt at conversation. He lighted yet another pipe. For the first time in his life he had come into contact with the Scotland Yard of France. Uneasy thoughts flitted through his mind. There was French procedure, as an example. In England a man had to be proved guilty; in France an accused had to prove himself innocent. And if he himself had by inadvertence or ignorance committed some offence against the law of the Republic, things might be just the tiniest bit difficult.

It was two-fifteen when he was summoned. With a second attendant accompanying, he was passed through to a small room where a couple of official-looking persons with gimlet eyes examined him from their desks. He was told to sit down. No sooner had he done that than a buzzer sounded, and he was told to get up again. In half a minute he was ushered into another room and left there.

This room was a not uncomfortable, if bare kind of study. It had some hundreds of volumes round its walls and a photograph or two. At one end sat a man with typewriter, pad and pencil, ready to take a statement in the approved Scotland Yard manner. At the far end an elderly gentleman was sitting behind a handsome desk. Above his head Travers saw the inscription of Liberty, Equality and Fraternity, and felt somewhat reassured. By the desk a third man sat, and he turned out to be the interpreter. And lastly, a fourth man was in the room, and that was the gendarme who acted as escort. He now took a seat just inside the door and remained there in the attitude of a benevolent museum attendant.

"*Asseyez-vous, m'sieur,*" said the old gentleman kindly. He seemed a man of fine culture and considerable courtesy.

"You wish an interpreter?" the old gentleman asked in quite good English.

"Yes," said Travers in French, and added: "Very good of you," in English. Already he was trying to make friends of the mammon of the law, and as for the services of an interpreter, heaven alone knew what technicalities and obscurities might otherwise pass over his head. Meanwhile the examining magistrate—which was what Travers imagined him—was stroking his white beard with one hand and holding in the other what was undoubtedly Travers's passport. The inquiry began.

Q. You are in possession of a passport which describes you as Ludovic Travers, British subject; author and company director, of St. Martin's Chambers, London.
A. Well, I was in possession of a passport like that.
Q. These statements are genuine and bona fide?
A. Most decidedly they are.

The examining magistrate stroked his beard again, laid aside the passport, and looked Travers clean in the eye. From then on he watched him like a hawk.

Q. Under the name of Ludovic Travers you booked a reservation in the fifteen-forty-five train from Toulon.
A. That's right.
Q. Your destination was London.
A. That is so.
Q. You have not in the course of your life met, or had dealings with, a man named Corley—Henry Corley?
A. (With a shake of the head.) Never heard the name in my life.
Q. This Englishman was also known as Thomas Cranbrook. Perhaps you knew him under that name?

The question was put that time with such a dramatic leaning forward that Travers had an idea he should have been either startled or confused. All he was, however, was hopelessly at sea, and he said as much. The examining magistrate nodded.

Q. What were your reasons for coming to Toulon?

Travers gave the facts at some length. His statement included the name of the Bandol Hotel, and an invitation to ask the management to prove that he had been there, that his conduct had been exemplary, and that he had only left it on the day stated.

Q. In your compartment were two people; a man known as Pierre Olivet and a woman—Marie Olivet. (Now, thought Travers, we are coming to it.) Have you any information to give as to any other names of these people?

A. I never saw them before in my life till they got into the train at Marseilles.

Q. M'sieur (earnestly), I think you will see on reflection that your answer is prevarication. You were not asked if you had seen them before.

A. Very well, then; I hadn't the faintest idea of their names till the *chef de train* took them this morning. I've never heard their names mentioned, and I know nothing whatever about them.

Q. You were very speedy in making their acquaintance as soon as they entered the train.

A. Was I? I think I was only being courteous in an ordinary way.

Q. It was you who took charge of Pierre Olivet when he became ill.

A. That was only common humanity.

Q. Was it common humanity that led you to follow him out to the platform at the risk of losing your train and your luggage?

A. Well, yes—I'm afraid it was.

The beard was stroked again. The examining magistrate looked away for a moment, then put a veritable facer.

Q. You yourself are not by any chance this Henry Corley, or Thomas Cranbrook, of whom we were speaking?

A. I'm afraid not.

Q. You wish to offer any statement on the events of that railway journey?

A. Do you mean, will I tell you anything suspicious that happened?

There the examining magistrate sat up and took notice. He said that that in effect was what he meant. Travers, only too delighted to tell tales out of school, began with his entry into the train, and his discoveries about the man Smith. There was the matter of false sunburn and the throwing of a guide-book into a tunnel. Even on such evidence Travers ventured to suggest that the man Smith might turn out to be the Henry Corley, *alias* Thomas Cranbrook, in whom m'sieur was so interested. And there was much more to come. The examining magistrate seemed interested in the information, but none too grateful. He leaned forward again, and Travers anticipated a further sensation in court.

Q. Would you be surprised to hear that it was this man Smith who laid information against yourself?

A. The hell he did! I beg your pardon. And is it permitted to ask to whom he laid information about me? And when? And where?

Q. (With courteous finality.) It is not permitted. But with regard to your own statements about yourself, have you any other confirmation to offer than the management of the Bandol Hotel?

There Travers thought very hard. He had plenty—so he thought. The question was, ought one to spread oneself? Was the blowing of trumpets absolutely necessary? He decided that for once in a lifetime, it was.

A. You will pardon me, but you are acquainted with Scotland Yard? You have had dealings with it?

Q. (With a dry smile.) Oh, yes, m'sieur; we have had dealings with it.

A. You know the name of the Commissioner of Police? You have met him?

Q. No, I have not met him. (Apparently he did not know the name, but he consulted a book. He evidently found the name. Travers went on at once.) He is, as you see, Sir George Coburn. He is also my uncle!

Travers received a quick look. For a moment he expected to hear the words: "And I, m'sieur, am the President of the Republic—or Charlie Chaplin," as the case might be. But all that came was a nod. Travers resumed:

"One of the superintendents of the Criminal Investigation Department—the one who has had most dealings with the French authorities over matters of mutual interest—is Superintendent Wharton." He spelt out the name. "If you inquire from either Superintendent Wharton or Sir George Coburn, I am sure you will be told that I am no suspicious character." He leaned forward with a courtesy that was charming in its irony. "The telephone number is Whitehall 1212."

He left it at that. The examining magistrate himself had written down the names. He contemplated them for a moment or two, and then he rose.

"You will remain here, perhaps, for some little time still, m'sieur, and we trust it will not be too inconvenient. At the very earliest moment we hope to conclude this inquiry."

Travers thought the *perhaps* was delicious. "And my telegrams, m'sieur?" he said. "Have they gone?"

"They have gone," he was told, "and the change from your note is available when you wish it."

It was only a quarter to three when Travers returned to his room. He was still there at four-thirty, when with a large abandon he ordered *café crème*—being suspicious of tea—and *brioches*. Then he sat on in the comfortable chair and read a periodical or two till five-thirty. Then he was again sent for, and this time to another room. A younger man, smart and official, saw him there. He spoke English exceedingly well.

"We regret, Monsieur Travers, the inconvenience you have suffered, but perhaps you will understand that sometimes these things are necessary in the cause of justice." Travers told Wharton afterwards that he there expected him to produce and wave a little flag. "We trust you will bear us no ill-will over the matter."

"None at all, my dear fellow," said Travers heartily. "Next time you come to London you will have to look me up. And"—with extreme beguilement—"I suppose you wouldn't like to tell me what it's all been about?"

The other shook his head. "At the moment, m'sieur, that is impossible. Later perhaps. You return to London?"

"Later perhaps." The retort had been obvious but with it there had come a changing of plans. A day or two in Paris would be amusing, and to cross that night was impossible in any case. Besides, if the police knew his Paris address, something might be forthcoming in a day or two.

"You can recommend me an hotel?—not too palatial a one?" he asked. The hotel was recommended. Travers asserted with no little emphasis that he would be there for at least a day and a half. And when he left the Sûreté, as far as he could see he was not followed. The law of the Republic had apparently no further use for him. Even the death of old Hunt had been no mystery, for never a question had been asked about it.

But the Travers who had left the Sûreté and the Travers who lingered that night over his dinner, were two vastly different men. The first had in him a strain of cussedness and determination; moreover he had been considerably annoyed. He had been thrust into a mystery and then kicked out of it, and, like the tent-maker of Tarsus, he resented being kicked out. And though he had no more use for snobbery than a Zulu for bed-socks, his personal pride had been ruffled. At the back of his mind was the thought that somebody was going to suffer. He had been made a fool of, and somebody else should experience the same feelings. And the fiercest resentment was against the man Smith, who had had the damnable audacity to cover his own tracks by the use of slanderous accusations against another man.

But the Travers who at eight-thirty that night sipped his liqueur and nodded with the orchestra, was another man. All the resentment had passed; what was left was a curiosity that fretted like a hair shirt. Some things he could now understand—the matter of a walking-stick, for instance, and a club-boot. Olivet had been smuggling something, and something of tremendous value and small in size. The stick had had a screw top and Smith had passed it out to a confederate to be searched. But the stick had been empty, and it had been the club-boot where the something had been concealed.

But there were problems, interwoven though they were, that were even more intriguing than that. The hidden something might be diamonds or jewels—Russian jewels, for instance, that were constantly being smuggled out by confederates of the old nobility. Smith was on the track of the jewels. He had escaped with Madame Olivet, and Madame Olivet had escaped with the club-boot. Then had Madame Olivet been double-crossing her husband? Was she in league with Smith? Was that why Smith had clumsily disguised himself—so that Olivet should not recognize him? Was that why Smith had shouted the name St. Raphael so persistently into Olivet's ear? And had the escape of Madame Olivet and Smith at Marignac been predetermined? And if so, had Olivet been murdered to facilitate that escape? Was that why Smith had told lies to Gallois about himself?

But these surmises left even more unexplained. Why had Smith thrown the guide-book surreptitiously into the tunnel? And—marvellous coincidence—another book had been torn up and thrown surreptitiously on to the permanent way. And thinking still in pairs, two men had died, and their bodies had been spotted. Brown had called Hunt's "indigestion spots," and had said they were not virulent. Yet young Hunt had caught them, or else why had he been rubbing his ribs? Or had he eaten of the same thing that had spotted his uncle? And how, in heaven's name, did that explain the spots on the dead Olivet?

And what of Gallois? He was a detective, and of some rank; there was no doubt about that. Then why had he been on the train, and in disguise? Above all, why had he been in the corridor outside that fatal compartment, when there was sitting room enough elsewhere? Had he been on the track of Olivet and the jewels?—the stolen jewels? And there Travers shook his head and left conjecture to itself. Since the Sûreté knew his whereabouts, the next day would surely bring some news. He would be sent for again—if only as the friend of Wharton and the nephew of Sir George—and questioned courteously on the happenings of that extraordinary night.

But as far as the next day was concerned, Travers might have been in Peru. Then the morning after that brought nothing from the Sûreté, and he sent more telegrams to announce his arrival that night. And since either Sir George, or Wharton, or both, had bailed him out at the Sûreté, he bought a couple of unpolished briars as presents before departing to the Gare du Nord. From Calais there was a perfectly superb crossing. The train was away on time from Dover, and it was six o'clock precisely when he came through the barriers at Victoria and saw his man Palmer with the Bentley.

As soon as he had bathed, he rang up Sir George. The Chief Commissioner was anxious, disturbed and inclined to be irascible. His nephew assured him that the affair was the most trivial in the world, and gave him a synopsis and multitudinous thanks. But there was no getting away from the fact that Sir George was a bit of a bore, and Travers said nothing about calling round. Palmer was instructed to pack up one unpolished briar, and a brief note was scribbled.

Dinner was early that evening. Before the meal was over the three evening papers arrived. Travers, having already cast his eye over the financial pages of the dailies, looked flirtatiously through general news columns for something more hectic. Then all at once he hooked off his glasses and polished them. He read the comparatively obscure paragraph again.

> "BURGLARY AT DEAD MAN'S HOUSE
> "VALUABLE SILVER MISSING
>
> "Following on the sudden death of Mr. James Hunt, who died under rather mysterious circumstances while travelling from St. Raphael to Paris, as was reported in these columns on Tuesday last, comes the news that at some time during the Tuesday night a burglarious entry was made at 'Marsh View,' the residence of the late Mr. James Hunt at Peddleby, near Rye, Sussex.
>
> "The discovery of the burglary was made by Thomas Brown, the valet of the dead man, who had proceeded straight to Rye after his master's death, to inform the household staff and make such modifications in the immediate household arrangements as were thereupon necessary. On opening the windows of the dining-room, Mr. Brown was surprised to see that a pane of glass had

been removed, and his attention was at once directed to the wall safe, the door of which was open. Private papers were also scattered about, but all that is at present known to be missing is a small collection of Georgian silver which had been placed in the safe before the party left for the South of France. The local police have the matter in hand, and developments are expected.

"Burglaries are common enough things, and the most uncommon feature of this particular case—and a rather disturbing one—is the enterprise of the modern burglar. The news of the death of a man is published one day, and forthwith the enterprising cracksman sees his chance. Police supervision of the house which took place while it was closed, was—as the burglar certainly guessed—relaxed when the staff returned again. The reader will find further comments on page seven."

The further comment, to which Travers immediately turned, was merely an article on the enterprise of the modern burglar. It conveyed little, but without it there was plenty to think about. Travers's fertile mind was at once seething with all manner of speculations. Russian jewels—the hollow walking-stick—two dead men with spots on their faces—the decamping of a woman with her husband's luggage—the breaking open, hundreds of miles away, of a safe, and all the score of curious and intriguing happenings of the last few days. And the death of Hunt was considered mysterious, it seemed. It was a Sunday when they had met in the train. On the Monday he was dead, and Brown returned to England—or he might have returned on the Tuesday. The same night the burglary took place. It was discovered on the Wednesday, and this was Thursday evening. And was the *Evening Record* wrong in its surmise? Had the publication of the death of Hunt had nothing whatever to do with the burglary? Was the burglar the elusive Smith, who had been in the compartment when the *chef de train* had been told the dead man's place of residence and had written it down?

He fidgeted in his chair for a minute or two, then announced that he was going out. It was great to be back again in London, he thought, as he caught sight of the Embankment trams. And at Scotland Yard they still seemed to know him, and there was no form to fill in and business to be stated. He felt the unpolished briar in his pocket as he inquired for Superintendent Wharton. The superintendent, he was told, was not in.

"What about Chief Inspector Norris?"

"He doesn't happen to be in either at the moment, sir," said the sergeant.

"A pity," said Travers. "Mind if I phone?"

He got Wharton's private address. Mrs. Wharton said that George was away on a case, and as far as she knew he would not be back in town till next day. Travers told her he'd enjoyed and profited by his holiday, and fancied he heard in her inquiry something more than polite solicitude.

He stood by the phone for a moment or two. There'd be plenty of time to see Wharton the following day. In the meanwhile, the pipe could be despatched.

"If Superintendent Wharton comes in tomorrow, leave word for him to ring me up and tell me his movements, will you?" he said to the sergeant.

Ten minutes later he was in his rooms again, and Palmer was packing the pipe. Ten minutes more and he wandered out again, this time towards Piccadilly. Outside a cinema a huge advertisement caught his eye.

ROME EXPRESS.

Travers smiled gently to himself. Somewhere or other he seemed quite recently to have heard that word "express" before. He fumbled in his small-change pocket and made his way in.

CHAPTER VII
DEFINITION OF MURDER

AT BREAKFAST the following morning Palmer put the usual question, if somewhat guardedly:

"The car will be needed this afternoon, sir?"

It was his master's custom to spend most weekends at his brother-in-law's place, Pulvery Manor, in Sussex. But Travers now looked pleasantly dubious. His mind conjured up immense accumulations of work at Durango House.

"I doubt we shall manage it," he said. "Still, we'll hope."

But when he arrived at Durango House he received a surprise that was rather disconcerting. His understudy had everything cleared up to the last signature; no decisions of grave importance were awaiting the cool judgment of Ludovic Travers, and though everybody seemed remarkably and unaffectedly glad to see him, it was only too obvious that Durangos Limited had survived his absence.

But he had an hour's conference with his own particular department, and mid-morning coffee with the Governing Director. Sir Francis pulled his leg about that Paris business, hinting at pretty girls and wanderings from the straight and narrow way. It was he, too, who remarked casually at the end of the pow-wow, that he supposed Travers would now be pushing off to Sussex. Travers, knowing that Sir Francis rarely talked, or even leg-pulled without cause, asked why.

"I thought after your experiences with the law, you might like to get out of Wharton's way," Sir Francis said. "He rang me up privately yesterday morning, and asked when you'd be back."

But if only for the sake of appearances, Travers hung about Durango House till lunch-time. At two o'clock he and Palmer were in the Bentley. Palmer, impassive as ever, made no sign when the car took the New Cross Road. He sat unmoved when it turned left at Lewisham clock, but when soon after it shifted a point or two still farther south-east, and in a direction that had nothing to do with Pulvery, he made an uneasy movement in his

seat. Travers, who had been waiting for that with quiet amusement, ventured to explain.

An old gentleman had died suddenly in the very compartment in which he was travelling—so suddenly and strangely, in
fact, that had Superintendent Wharton been in town, he would
have been asked about it. The papers had also announced something unusual in the death. Now there had been a burglary at the
dead man's house. What he himself was going to do was to round
off the experience. He had come into contact with the dead man,
and had been interested; now he would like to cast an eye over
his environment. A matter of five minutes, perhaps, and then
full speed west for Pulvery. Travers himself thought there was
often a great deal of reliability to be placed on outward appearances. One might learn quite a lot about a man from the kind of
house he lived in.

"I suppose you can, sir," said Palmer, but none too heartily.

"You don't believe it?"

"Well, sir," said Palmer, with the gravity of sixty that remembered his master in a pram, "I've known exceptions, though not
in the same way, sir."

"Such as what?" went on Travers remorselessly.

"Well, sir, a man just came into my mind as you mentioned
the matter. In my younger days it was, sir. He was a singer;
privately, of course, sir. A very fine bass. Very fond of nautical
songs, sir. *King of the Deep am I* was what might be called his
masterpiece. Perhaps you know the song, sir?"

"Can't say I do," said Travers.

Palmer nodded. "Well, that was his favourite song, sir. And
then one day, sir, a party of us went down to Hastings for the
day, and would you believe it, sir, he turned all giddy when he
looked into the water off the end of the pier? We had to get him
away. Couldn't stand the sight of the water, sir."

Travers smiled. "That's convincing enough. And I suppose
you've never in your travels run up against a valet, or personal
servant, of the name of Thomas Brown?"

"Brown, sir?" said Palmer, and harked back to the past
again. But he could find no man of the kind Travers described,

large though his experience was. But Travers loved to get the old fellow to talk, and they were still talking when the car came into the village of Peddleby. As they slowed before the post office to ask the way to "Marsh View," a large blue tourer passed them. When they moved on again along the village street, there was the tourer drawn up in front of a comfortable-looking inn. Palmer suddenly leaned across.

"Pardon me, sir, but I believe that was Mr. Wharton coming out of the inn door."

"Wharton!" Travers clapped on the brakes, stopped and looked out. There was no mistaking that grizzled face with its vast, weeping-willow moustache. Travers was smiling as he reversed the car and got it round.

Wharton was speaking with what seemed considerable earnestness to a couple of men who had got out of the tourer. He gave a little gasp as he caught sight of Travers. He nodded as a kindly father might when his offspring arrives home with the seat torn out of his breeches.

"Perfectly amazing!" began Travers, thrusting out a hand. "And how are you, George?"

Wharton still seemed to be recovering slowly from the shock. He was used to the ways and dramatic appearances of Ludovic Travers, but this was beyond him. He said he was pretty well, and that Travers was positively robust, and that it was a hot day.

"You weren't so anxious to know my whereabouts merely to tell me that," said Travers.

"No," said Wharton. His later stupefaction had been a cloak to cover some quick thinking. "And what brings you this way?" Without waiting for an answer he introduced the two strangers. Walker, Travers did not know, but Holt he had met before, and the two smiled pleasantly at each other.

"Locks, bolts and bars soon fly asunder, what?" quoted Travers with fatuous flippancy.

"I don't know about that, sir," said Holt modestly.

"Well, I'll leave you three to it," went on Travers. "As soon as you've finished, George, you and I'll unburden our souls."

He moved over to the Bentley. Palmer was told to move the car into the inn yard and make arrangements for his own tea. A wait of an hour or two was anticipated. He stood by till Holt and Walker had moved off in the direction of "Marsh View."

"I won't keep you ten minutes," began Wharton.

"My dear George, why dissimulate?" Travers smiled at him. "You know perfectly well I'm bound for 'Marsh View'—and so are you. What about going together?"

Somehow Travers had the idea that the old General—as the Yard had nicknamed him—knew a tremendous lot more than he cared for the moment to admit.

"And what's the attraction of 'Marsh View'?" Wharton asked.

Travers said he had seen things in the papers. He let out further that the business about which he had been questioned by the Paris police had really been vaguely connected with the death of the very man who owned "Marsh View." Hence the natural interest. Moreover, he had a whole series of the most amazing happenings on which to ask Wharton's advice. Wharton nodded, and made grunting noises.

"As a matter of fact," he said, "we were informed yesterday morning that you were concerned with that. I tried to find out your movements from Durango House. Shall we go along?"

He set off at once. Travers was used to Wharton's little tricks of secretiveness. In good time he knew he would be told at least most of what was in the General's mind, and that that was something very much out of the ordinary was only too apparent. County authorities are not in the habit of calling in Scotland Yard to inquire into burglaries, and even if the Yard had been called in, the highest member of the hierarchy to have been dispatched would have been a chief inspector—and here was a member of the Big Five! What was more, from the fact that the place of meeting had been the inn, Travers deduced that Wharton had been in Peddleby for some time.

"Marsh View" was five minutes' walk from the inn, and Travers occupied most of it in relating what he knew of James Hunt. At the very end, as they turned into the drive to the house, he had his first facer.

"I see," said Wharton calmly. "That's roughly what Brown told me. And, by the way, have a talk with Brown yourself as soon as we get inside. I want him out of the way."

He rang the bell. Travers looked up and round. "Marsh View" was a fairly modern, roomy house, gloomily secluded and yet close to the village. From the ridge on which it stood one could see miles across the marshes, and a faint grey line showed the Channel.

Brown opened the door. His eyes goggled at the sight of Travers.

"Extraordinary coincidence, seeing you again," Travers smiled.

"Yes, sir, it is," Brown said limply.

"I'll go straight through," said Wharton, and went off along the passage. Evidently, thought Travers, he knew his way about. Brown was still recovering from the shock of seeing Travers.

"The superintendent happens to be a friend of mine," Travers explained. "Also I happened to see the account of your burglary, and as I had business this way I thought I'd call and see if there was anything I could do."

"Very good of you, sir," said Brown, still dubious, if not suspicious, as Travers could see. They passed the open door of the drawing-room, and Travers saw something. He stopped, then went inside.

"Quite a fine old clock, if I may say so." He nodded benevolently at the rather trivial grandfather, and then, naturally enough, flopped down in a handy chair. "Very hot to-day. Fatiguing, in fact."

"It is hot, sir," said Brown.

"Sit down for a moment, won't you?" went on Travers. "And when do you expect Mr. Hunt's—er—remains to come over? They're burying him here?"

"That I don't know, sir," said the valet. Travers was finding it more and more hard to think of him as that. Granted that servants in time assume the dignity and bearing of environment, there was yet something of quality about Brown that was elusive and somehow disturbing.

"You've had no news?"

"Well, some news, sir. There seems to be some difficulty over there and the master may be buried in Paris. That will probably depend on Mr. Leslie, sir."

"Quite," said Travers. "You're fond of him? Mr. Leslie, I mean?"

"I am, sir," said Brown, and for the first time, emphatically. "A complex character, if I may say so. Always very shy and nervous. He was not allowed out enough, sir; not with those of his own kind."

"Between ourselves you mean he was bullied," Travers suggested calmly. "Like yourself, if you'll forgive the remark."

Brown hesitated. "I think you're right, sir. It was difficult living here. If it hadn't been for the young master, I might have gone long ago."

Travers nodded sympathetically. "What caused the irritation, do you think? Something constitutional?"

Brown shook his head. "I can't say, sir. I've often thought about it myself. He seemed to delight in deliberate provocation. He had a cruel tongue." He shook his head again. "I admit he suffered considerably—with his throat principally. The local doctor found him a great trial, sir."

"I expect he did," was Travers's comment. "But it wasn't throat trouble that caused the spots?"

Brown looked surprised for a moment. He thought the matter over, and then shook his head. "I imagine that was digestive trouble, sir. If it hadn't been for those spots we should have travelled back by road. As it was, the car was sent on to Calais. I believe the chauffeur had orders from Mr. Leslie to bring it back to Paris again. It's there now at any rate, sir."

"And what happened to you exactly, in Paris?"

Brown smiled wearily. "Nothing particular, sir. I wrote a statement of what I knew. I also gave them the bottle with the rest of the lotion in it. Why they should think that had anything to do with the master's death, I don't know."

"Neither do I," said Travers hypocritically, and he blushed slightly, for in his mind had been the thought of the lotion too.

"There was no difficulty made about my coming on here," went on Brown, and Travers pricked up his ears. Something curious had happened there. "Naturally I'm somewhat anxious to see the young master again, sir."

"You'll be glad when everything's settled," added Travers, and nodded. "And what are you going to do with yourself? Stay on here?"

Brown hesitated again for the merest moment. There was always something extraordinarily sympathetic about Ludovic Travers; something that invited confidence and inspired trust. Brown had felt all that, and he knew his listener had the stamp of breeding and quality.

"To tell you the truth, sir," he said, "I don't think I shall stay—not when everything's settled. Mr. Leslie has often talked it over with me. I think we shall go abroad, sir; to the Colonies most likely, and Kenya for preference."

Travers suddenly got out of his chair and went over to the window. "You've both been a bit stifled," he said, and then his hand went out to the view away across the marsh: the endless flat pastures with sheep dotted smaller and smaller to the pearly grey horizon above which great clouds floated. "No boy could see that sort of thing every day without wanting to get away somewhere."

Brown nodded gravely. "You're right there, sir. It calls, as they say."

Travers turned back to the chair again. "Mr. Leslie Hunt the only relative? I mean, he's likely to inherit?"

"That I can't say," said Brown. "There is a brother of the late master, but they weren't on very good terms. And the late Mr. Hunt was not communicative. He delighted, if I may say so, in using his money as a kind of lever. He used to threaten the boy that he'd be a pauper if it weren't for him."

"I know," said Travers. "As man to man, Brown, you haven't much of an opinion of your late master."

Something like a scowl went over the valet's face. He spoke the words with such passionate intensity that Travers was startled.

"Not much of an opinion, sir? I've this opinion—and I don't care who hears me. He was inhuman. He had a diseased mind; a cruelty complex I've heard it called. He tortured that boy and he tortured me." He broke off. "I'm sorry. I oughtn't to have told you that—I mean, a stranger."

Travers clapped him on the back. "What's on the mind is best off it. I saw a little in the train that evening. But I'd forget it if I were you. Put it behind you. The future's in your own hands." He moved over to the door. "Now I wonder if I might join Superintendent Wharton?"

"Certainly, sir." Nevertheless at the door the valet stopped again. "I suppose you haven't had any news from Paris, sir?"

"I'm afraid I haven't," Travers told him.

"What I was interested in, sir, was that extraordinary case of the man—that Frenchman—who had some sort of an attack. I just wondered how he got on."

"He died," said Travers. "Simply collapsed and died. A remarkably queer thing too was that he was beginning to be covered with spots, something like those Mr. Hunt had."

Brown bit his lip, "Spots! A remarkable thing, as you say, sir. And they didn't know what he really died of?"

"Not when I left them," said Travers, and smiled reminiscently. He followed on Brown's heels to the dining-room door. Brown tapped, and then turned the handle. The door was locked. Almost at once a voice—Wharton's voice—was heard from the other side.

"Just one moment and I'll open the door."

The moment was best part of five minutes, and when Travers stepped inside the room there was nothing particular to be seen. Wharton explained—and it seemed for Brown's benefit—that he had been going over the floor for footmarks. Travers saw the safe, a small one, set in the wall in a corner, and on the floor stood a mediocre oil-painting which usually hung above it as a camouflage.

Wharton rubbed his hands together. "Well, I think that's all, Brown," he said. "You've got that inventory of the silver for me?"

Brown produced it at once. "There may be some small difference in the one I gave the local police," he said, "because, as I told you, sir, I wrote from memory."

"That's all right," said Wharton. He held out his hand. "Well, I think we'll be going. Thank you for helping us. As soon as we get the malefactor we'll let you know."

The remark was uttered with such deliberate flirtatiousness that Travers knew that Wharton had something up his sleeve. And when they got out of earshot of the house again he was just about to put a question when Wharton got in first.

"How'd you get on with Brown? Learn anything new?"

"Quite a lot," said Travers. He gave the General a look of humorous reprimand. "The trouble is, George, that it won't be new to you. Before I've said two words you'll tell me young Hunt told you that."

"But I haven't seen young Hunt," said Wharton with a look of real amazement.

"That's all right then," said Travers. "If you ever do see him, you'll acknowledge, in the description I'm now about to give you, the hand of a master." The description thereupon followed.

Wharton grunted. "Not a very attractive character, as you say. But where's the bearing?"

"Only that Brown's so fond of this unattractive young man that he put up with a dog's life here so as not to be away from him. I know that people lavish affection on strange objects, but honestly, George, Brown's story read like a tupp'ny novelette."

Wharton smiled wryly. "Before we reach this pub you'll be giving me a cast-iron theory that Brown was old Hunt's illegitimate son, and that young Hunt is Brown's son—"

"Don't be immoral, George," cut in Travers. "We want to keep this case pure. And to be perfectly serious, Brown—as you've probably found out for yourself—is a man of considerable education."

Wharton gave a deprecatory shrug of the shoulders. "He speaks well enough. All these superior servants do."

"Oh, no, they don't, George," countered Travers. "But you've got to take my word for what I've said. Brown's exceptional.

Where's your ordinary butler or upper servant who's conversant with the correct handling of a gerund?"

"A what?" But they were at the inn and Holt and Walker were waiting. That turned out to be a pity because Travers's dissertation—never delivered—on certain rules of correct speaking, might have led to a few short cuts. And when five minutes later, the other two had started off back to town, it was Travers who asked questions instead of developing theories.

"What's happened with your two experts, George?"

"Not too much," Wharton told him. "I was down here yesterday afternoon, by the way, to meet the local people—"

"At their request?" broke in Travers.

Wharton made a face. "Well, no. At our request. Still, I met them and looked the ground over. There was a perfectly good entry made by the burglar from outside and the safe lock showed scratches, so that the local people knew it had been picked. There were quite good footprints which didn't tally with Brown's—"

"You had an idea the burglary was a fake?" cut in Travers again.

"Not necessarily," said Wharton. "You ought to know enough to know that everything's got to be thought of. However, I got my glass on the scratches and thought I'd like to know more about them. It was none too early by then, but I got into touch with Abnetts, who make that kind of safe, and arranged for a man to come down. They suggested Walker, though he couldn't get here till this afternoon; so I said we'd be glad to wait for him, and I had Holt wait accordingly. Walker says the scratches are—scratches, and that's all he knows about 'em. On the other hand he and Holt are plumb certain that the lock was opened with a key. In other words, the scratches are fakes."

Travers pulled a face. "That can only mean Brown."

"Not at all," said Wharton. "We've no fault to find with the entry. If the thief had some special knowledge or was in the know, he might have had a key, and it might have been to his interest to make himself out, by faking, to be a common or garden picker of locks. Also there's three women in that house—

housekeeper and two maids; though"—and he smiled somewhat ruefully—"from what I've seen of them there's damn little they'd open, unless it was a tin of sardines."

"Yes, but why did you come down here at all?" began Travers. The question was left in the air. The landlord came out to the garden with the information that Mr. Wharton was wanted on the phone. Travers sat on and speculated. It was a quarter of an hour before the General was back. There was something about him that was different. Travers smiled ironically.

"What's happened, George? Seen your name in the birthday honours?"

"Not at the moment," said Wharton imperturbably. "But about this week-end of yours. I suppose it isn't a matter of life and death?"

Travers looked hard at him. "You want me to stay down here?"

"Not exactly," said Wharton. "The fact is I'm flying to Paris first thing in the morning and I'd like you to come over."

"Then you must want me devilish bad," Travers told him. "This is the first time, George, in all our long and affectionate associations, that you've asked me to join the inner ring."

"But you'll come?" Wharton's eyes twinkled.

"Of course I'll come," Travers told him. "Where's the rendezvous?"

"We'll see to that later," said Wharton. "First thing you're going to do is to give me an extract or two from that diary of yours. I'm afraid that means going back to the Yard at once."

"Right-ho," said Travers, with what he tried to make resignation. "And now perhaps you'll tell me just what's been happening."

"Exactly," said Wharton, and rubbed his chin. "Hunt died on Monday, didn't he?"

"Either then or Sunday night," said Travers, wondering what was coming.

"Yesterday morning we had an inquiry," went on Wharton. "The Sûreté wondered if we knew anything about Hunt. It seemed there were various complications arising out of his death. All we knew was the burglary here, and our source of information was the same as your own—the papers. If the case developed I should probably be the one to work with the French authorities, and that's why I came down here to get all the news from Brown—and see the burglary affair." The General lugged out his pipe. The pause satisfied his small qualms about giving too much information at once. Travers recognized his own cue.

"And what's happened now?"

Wharton smiled provocatively. "Well, they wanted to know if we could put our hands on a gentleman by the name of Travers, who had just left Paris but who might be a material witness in the case. I said it was difficult but it might be managed."

"Yes, but what case?" persisted Travers.

"Why, the death of James Hunt," Wharton told him innocently. "Murder, I ought to have called it. That's the usual term when a man dies from someone sticking a hat-pin in his heart."

CHAPTER VIII
TRAVERS HEARS THE NEWS

ALL THAT WAS WHY Ludovic Travers found himself, at midday on the Saturday, at the very last place he would have guessed had he been given a hundred chances twenty-four hours before—at a Paris restaurant, having lunch. A couple of hundred yards away Wharton was talking things over with his colleagues at the Sûreté, and it was not unlikely that in an hour or so Travers himself might be summoned to the inner circle.

And it was time, he thought, that something really sensational should occur. Precious little had happened since Wharton had made his announcement at Peddleby. The news that old Hunt had been murdered ought to have been sensational enough, and yet somehow it was not. It was the manner of his killing that had taken the edge off Travers's inquisitional appetite. Everything seemed so obvious. Marie Olivet had jabbed in the hat-pin. She had remembered the insult the irritable old fool had given her, though ostensibly when she and her husband had gone to sleep it had been with no hoarded grievances. But in the night an opportunity had presented itself—and Travers even thought he could guess when that moment had been. As she had worked it out, the mark made by the hat-pin should have been invisible; and then, later in the morning when her husband had died, she had taken fright and disappeared.

Wharton had listened politely enough that previous day to Travers's theories, but what he could not understand—and he said so frankly—was the attitude of the French authorities. If everything were so absurdly simple, then why request the urgent presence of a responsible and competent official from Scotland Yard? And there the General had left the matter for the moment, and while he saw his man and arranged for Palmer to be taken back to town. Travers returned to "Marsh View" to obtain from Brown the name and address of the dead man's solicitors. Brown gave particulars at once; Forthright and Hughes of Hastings—and added, with what was either disquiet or curiosity, that he had been in communication with them himself on behalf of the young master.

Wharton, for all his dislike of what he termed Travers's hell-wagon, was thereupon driven in it to Hastings and interviewed the solicitors himself. Travers waited in the car and wrote a note for his sister, and when Wharton reappeared half an hour later, the Bentley was headed for London, and Travers heard the latest.

Old Hunt, Wharton had learned, sprang from good stock. Fifty years and more ago he had come straight from a public-school to his father's flourishing business of tea-merchants, with shops in Cheapside and the Strand. When James was thirty his father died and then the business was sold and James retired on the proceeds to live at Buxton a life of comparative seclusion. His two brothers had been extremely hostile when the sale was mooted, but James was master and they had their share. One was a parson at Tunbridge Wells, and Leslie was the son of his middle age. He had lost his money by foolish investments and had died with precious little to his name; whereupon James had adopted his son.

The other brother, Charles, had launched out into a shop of his own at Hampstead. Lately, however, on account of the pressure of monopoly businesses and the bad times, he had been feeling the pinch. At the very first he had been on tolerable terms with James, then there had been a long enduring quarrel. Two years before there had been a reconciliation—but only till James had discovered that what Charles wanted from him was not so much brotherly love as a loan. Strangely enough, only two weeks previously Charles had written to the solicitors to inquire after James's whereabouts, and had been given the St. Raphael address. Charles, the solicitors understood, had proceeded to Paris as soon as he had heard, in a telegram from Leslie, of his brother's death. Presumably he was there at the moment. Charles, by the way, was married and childless. James had been a widower for some years, and he too had no children. The Hunts, as Wharton remarked, seemed an unfertile folk.

As for the will, James had made a new one when two years before he had become temporarily reconciled with Charles, and under it Charles received a good sum. But when James discovered what he deemed to be his brother's duplicity, that will was cancelled and he made what the solicitors had every reason to suppose was the one under which the estate would be administered. Leslie was to receive twenty thousand; Brown, if still in the employ of James Hunt, the sum of two hundred; the rest went to the Royal Geological Society, of which deceased was a member. The estate, after settlement, would be in the neighbourhood of a hundred thousand pounds, and at the mention of that sum Travers had whistled.

All that information had naturally been given in the strictest confidence, and Travers had smiled to himself as he imagined the General extracting it piece by piece. Guy Hughes knew "Marsh View" well. He had a high opinion of Brown, though it had been easy to see that he had considered his master a difficult client. For Leslie he had felt sorry. His uncle had used him as a combination of errand boy and secretary.

"Brown told me as much yesterday," Wharton had said to Travers. "I think that might explain the rather curious affection he felt for him; don't you think so? What's the poet say? Pity is akin to love—or something of the kind?"

But if Travers had been interested in Wharton's discoveries at the solicitors' office, Wharton had been flabbergasted at the tale of Travers's adventures in the Paris express. Every now and again he had cast a look which plainly hinted at leg-pulling, but the face of the narrator had been so solemn that Wharton had reluctantly recognized that Travers had not suffered from some amazing nightmare.

"So you see what I meant when I said the death of Hunt looks like falling flat," Travers had said. "Now if it had been an inquiry into the death of that chap Olivet, there'd have been something really worth while. You got any ideas?"

Wharton had had none. He was feeling, in fact, rather stupefied, and he had said so. And curiously enough, what Travers had said to Wharton as the Bentley had hurtled along between Tonbridge and Sevenoaks, was what was obsessing his mind as he sat over his lunch in the Paris restaurant that Saturday morning. If only there were to be an inquiry into the death of Pierre Olivet! If one could learn, for instance, the whole history of a walking-stick, a missing club-boot and a missing wife; a face that was white and then hectic red, and a delirium that had been ghastly and a death that was terrifying to recall! And with it there would be the curious history of Smith, the man with the sunburned face who threw a guide-book into a tunnel, wiped his face with a white handkerchief in private and with a green one in public, and took a nocturnal interest in walking-sticks and a daylight one in another man's wife.

Just short of one o'clock, Wharton turned up. Travers, who had settled the bill and was pawing the ground restlessly, was off the mark at once.

"What are they likely to ask me?" he said to Wharton.

"Nothing at all," said Wharton. "We're going down to St. Raphael with your friend Gallois by the four o'clock and we'll do all the talking then."

"Who *is* Gallois?" asked Travers, and he had rarely been more anxious for a definite answer.

"Inspector Gallois of the Sûreté Générale, if that's what you mean," Wharton told him. He added a look that was extremely puzzling. "Even if the opportunity occurs, don't mention anything outside our own particular case. The Olivets and your friend Smith, for instance."

"Right-ho," said Travers airily. "My secrets will die with me, and then one day, George, you'll be sorry. And if I'm not going to be asked any questions, what am I going with you for?"

"They're turning young Hunt loose," said Wharton. "The old man was buried the day before yesterday, here in Paris. Then there's the Charles Hunt, who's over here, and the chauffeur. If anything suspicious arises out of our inquiry, there'll be an eye kept on the three of them when they get back home. All that's happening now is that they're being called in to be told officially that they can go. We're not too keen on any of them seeing you here, so you'll be in a handy room to give your usual series of impressions. That all right?"

As Travers knew well enough, it had to be all right—and it sounded interesting. More interesting still was the meeting with Gallois, who was waiting for them. He shook, hands most energetically with Travers, and it appeared that his English was much better than Travers's French. And he had—as Travers had once deduced—a humour of his own, and for the moment it consisted in a description of Travers's fluency as a poet. Travers promised him a copy of the Ode to the League of Nations—when it should be printed. Then the face of Gallois straightened. He took his seat behind the official desk, with Wharton at his right hand. Travers was given a seat in the next room, the door of which was ajar. A bell was pushed, and in a few moments young Hunt was shown in.

In his black he looked rather appealing, but there was no getting away from that receding chin. His voice, baritoned by the occasion, was no longer an irritable squeak. Travers felt sorry for him, and he wondered what he would do with that twenty thousand.

And then suddenly Travers pricked his ears. More than once before in his life he had startling experiences of the tenacity of

Wharton's memory, but nothing like what he now heard. When the story of the Paris express had been related, Wharton had been fascinated enough, but he had made no comments and taken no notes. It was after Gallois had spoken officially in rather formal English that Wharton chimed in. He had been sitting with his hand cupping his chin and moustache, not wishing apparently too much of his face to be seen.

"I suppose you yourself didn't catch any of those spots from which your uncle suffered?"

Young Hunt looked surprised. He hadn't a sign of a spot, he said.

"Not even a reddening of the skin—or an irritation?" asked Wharton.

"Oh no, sir," said Hunt.

"That's capital," said Wharton. "We feared it might be catching. But about the lotion your uncle had applied to him. Surely he took some internal medicine as well?"

"Oh yes, sir, he did," Hunt told him, and with no hesitation. "He took it last thing at night—I mean, I suppose he did. Brown probably gave it him the last thing, after he'd put on the lotion."

"You mean in the lavatory," said Wharton bluntly.

"Yes, sir; in the lavatory."

Wharton gave a quick glance at Gallois, then rose with his hand out.

"Well, Mr. Hunt, I'm sure we both wish you well. You've had a very trying time, but those things can't be helped. What do you think of doing with yourself now?"

Hunt looked relieved that everything was over. He licked his lips, it was true, but he was trying to smile.

"I might be going to stay with my uncle for a bit, sir."

"An excellent idea," said Wharton paternally. "Well, good-bye. Don't be ill on the crossing."

Out went Hunt, all smiles and gratification. In came Travers.

"Why that question about the spots, George?"

"Didn't you tell me he had rubbed himself that night when he came out of the lavatory?" countered Wharton.

"Yes, I did," said Travers slowly. "And what was the idea of the medicine?"

"That we'll go into in the train," Wharton told him. "Now we'll see the brother."

Charles Hunt was an elderly man, remarkably well preserved. He had an ugly growth of extremely short, grey beard; or else that torpedo-shaped beard had been too closely clipped. He was in the room a couple of minutes only. Gallois told him he was no longer needed, and offered official thanks. Wharton said the nephew had told them that he might be staying with him for a bit, and was informed that that was so. More hand-shaking, condolences and good wishes, and Charles Hunt went out. Travers, hardly able to contain himself, burst into the room almost before the door had closed.

"I say; stop him!" he said to Wharton. "He's that amazing old cuss I told you about; the one I barged into twice in the train. The one who was so anxious to know if the man in our compartment had smallpox!"

"Right!" said Wharton grimly. He gave a look at Gallois, and the bell was pushed. Travers retired, and in a minute Charles Hunt reappeared. Wharton, who had whispered to Gallois, did the talking.

"Sorry to trouble you again, Mr. Hunt, but there's a little matter we'd like cleared up. Where exactly were you when you heard of your late brother's death?"

Travers was too far off to catch the expression on Hunt's face, but he seemed to detect some apprehension in his voice.

"Why, I told you; I mean I told this gentleman here. I was at my house, at Tufnell Park."

Wharton smiled reassuringly, and he rounded on the unsuspecting Gallois. "I told you Mr. Hunt had said so—and I was right, as you see. But what we were wondering, Mr. Hunt, was if you were very surprised that your brother was in a train. You expected him to make the journey by road, in his car."

"I *was* surprised," Hunt said frankly. "What I imagined, gentlemen, was that his car had broken down."

Wharton leaned across the desk till his face, with its ironical smile, was not a yard from the startled Hunt.

"You are quite sure, Mr. Hunt? You weren't, for instance, on that train yourself?"

The indignant denial hesitated on Hunt's lips. Wharton's look was too much for him. He shuffled his feet.

Wharton's tone changed to the contemptuous. "We've given you considerable rope, Mr. Hunt. We've let you tell your story in your own way. Now we want the truth. Tell us why you were on that train, and why you had shaved off your beard and disguised yourself with yellow-tinted glasses. And the whole truth this time, please. Otherwise we shall have no compunction in putting you under lock and key."

Hunt shuffled again. "I didn't mean to deceive you, gentlemen. I didn't think it was important..." "Never mind about that side of the past," broke in Wharton. "And we're busy men. Get on with the story."

The gist of it was that Charles Hunt had long pitied his nephew—since he had clapped eyes on him, in fact, those two years before. He had tried to induce James to let the boy stay with him, but had had no answer to his letters. But ten days ago, Leslie had reached his twenty-first birthday. Charles Hunt had therefore determined—after talking the matter over with his wife—to go to St. Raphael and obtain a surreptitious interview with Leslie, and inform him that he was of age, and could exchange uncles at any time he liked. But the opportunity for the interview had not presented itself, in spite of the harmless and effective disguise which he—Charles Hunt—had adopted. He had, however, made himself known to Brown, under a pledge of strict secrecy. Brown, he said, had given him the information about the train journey, where he had still hoped for that interview with his nephew. And that, Charles Hunt said, was the honest truth and all of it—so help him God.

"I see," said Wharton. "But there's still a point or two to clear up. Why couldn't your nephew leave his uncle of his own free-will? Was he his legal guardian till he came of age?"

"He wasn't that exactly," said Hunt. "He had a hold over him. You might say he mesmerized him. And he used to keep telling him about the money and what he'd have. Also, I'm sorry to say that my nephew hadn't much courage. His spirit seemed to have been sucked out of him, sir, if you see what I mean."

"Quite!" said Wharton. "All the same, why couldn't you wait till your brother died? He was an older man than yourself. His health was none too good."

"That's where you're wrong, sir," put in Hunt quickly, "if you'll excuse my rudeness. My brother was a hypochondriac. Half his troubles were his own imagination, and brought on by silly worry. And what's more, sir, I happen to know that the doctor only sent him to France to get him out of the way; and he told him that he was good for another twenty years."

And there ended, more or less, the gospel according to Charles Hunt. Wharton twisted his tail good and proper.

"We've heard this latest story of yours," he said, "and what action may be taken against you will depend on your future conduct. Perjury's a dangerous thing, and people like yourself have got to be taught it. And supposing you are now allowed to return to England, you are proceeding straight to Tufnell Park?"

Hunt swore by all the gods that he was.

"There I should advise you to remain for a bit," said Wharton curtly. "You may be under police supervision from the very moment you leave this building—and you've brought it on yourself."

Travers sat on in the inner room, too busy recalling just what had happened with Charles Hunt in the Paris express. He saw, of course, much that was self-explanatory; the constant hanging about of the man in the neighbourhood of the connecting bridge of the two carriages, but what he still found difficult to dismiss from his mind was that matter of the spots. Deep in his mind was still the hunch that those spots had played some part in the murder of old Hunt, and if that were really so, then the questions of Charles in the train, and his mention of smallpox, might have had in them far more than had been intended to reach the ear.

The chauffeur was now in the outer room. He was the usual type, clean-shaven and in blue suit, and holding his peaked cap in his hand. Gallois informed him that he now had full permission to proceed to Calais with the car. Wharton took over.

"You were expecting to travel pretty fast in order to get to Calais by the time the express reached it, weren't you?"

The chauffeur grinned. "I certainly hadn't got to lose no time, sir. But they weren't coming straight through, sir. The boss was staying in Paris for a bit to give me time, and then coming on for the evening crossing."

From something in the General's tone, Travers guessed that that information had already been in Wharton's possession.

"I see," he began, but the chauffeur cut in ahead.

"Not only that, sir, I didn't follow the same road what they did. I had the *route nationale*, as they call it, and didn't go nowhere near the sea. I went right across country through Aix."

"Quite!" said Wharton. "And that brought you out at Avignon, without going anywhere near Toulon or Marseilles or Arles."

"That's right, sir." The chauffeur grinned again.

"And you got to Paris—when?"

"Just about two o'clock, sir. Might have been a bit after."

"And were you ever actually ahead of the train?"

"At Avignon I was, sir. Stand to reason, sir, with that short cut I told you of, and them stops they had." He looked inquiringly at Gallois. "I told this gentleman all about that."

Wharton smiled his thanks. The witness had been a good one. Then his face straightened.

"Between ourselves, you found the late Mr. Hunt a good master?"

The chauffeur shook his head at once. "No, that I didn't, sir. What's more, sir, I made up my mind I was giving in my notice as soon as I got back home. He used to speak to you like a pig, sometimes he did. He did to everybody, for the matter of that."

Wharton had been nodding away in approval and sympathy. "What people was he rude to?"

"Brown, sir, for one; as nice a fellow as you want to see. And the young boss, as he is now, sir—least, I'm taking my orders from him."

"Exactly," added Wharton. "You hadn't been with his uncle very long, had you?"

"Just over a month, sir," said the chauffeur, "and that was about thirty days too long."

The chauffeur departed, and Travers emerged. For some minutes he studied the photographs on the walls, while Gallois and Wharton wrote things down and conferred. Then Wharton looked at his watch and said there wouldn't be too much time unless he was lucky with the phone. Then Gallois disappeared, and Travers was left to himself for best part of half an hour. Wharton came back first. "Gallois won't be five minutes now," he said, and pulled out his pipe. "You're ready, I suppose."

"Heady enough," said Travers. "But what is it we're going to inquire into down there, George? Anything else besides the death of old Hunt?"

Wharton smiled enigmatically. "Why disparage the death of Hunt? Isn't one perfectly good murder enough?"

"I didn't mean it like that," Travers told him. "All I meant was that to inquire into the death of Hunt a few hundred kilometres from where it took place, wasn't quite expected—unless you're looking for motives."

"Motives!" said Wharton, and grunted. "We've got a carriage full of people with motives." His eyes twinkled. "What you're driving at is that you're far more interested in the death of your friend with the red face."

"And why not?" demanded Travers. "Aren't you interested in it yourself?"

Wharton waved a placatory hand. "To tell you the truth, I'm even more interested now I know what he died of, than I was when I only knew as much as you do."

"What he died of?" Travers stared. "And what did he die of?"

"He was poisoned," said Wharton. "Poisoned with atropine. And it was jabbed into his arm with a syringe."

CHAPTER IX
TRAVERS JOINS THE FOOLS

NO SOONER DID they mount the steps and enter the corridor of the train than Travers made a great discovery. And when Gallois led the way to a second-class on which a reserved ticket was prominently placed, he was not so surprised as he might have been. It seemed that the journey to St. Raphael was to take place under much the same conditions as the one from there to Paris. The carriage had mixed thirds and seconds, and the second-class which the three had to themselves occupied precisely the same relative position as the one in which Travers had travelled that tragic night. And for all he knew, the carriage was the identical one in which the murders had occurred.

But when Travers ventured to mention that fact to Wharton, the General assured him that the reconstruction of the crimes was not quite so perfect as that. Not that he was worrying about crimes at that moment; he was too busy stowing away his bag and donning a tweed cap in place of the felt hat. The seat he had chosen was the window corner, corresponding, in fact, to that which had been occupied by James Hunt. Travers had his old place just inside the door, and Gallois faced Wharton, as Leslie Hunt had faced his uncle.

The train moved off, and for some minutes the talk consisted of generalities. Wharton and Gallois slipped more and more into French, and Travers gradually retired from the conversation, and spent his time in watching the country-side—or so it seemed. His mind ran back to what Wharton had said about the death of Pierre Olivet, and again—but for the manner of the killing—he saw the solution with a plainness that threatened to make inquiry a fiasco. Who could have killed Olivet but Smith— the man who disappeared with his wife?

And then, as Travers began to fit round pegs in round holes, something went wrong. Smith, he assumed, had injected the drug as a soporific—but atropine, if he remembered rightly, was nothing of the sort. Smith, therefore, could not have administered the drug in the hope of putting Olivet to sleep and so facilitating an escape with luggage and wife. And there could surely be no sexual intrigue between Smith and Marie Olivet, who had looked almost old enough to be his mother. And as he thought of that, Travers grunted. He had been making little noises for some time, but now Wharton turned on him a quizzical look.

"Well, discovered the mystery?"

Travers started. "Mystery? Oh yes—I mean no." He smiled sheepishly. "Just thinking things over, you know. You'll laugh at me, but I can't for the life of me get far away from that bloke Smith."

Wharton looked down at his tobacco pouch, and he made a most peculiar face. What he ultimately said was so far from the point that Travers looked hard at him.

"Was it Mark Twain who remarked on the various kinds of fools, and said he'd been the whole lot and then some?"

"Can't say," smiled Travers. "But judging from my own experience, the statement was not as modest as it sounds."

"Yes," said Wharton in his best enigmatic manner, "I suppose you're right. I've been most of the kinds there are. I was one yesterday when you told me your experiences in that hell-wagon of yours."

"And how was that?" asked Travers guilelessly.

It was to Gallois that Wharton referred before he answered. "Have I your permission, my friend, to tell our colleague the history of the strange affair of Pierre Olivet?"

Gallois spread his hands to indicate that nothing would give him more pleasure than that Travers should be informed of anything which the Superintendent should deem necessary.

"*Alors*" said Wharton, with a shrug of his own, "I thank you, my dear Gallois, and I will inform the world why I was a fool." But world or no world, it was to Travers alone that he told the tale.

"The whole thing was very simple," he began. "The drug squad were acting in the Olivet affair in conjunction with the Sûreté Générale, much as the Special Branch at home acts in conjunction with us. Smith was a League of Nations man. It was the League who got wind of the way drugs were being taken across the Channel. Two suspicious persons were interrogated and a house was raided, and I believe a document of some sort was found..."

"A letter," broke in Gallois.

"A letter was found which alluded to someone known as the Cripple and also to an Englishman—the *Anglais*, as he was referred to and not given a name, though the Drug Squad thought they had run across him under the names of Corley and Cranbrook. Now the only cripple that had ever come under the notice of the customs authorities was a man with a club-foot, and when I say 'come under their notice' I simply mean they remembered him as a man who had made frequent crossings accompanied by his wife.

"Still, all that's comparatively irrelevant. It was ascertained that this particular cripple had bought a ticket for London and reserved the seats. Smith—we'll call him that—thereupon went from Marseilles to take the express at St. Raphael. It was a wild hope that the unknown Englishman would be on the train, and if he were he would certainly by some look or sign, show connection with the Olivets.

"Now Smith's peculiar part was to be an Englishman who had been at St. Raphael on holiday, because the Olivets were to be followed by him right to London. It was more important that we on our side should know who was in the traffic than that the Olivets should be arrested and searched on suspicion. Smith laid himself out therefore, as I said, to be an English tourist. He sunburned his face, and as he didn't know a thing about St. Raphael he learned it up from a guide-book in case there should be any questions asked.

"At Toulon, you entered the train—and you were an Englishman. Now you pride yourself on your utter lack of snobbishness. You talked to Smith and you behaved generally quite differently from what Smith had taken you to be—an Englishman of the frigid class. What should have been your virtues, proved your undoing."

Travers smiled. "Damn good, that!"

Gallois looked slightly puzzled. Wharton explained. Gallois nodded benevolently.

"In other words," went on Wharton, "Smith began to wonder. He put away surreptitiously the guide-book which might have aroused your suspicions, and at a suitable moment he chucked it out of the window into the darkness of a convenient tunnel. Later, when your well-known passion for the study of humanity had led you to fraternize with the Olivets, he was more than suspicious; he was almost sure—and he passed those suspicions on to our friend Gallois. And you even attempted to begin a conversation with him!

"To go back to Marseilles. Smith indicated the whereabouts of his compartment to Gallois on the platform and that enabled Gallois to be actually in the corridor before the arrival of the Olivets. He was so admirably disguised and with such a perfect minimum of effort—that you took him for a humble inhabitant of our dear Provence." Wharton bowed slightly to the obviously gratified inspector.

"Not only that," said Wharton. "In the meanwhile our friend Gallois had recognized in the woman, Olivet, a woman who under the name of Louise Battrigny had been convicted and sentenced four years previously for an offence that had to do with the White Slave Traffic. A highly dramatic stage was set. In the corridor our friend Gallois remained a comparatively unnoticed and not uncommon type of traveller. Inside the compartment Smith had to convince you and the Olivets that he was what he seemed to be, and he talked a lot about St. Raphael, and he took good care—as you yourself noticed—that the Olivets should hear it all.

"When night fell and that quarrel occurred, Gallois was frightened—and I don't wonder. He was frightened that something had happened before it should have happened, and when he peeped in that window and saw the face of Louise Battrigny, he says he thought for a moment the woman had gone mad and that she certainly was going to jab that pin in old Hunt's belly. But the quarrel died down—and if you will pardon my saying so, that was the one flaw in your otherwise marvellous observation. And, dare I say it—?"

"Don't be an old humbug, George," laughed Travers. "You know you're damn well going to say it—whatever it is."

Wharton's eyes twinkled. He knew Travers would take it like that. "Then I will say it. You gave yourself—your pacific efforts—the credit of calming down a lot of angry people. That was why you did not notice that the calm came a little too quickly. You see, it was to the interests of the Olivets—even considering the provocation—not to draw attention to themselves. Already they realized they had made a mistake, and I rather imagine they were a bit suspicious of old Hunt and circumstances generally. The carriage was not the friendly place it had been, and friendliness was essential. So, as I was saying, the Olivets composed themselves and prepared for sleep.

"There could be no more people entering that compartment because though two places ostensibly had not been taken, that had all been arranged, and the *chef de train* had had orders not to allow those two vacant seats to be taken by a passenger entering at a later station. When everybody appeared to be asleep, Smith passed out that rather too massive walking-stick. It was examined by our friend Gallois and found to be genuine. Smith would have liked to pass out the luggage but that was absolutely impossible. Later, Smith confirms that old Hunt gradually got in his sleep away from his corner and that Olivet got nearer the corner till the two rested on each other. Olivet moved back to his place and Hunt still leaned on him. Smith confirms that Olivet thereupon changed places, and it was as the train entered Dijon. But more of that later.

"We'll say simply that in the night Hunt was stabbed with a hatpin and Olivet was given an injection of the drug that killed him. The death of Hunt didn't matter to the Olivets because at the same time they were aware of it, there took place something much more important—the illness of Pierre Olivet and the natural acute anxiety of his supposed wife. Gallois soon entered the compartment while Smith waited outside. You took an interest in Olivet, and confirmed the suspicions against you. You followed him along the platform, and Gallois therefore followed you. Smith took over in the train and saw to the luggage and the supposed Madame Olivet. Madame later decamped and—through no fault of our friend Gallois here—took with her the club-boot in which undoubtedly the drugs had been concealed. I may say that it has been worked out, and calculated that at retail price the value of the cocaine that could have been concealed in that enormous boot was three thousand pounds; quite a paying proposition, even if there were no other hiding places.

"When Madame decamped, Smith, who had been going through her luggage and your own, went after her. He was inside that saloon car you saw. So far no trace of her has been picked up though it is almost a certainty that she is in Paris. That concludes the case of the two Olivets. It also explains—" and Wharton made a gesture of the most hypocritical humility, "—why I made myself a new kind of fool."

Travers laughed. "There's one place for you, George, and that's the stage—"

"Give me time," protested Wharton.

"Don't add complacency to hypocrisy," went on Travers. "You've been telling me under the guise of your little allegory, that I'm several kinds of a fool. You were misled by my enthusiasms—otherwise lord knows what might have happened."

Wharton nodded heavily. "Well, we've had our little joke and a joke's always a tonic. And now I'll say this. I don't know, outside the profession, two men who'd have observed so much or as accurately as you. If ever you go into the drug trade, we'll have our hands full; isn't that so, Gallois?"

Travers leaned across to the inspector. "I must congratulate you on the delightful way you pulled my leg on that journey. Amazing good work, if I may say so."

"Pulled my leg?" repeated Gallois, who knew that he ought to be pleased about something and hardly understood what. Wharton explained the slang. Gallois beamed at Travers. Travers offered his cigarette case and the compartment was on good terms with itself.

"To be very, very serious, George," said Travers suddenly, "I can't disguise from myself that I'm feeling the least bit depressed. Everything that I made fit in, seems out of place. Take those spots, for instance. There never seemed a more promising line of inquiry than the queer fact that two men had spots and both died suddenly."

"And why shouldn't it still be so?"

"Well—" Travers smiled deprecatingly "—if a man's stabbed to death and another's poisoned, why worry about spots? I mean you might just as well be anxious to know what their ideas were about stamp-collecting."

Wharton smiled with an irritating secretiveness. "There are going to be quite a lot of queer connections in this case before it's over—eh, Gallois? The spots may not be so unimportant as our friend thinks." He turned to Travers again.

"You worked with Norris over the April Fools Case?"

"That's right," smiled Travers.

"You know that Norris has provided himself with a perfectly good slogan of his own?"

Travers thought back. "Well, I wouldn't call it a slogan, but I know he's rather fond of pouring scorn on flimflams and flummery."

Wharton nodded. "Now you say you feel depressed." He spoke slowly for the benefit of Gallois who was following the conversation with strained interest. "You're inclined to think that what I've told you about the Olivets has what we might call spoiled the case."

"Not quite that," said Travers. "I do say that all the romance has gone out of it. The whole bottom's been kicked out of it."

Wharton grinned hugely at Gallois. "Romance. Ah, when we were young, my dear Gallois, you and I, how we loved that word romance."

Travers was amused. The old General was enjoying himself enormously and he had in Gallois an audience after his own heart.

"But as I see it," Wharton went on, "the discoveries of the French authorities and of our friend Gallois here in particular, put that romance into the case. As Norris would say, away with flimflams and flummery. We've got rid of the rubbish. We've got rid of embarrassments. We know that two men were killed in a certain compartment of a railway carriage. Six people were in that compartment. You, Mr. Travers, killed nobody. Mr. Smith killed nobody. Did those two dead men kill each other? If not, only two people remain to do the killing—Madame Olivet and Leslie Hunt. Madame Olivet daren't have killed anybody—considering what was in her so-called husband's boot, and considering her own precious record. Young Hunt looks as if he hasn't the guts to crack a flea. Nobody else entered the compartment since it was under the direct observation of Smith and yourself." Wharton waved his hand at his twin audience. "Isn't that a case for you? Isn't that what you'd call romance?"

Travers clapped his hands with gentle irony. "Bravo, George. That's the best show I've seen you put up."

"Good," said Wharton, and got to his feet. He addressed himself to Gallois. "Shall we make a beginning of those researches we propose to undertake?"

Gallois hopped up at once. "I will see a *sous-chef de train*. If he is stationed outside the door there, we shall not be interrupted by those who imagine a beneficent government is enlivening the journey with a circus."

"Got those notes of yours handy?" Wharton asked.

Travers produced them from his case. Under his directions that same suitcase was placed above where Olivet might be imagined to be sitting. Wharton did things with a newspaper and Travers had to smile somewhere inside when the General explained that it represented Hunt's white waistcoat. Then Gallois came back; the corridor curtains were drawn and the show commenced.

It was a show that had other incongruities than Wharton's waistcoat. All the time, for instance, Wharton and Gallois had notebooks and pencils in hand, and wrote even when they were supposed to be dead. There was Smith's statement that had to be consulted from time to time, and Travers who had to be referred to at every few moments, and yet in spite of incongruities, the proceedings had a certain solemnity that seized on Travers's mind till to have smiled would have seemed incredible.

"What's the time supposed to be?" Wharton asked.

"Ten forty-five," Travers told him.

Wharton settled to his corner and Travers placed him ready for sleep with the white waistcoat at the correct angle. Gallois came over and took the place occupied by Olivet.

"One thing we've got to imagine," said Travers, "and that's Madame Olivet's hat." He screwed up a newspaper and placed it on the rack where she had placed it that night—between herself and Leslie Hunt.

"And when did you go to sleep?" asked Wharton.

"I don't know," Travers confessed. "All I do know is that I woke up again at eleven thirty-five."

"Something happened during the time you were asleep," said Wharton. "You remember, Gallois? The suitcase."

Gallois got down the case from the rack and placed it on the seat at his left hand.

"Most important, that," said Wharton. "Smith saw him do it, and it gave him the idea that Olivet was anxious about what was in it. As it turned out, all he used the suitcase for was an arm rest. It makes all the difference."

"Very comfortable," agreed Gallois. "And what happened next, M'sieur Travers?"

"First the walking-stick was passed out," said Travers. "I work that out as having taken ten minutes—I mean till it was back on the rack again. Then young Hunt went out to the lavatory and I went out too. I reckon it was a quarter of an hour before I got back here again. That makes it approximately midnight. I should guess it was another ten good minutes before I went off to sleep again."

Wharton indicated Gallois. "Our relative positions were unaltered?"

"As far as I can remember, yes. If that white waistcoat had moved I'd have noticed it." He looked at his notes. "When I woke again at one twenty-five, I ought to say I was very drowsy."

"And what happened?"

"Mind if I come over?" Travers said. "I'll show you by placing you. You've got to move out of your corner and M'sieur Gallois has to lean towards you so that you roll against each other." He supervised the positions.

"Wait a moment," said Wharton. "How on earth should a man leave a perfectly good corner and lean over here? It's exchanging comfort for damn discomfort."

"The spots made him restless," suggested Travers.

"Maybe," said Wharton. "Much more likely it was unnatural sleep brought on by some dope put in his final tot of medicine."

Travers frowned. "Aren't you getting on rather a long way ahead? Doping the medicine's a new one on me."

"Purely a surmise on my part," said Wharton airily. He got back to the discomfort of leaning against Gallois.

"Now," said Travers, "don't forget that Hunt was sleeping with his heels tucked under the seat." Wharton drew his heels in. "And now you move slightly forward, M'sieur Gallois, so that both of you are leaning on the suitcase; you in the front and Wharton behind. Now, George, you take the strain and lean back too. M'sieur Gallois, you go forward and abandon your case altogether. Now get up quietly and get into the corner. That's right, but what about doing it all over again?"

It was done again. Gallois settled into the corner and Wharton slept with his right arm over the suitcase. Gallois snored gently and wrote something in his notebook.

"Splendid!" said Travers. "Now we go on to one thirty-eight. That's when Olivet suddenly woke up and felt too much of a draught and closed the window."

Wharton sat up and watched the closing of the window and Gallois settling himself again to sleep. The General shook his head.

"It isn't right. Or rather it is right." He explained himself. "If there was one thing that would have woken up Hunt it was the closing of that window. You said it went up with a click and yet he didn't hear it."

"You mean you think even more strongly that his last dose of medicine was drugged?" Travers asked bluntly.

Wharton suddenly dried up again. "We'll know more when we're in the train on the way back. And what happened next?"

"The next thing strikes me as the most important of the lot," said Travers. "I woke up again at two fifteen and I can't say for certain that things were as I saw them. All the same I'd be prepared to swear that Hunt and Olivet had changed places again. But before we deal with that, may I say that while you're where you are now was the best time for Madame Olivet to stick in the hatpin—if she did it. I suggest that a pin from up there got loose from the hat and fell to the seat. When she woke up, her hand closed on it." He frowned. "It's a pity the exact time of Hunt's death couldn't have been accurately determined. Did he die at once?"

"As soon as the pin entered the heart," said Wharton. "And it was a frontal thrust. It didn't penetrate sideways. But if you say that Hunt and Olivet changed places again, how could Hunt have been dead?"

"It might have been the dead body that fell—so!" Gallois drew Wharton towards him. "Then that woke me, and I got up angrily, like this, and you fell."

"But I fall along the seat," objected Wharton.

"And I push you to the corner because you are still an obstacle," said Gallois, and tried to do it. Wharton took some moving. Travers admitted that the noise ought to have awakened him. Perhaps, after all, Hunt was alive at two-fifteen.

"What do Smith's notes say?" he asked.

"Smith hasn't any from then on," said Wharton. "It was his turn for sleep, and Gallois here kept watch outside."

"Good lord!" said Travers. "So we both went to sleep. I didn't wake till gone half-past five, and anything might have happened." A look of relief went over his face. "But there couldn't have been any noise, or I'd have woken up."

"As you say," was Wharton's ironic comment. "Anything might have happened. Two men might have been killed, for instance."

Gallois spread his hands. "But Smith, he woke up earlier than M'sieur Travers." He grabbed the notes, and found the entry. "He woke at four and saw nothing. He heard the breath of Olivet."

"Exactly," said Wharton. "Olivet had already been drugged, and was feeling the effects of the atropine. The first sign is restricted breathing. That gets worse and worse, and the speed depends on the dose. Some hours after, the eyes bulge and there's delirium. If that gives place to coma, the patient may or may not recover. If a second delirium arrives it's all right; if the coma persists then it's all wrong. The face is more violently flushed, and is often spotted with a red rash. The patient sinks, and dies from breathing failure."

"Spots," said Travers. "Funny, isn't it, how we always get back to them?" He shook his head, and left it for the moment at that. "But about the death of Olivet, George. Which arm was he punctured in?"

"The left," Wharton told him. "The forearm it was."

Travers frowned. "That ought to be easy enough. I mean, it couldn't have been a person entering from the corridor who did it. He'd have punctured the handier arm—the right one." He frowned again. "Any of the other three might have done it—and yet they didn't."

Gallois cut in. "The Battrigny woman would not do it. Besides, consider how surprised she was and how helpless when she saw him ill."

"Young Hunt wouldn't have done it," said Wharton, "even if he had a syringe on him, and that's preposterous. Old Hunt was different. If he was a hypochondriac he might have had a battery of medical gadgets on him. All the same, I'm plumb sure he wouldn't have murdered Olivet. And, if you ask me, there'll be the devil of a lot of deep digging before we find out who did."

"About that injection," said Travers. "Would anybody feel the needle when asleep?"

"Depends on the sleep, I'd say," answered Wharton, reaching for his case. He showed what he had in his hand. "Still, we can try it. This little chap will soon prove that."

Travers took the small syringe and tried the plunger, and he winced at the sight of the wicked-looking needle. "How're you going to try it, George?" he asked.

Wharton explained. "Why not draw for it? The one who wins tests it on the other two some time to-night when we're asleep."

Travers suddenly smiled. "Isn't worth the trouble, George. You've placed me in the noble company of fools. Let me put myself in the glorious army of martyrs. Try it on me tonight—only for the love of heaven be sure I'm asleep."

"I'll make sure of that right enough," Wharton assured him. He put the syringe back in its box, and then included both Gallois and Travers in his gesture. "And now we will let the case rest till the morning. By then perhaps something else will have solved itself."

"The night brings counsel," added Gallois in French.

Travers smiled dryly. "It's going to bring me more than that." And in sudden alarm. "You've got something to sterilize the needle, George?"

"We'll find something," said Wharton, "if it's only a perfectly good flame of a match. And we'll choose a soft part."

But when Travers woke up just before five in the morning and stared straight into the eyes of Wharton, he knew the experiment had been a success from the General's point of view. Moreover, Wharton had been a generous experimenter at Travers's expense. Not only had he tried a soft spot—the thigh—but the rigid muscle of the left forearm as well, while its owner supported himself on it in sleep. And though Gallois had also been asleep and unable, therefore, to confirm the experiments, Travers knew from the slight itchings left by the penetration of the needle that Wharton had pierced with a sure hand.

CHAPTER X
WHARTON IS ABSENT-MINDED

IT WAS A GREAT journey and a great experience. Travers knew he ought to be grateful, and indeed he was; not only for the always exhilarating company of George Wharton, but for the rarer privilege of working with a latter-day Lecoq in the person of Inspector Gallois. And yet his satisfaction was always being chastened with doubts. Wharton and Gallois had all the known facts in their possession, and though there might be nothing churlish in their apparent assumption that he knew them too, his small gratification was not enough compensation for the ignorance he was feeling. And after breakfast, while Wharton and Gallois were chatting amiably together, Travers wrote down the salient matters about which he would like a little more information. He was so engrossed in his writing that the joke was almost over before he recognized that it was to himself that the two were referring.

"Our friend continues the composition of his ode," said Gallois, nodding across at Travers. "The League of Nations is a formidable subject."

"It is the fresh air of the morning," said Wharton. "To vulgarians like us it gives appetite; to the poet—inspiration."

Travers saw them laughing, and gathered the purport.

"Speaking as one fool to another," he said to Wharton, "I wonder if I might raise a point or two?"

"Why not?" said Wharton, and winked at Gallois as if loath to leave the joke.

"Well, then, that chauffeur business. I can't get the hang of it. I understand he gave a lot of information to the inspector here, but why did you question him about the journey, and ask when he was ahead of the train?"

"Why?" repeated Wharton with the most innocent air in the world. "Well, principally to hear him talk and be able to sum him up better. I admit I was interested in his alibi."

"And had he got one?"

"Unless he bribed his passenger pretty heavily, he had."

"His passenger!" Travers stared. "That's a new one on me."

"The passenger was the chef's brother—"

"Hold on a moment," cut in Travers with humorous exasperation. "I wish to blazes, George, you wouldn't keep producing new people like rabbits out of the hat. Who's this chef?"

"The chef worked at the villa," Wharton told him. "Our friend Gallois will tell me if I make a mistake, but I gathered that the chef, and a woman to do some housework, were supplied with the villa, as was a gardener. The chef's brother was also a chauffeur in the town and temporarily out of a job, and he was a pal of Ellman—Hunt's chauffeur—and when he knew that Ellman was going to Calais by road, he asked him if he might go as far as Paris with him to save the fare."

"He proposed to stay there for some days to search for work," added Gallois.

"That's right," went on Wharton. "Old Hunt was told nothing about it. Ellman and his pal took turns at the wheel, and their stories have been checked one against the other." Wharton smiled suggestively. "From the way you were consulting that guide-book, I take it you were working out the speeds."

"Right first time," said Travers. "And as I work it out, Ellman got to Avignon by about six. We left at about seven, so he had an hour's start of us. In other words he might have been on the station at Lyons, which was our next stop—or even at Dijon."

"Well, you're not far wrong," said Wharton. "They got to Avignon at ten past six, and pulled up half an hour for a meal, so they actually left again twenty minutes or so before you did. Ellman's pal drove the stage to Lyons, and then Ellman took over. They admit they went hell-for-leather and were still ahead of the train. But the trouble begins after Lyons. Ellman's pal swears he slept like a log till they were going through Dijon, and even then he didn't know what time it was. Ellman says he doesn't know either, only he was going at the devil of a lick because he wanted to get to Paris early to spend a few minutes with a little girl his pal had told him about."

"I see." Travers nodded. "What it amounts to is that Ellman has no alibi."

"Well"—the General pursed his lips—"that's just what it does amount to. All the same, assuming the *route nationale* passes right by the station at Dijon, and assuming that Ellman might easily have been on that station when your train was there, how in the name of sanity could he have got inside your compartment and killed a man—or two men?"

Travers smiled. "Lord knows. Still perhaps the answer's something else you've got saved up for the return journey. And any point in asking how you found out all about Ellman's pal?"

"Gallois here went straight down to St. Raphael on the Monday night," said Wharton. "He saw the chef, made certain inquiries and instituted others, such as checking up on Ellman's meal at Avignon. The chef gave his brother's Paris address. The rest was easy. And anything else you'd like to know?"

"About Hunt's wound this time," Travers told him. "Why didn't I see a blood-stain on his waistcoat?"

"There wasn't any blood," said Wharton. "Death was instantaneous—from shock, if you like—and however quickly the pin was withdrawn, there couldn't have been any bleeding."

Travers nodded. "And in much the same context, why didn't the stomach content settle what you're anxious to find out—I mean whether his last dose of medicine was drugged?"

Wharton made a face. "Unless there's an exhumation his stomach content won't be known. The doctors determined the cause of death as from a long, extremely fine, circular instrument with a sharp point. Young Hunt and Smith had mentioned the quarrel, and a hat-pin was deduced and it fits the case. But there was no point in an examination of stomach content for that."

"I see," said Travers. "And about the death of Olivet. Why the choice of atropine? I mean, is there any connection as there seemed to be over the spots? Olivet was almost certainly carrying cocaine. Is there any connection between that and atropine?"

Wharton seemed struck by the idea. He thought for a moment. "I wonder now. Atropine's the same family, so to speak. It affects the same part of the brain. It causes the same bulging of the eyes—though much more than cocaine, of course. And what was the exact inference?"

"There wasn't one," said Travers frankly. "If atropine's smuggled—as cocaine is—then Olivet might have been carrying it. He might be a drug fiend himself. He might have doped himself with it and given himself an overdose."

"He was a drug fiend right enough," said Wharton. "But the drug he carried was in powder form, and I've never heard of addicts taking atropine—have you, Gallois?"

Gallois said it was outside his experience. Wharton pontifically agreed) and he added that no syringe was found on him, unless of course, the woman took it.

"That settles that then," said Travers. "Now something else. I admit the practical impossibility of anybody entering the carriage without Smith or myself knowing it—let alone M. Gallois— but what I'm getting at is this. Could any of Olivet's enemies or rivals have got at him and given atropine, knowing it might have been mistaken for cocaine?"

"Far-fetched, even if you omit the difficulty you raised yourself—that of entry," said Wharton bluntly. "Also the essential differences between the two drugs were such that no doctor would have been deceived, and any enemy of Olivet would merely have killed him, without giving a damn how."

"I take your word for it," said Travers, "and I'm sorry to be such a nuisance—"

"Not at all, my dear fellow," Wharton assured him with a large gesture of disagreement. "And you were going to add?"

"I was going to ask if atropine was easily get-at-able."

Wharton pursed his lips. "I think so. It's belladonna, you know. You could scrape it off the usual plaster. Also it's used for eye-drops."

Travers nodded again. "Then that's the lot, I think. Except"— and he spoke directly to Gallois—"that I was wondering if it would be the intention of the French authorities—when they ultimately catch the Olivet woman—to give some sort of amnesty over the drug offence on condition that she tells what she saw in the train. She mightn't have seen much, but it might make all the difference."

Gallois shrugged his shoulders. "If she was asked about the death of Hunt she could tell nothing. If we told her he was killed with a hat-pin she would suspect a trap—and she would lie. We do not wish to tell that."

Travers was surprised. "But doesn't everybody know how Hunt was killed?"

"Nobody knows," said Wharton. "Young Hunt doesn't know. We let them think what they liked in the hope they'd let something out, but all they do know is that he died suddenly, and there had to be a stringent inquiry. Secrecy is half the battle in a case like this."

"How do you say it?" added Gallois, and grinned. "Forewarned is forearmed?"

"Precisely," said Wharton, with a commendatory clap on the knee. "So you see the Olivet woman won't be much good to us, unless she volunteers a statement. As for the man supposed to be her husband, it's far more important that the police should get information about the drug business than find out who killed the man—unless it's all the same thing."

"There is only one pity in the death of Olivet," said Gallois, and it was very earnestly that he spoke to Travers. "If he had remained alive he would have told us many things. Now he is dead he is useless. He is a carcass. Men such as him are better dead. A murderer kills one man, but these men—these Olivets—kill many men. For the information, it is a pity he is not alive, but now he *is* dead?"—and he shrugged his shoulders.

"I'm with you there every time," Wharton told him. "If it weren't for the information they indirectly give you, such men ought to be killed on sight. And if anybody did kill him as a kind of punishment, what I say is he ought to be rewarded."

"All the same, murder is murder, and nobody knows it better than you," said Travers. "And just as a very last suggestion, I suppose you've decided that it's impossible to search a few hundred kilometres of permanent way for a syringe, even though we could determine from where it was found just when the murder was probably committed."

"It's being done," said Wharton, "though it's hopeless, as you say. If anybody threw away a syringe, it'd have been thrown a pretty long way."

"And that book young Hunt tore up? We do know almost to a mile where that ought to be."

"That, too, has been arranged for," said Wharton, and Travers suddenly blushed, remembering that yellow-backed guide-book which had been hurled so mysteriously into a tunnel—the book which formed a curious pair with the thriller of Leslie Hunt. Wharton's eyes twinkled as he obviously remembered that, too, but all he did was to fish for his pipe. "And now what about assigning our various jobs for when we get to St. Raphael?"

The compartment forthwith went into conference and by the time the train drew in it was all mapped out. Travers fixed up rooms for the night and the other two went off to interview the local police. It was well on the way towards lunch when Wharton turned up at the hotel. Gallois was already at the Villa Marguerite, he said, and on what he learned might depend what they had to find out themselves.

"All the same, we might just as well go along and see this chemist," he ended. "Not very far, so they tell me."

"What are you hoping to learn?" Travers asked him as they set off.

"Well, we've got the analysis of what was left of the lotion, and we might see if that was tampered with. And we've what was left of the medicine too. That shouldn't have been tampered with because Hunt kept it himself in a flat pocket flask."

"Funny thing to do, wasn't it?" remarked Travers. "The man keeps the lotion and Hunt keeps his own medicine."

"I don't know," said Wharton, and he said it so warily that Travers had an idea that he was thinking of something else. "After all a man knows when to take his medicine but he doesn't know when he's likely to itch sufficiently to be lotioned. Also you can take medicine in public whereas you can't very well strip in public."

They passed the shop before entering and Wharton ran his eye over it. In the window was an announcement that English was spoken. And when they entered, it turned out to be the proprietor himself who spoke English. He told them that he had spent two years in London. Wharton produced his French credentials and recalled the visit of an English valet to purchase some lotion. The proprietor remembered at once. He also knew the master. Wharton was plainly surprised.

"Yes," he was told, "he came often into the shop here. I knew soon that he was what we call an imaginary invalid." He smiled. "It was not for me, of course, to tell him that."

"Of course you wouldn't," said Wharton. "People like him are good for trade. And what were his special ailments?"

The proprietor shrugged his shoulders. "He had many ailments, m'sieur. It would be a pain here and a pain there—and all nothing. In England he told me he suffered with the throat. The doctor made him sleep with the window open. Now he is almost cured of that. He is a man who likes to be ill and, when his throat is better, he must imagine he is ill in some other part of his body."

Wharton nodded. "Well, he won't have any more delusions of that nature." He gave the startled shopkeeper the reasons and the atmosphere immediately became congenial for inquiry.

First of all came the lotion. Brown had come for it the first thing on the Friday morning. The chemist had suggested an ointment, but Brown had preferred a lotion. He had also suggested calamine and sugar of lead, which was what the chemist would have given him even if he had not suggested it. Wharton showed Travers the analysis of the lotion that had been left in Brown's bottle. It was the same.

But when it came to the medicine, things were a little more complicated. Brown had apparently been suspicious of French pharmaceutics and there had been quite an argument about its composition. Moreover, as Brown had said, he knew his master and his symptoms and vagaries, and the chemist did not. But when the final composition of the medicine had been settled, both Brown and the chemist had agreed that it should do the patient good. It had consisted of merely soda and magnesia and tincture of rhubarb, with a little chloroform water—up to eight ounces.

"I know that prescription," nodded Wharton. "It's the usual one. Three times a day, after meals."

Again he showed Travers the analysis of what had remained in the flask. Everything seemed correct. And before resuming his inquiry with the chemist, Wharton asked a strange question.

"Notice anything peculiar about all this?"

Travers shook his head. "Can't say I do."

Wharton gave a little shrug. "Then it may be my imagination." He turned to the chemist. "And that was all, m'sieur? There was no request for a sleeping draught?"

He received a perfectly amazing stare. "But how did you know that, m'sieur?"

Wharton chuckled. He said there were ways and means of finding most things out. Then his face straightened. When was it that Brown asked for the sleeping draught? And had his manner been secretive?

The chemist gave a look even more astonished than the last one. "But it was not that Mr. Brown who ask for the sleeping draught. It was the other one—the master."

"The master!" echoed Wharton, and appealed dumbly to Travers. The chemist explained.

Brown, as he had said, had come into the shop at about ten o'clock on the Friday morning. At about noon, who should come in but old Hunt. He seemed anxious to know if the lotion and the medicine were all right and he exhibited the incipient spots which he said were due to something he had eaten. He had had an attack of the same kind before. Pajou—the chemist—knew Hunt for the hypochondriac that he was, and he saw nothing unusual in the questions or the spots, and he thereupon said what was the nature of both lotion and medicine.

And then Hunt said that the last time he had had a similar attack, the spots had troubled him considerably at night and might he have a soporific. Pajou suggested powders, but Hunt said he preferred something soluble in the medicine and he would take the soporific in the last dose of medicine before going to sleep. Pajou had therefore given him three doses, which Hunt had said would be enough till he got back to England and saw his own doctor. The total—to be divided into three doses—was only thirty grains of chloral in solution.

"And suppose he took the lot?" asked Wharton.

"That would be no harm," said Pajou. "Chloral is not safe in large amounts. Sixty grains is a large amount, but thirty is not large. The ten grains which he was to take were small."

"But it would make him sleep?"

"But certainly it would make him sleep!" said Pajou with an emphasis that assured Wharton that he knew his own job.

That virtually ended the inquiry. When Wharton left the shop he walked the first few yards in the direction of the hotel like a man in a dream. Then he gave a series of nods as if his mind were quite made up.

"What do you make of it all?" he asked Travers.

"I think Hunt was a silly old fool," said Travers promptly. "Hypochondriacs, I imagine, always are. But the chemist's statement fits in all right."

"How?"

"Well, there wasn't any bottle of chloral found on Hunt for one thing. He took the two doses and one was left for that last night in the train. After he'd taken that last dose—which was in the lavatory where Brown had dressed his spots—he threw the bottle out of the window. Brown should confirm that."

"I suppose that'd be it," said Wharton, and again his thoughts seemed to be miles away.

Nothing more was said till during lunch. Gallois had not come in, but Wharton had expected his inquiries to be protracted in any case. And when the question was put to him, Travers could see that Wharton was considerably troubled in his mind.

"I'd like to mention a possible theory," the General said, and he laid down knife and fork and leaned forward across the table. "Am I right in deducing that Hunt was suspicious of Brown? Did Hunt really think his valet might poison him?"

Through Travers's mind there ran like lightning what Pajou that morning had mentioned and implied. And his mind flashed back to something else.

"Do you know, George," he said, "I think you're right. Hunt knew the lotion must be all right and he let Brown take charge of it. But he hung on to the medicine himself. And there's more to it than that. Do you remember that extraordinary scene in the train? How old Hunt sneered at Brown, and how he didn't do his sneering direct but sneered at him through Smith and myself?"

Wharton nodded frowningly. "Tell me again."

"It was diabolical," went on Travers. "He peeped round to us two and you know there was a double meaning in every word he said. It was meant to lacerate and all the while he was pretending it was a joke. He asked Brown—all the time talking to us—if the lotion weren't poison. He said it was dangerous to poison people. Poisoners got landed in jail and were hanged by the neck."

"And how did Brown stand it?"

"As far as I could judge, he didn't move a muscle. That made me think he'd been used to such scenes before. Even Smith said that if he'd been Brown he'd have hit the old swine across the mouth."

Wharton nodded heavily. "As soon as I know one or two things, we're going back home. That's where most of the truth of this case lies. The trouble is that we'll have to go so damnably careful."

Travers agreed. He knew the rulings on the obtaining of evidence only too well. If Brown—or any other suspect for that matter—cared to shut his mouth with a snap, it was more than the police dared do to prise it open. Wharton picked up knife and fork again but the enjoyment seemed to have departed from his meal. He was still gloomy and uncommunicative as they sat under the trees with their coffee, and Travers was glad when he caught sight of Gallois coming jauntily along the pavement and up the hotel steps. The inspector cast a quick look round and when he noticed them, came over at once. Travers had a chair drawn ready. Gallois sat down with an air of mystery.

"Well, my friend," he said to Wharton, "I have discovered what made the spots which give us all this trouble."

He waited complacently for Wharton's question.

"And what caused the spots? Some strawberries that the foolish Mr. Hunt insisted he would eat."

"Strawberries!" said Wharton. "You mean wild strawberries? The little ones as big as that?"

Gallois shook his head. "It was your English strawberries. Large ones like that. Strawberries of the garden—not of the woods."

Wharton clicked his tongue. "Now, why the devil didn't I think of that?"

CHAPTER XI
THE COAST IS CLEAR

WHARTON TONED DOWN the extraordinary in the statement by an explanation. There were a lot of people who couldn't eat strawberries, he said, and he himself was one of them. The twice or thrice he'd tried of recent years he had forthwith been covered with an annoying rash. But he was anxious to know just how Gallois obtained the information.

That had been easy. Gallois had seen the chef and talked a lot about the mysterious something that had disagreed with Mr. Hunt, and the chef could attribute it to nothing else but the strawberries. And a piece of corroborative evidence was added. Brown had purchased the strawberries and even before they were put on the lunch table he had confided in the chef that the master oughtn't to eat them. He had had a rash once before after eating strawberries, said Brown. But Hunt had eaten and what had happened was his own fault since Brown had taken the liberty of cautioning him—at least that is what Brown told the chef. A good few of the strawberries came back from the lunch table, however, and both the chef and Brown had eaten them with no ill consequences.

The rest of what Gallois had picked up was less important. Old Hunt had passed his time in expeditions up the mountains in the car and there he had chipped rocks and explored and enjoyed himself highly. Leslie always accompanied him. Of an afternoon, however, the house took its siesta, and often of an early evening Hunt and his nephew went down the few yards to the sea and sat under a gaudy umbrella watching the world at play. Dinner was always at seven and. as far as Gallois had been able to ascertain, young Leslie had never gone out after that. The story of Charles Hunt that he had been unable to get an interview with his nephew, seemed therefore to be confirmed.

Gallois went off to his meal and the other two lingered on in the shade. It was a day of intense heat. The sun shone out of a sky of lead, and Travers was not at all hurt in his feelings when the General suggested that the shade was a good place that afternoon and it was a pity that he himself had to go out into the sun to have another word with M. Pajou. Of what that word was he gave no hint and it was an hour later before he returned. Then he went in search of Gallois and when the two came back the inspector announced that he had to go to Marseilles at once and confer with Smith about the Olivet affair. He was proposing to take the four o'clock. If Wharton took the eight o'clock night express, he would rejoin him and Travers at Marseilles. And if Mr. Travers would accompany him to the station he would arrange special reservations for the journey.

Wharton said that would suit him admirably. He had to get a message through to London and he would also like a word with that chef, who hadn't better be disturbed at his siesta. But Wharton must have spent a lot of time at something for Travers saw no more of him till dinner and the case was not referred to till they had taken their seats in the train. Again they had a second-class to themselves, though there were no thirds in the carriage and the position of their own compartment was different from that of the one in which they had travelled down.

"What's your opinion of Brown?" Wharton asked when the train was on the move and they had got their pipes going.

"Don't know," said Travers. "In some ways he's got me beat."

"I know," said Wharton. "If you'd put me the same question, I'd have given the same answer. But tell me this. Why did old Hunt need a valet?"

"Don't know," said Travers again. "But a lot of people have men servants in preference to women. It's become quite a habit."

"You're thinking of men parlour-maids and such-like," retorted Wharton. "Brown spoke of himself as a gentleman's servant and that's what he was pure and simple. Old Hunt might have had money, but all the same I don't see why he launched out into that excrescence of snobbery—the valet. Hunt was middle-class, whatever his education."

"There's something in that," agreed Travers. "But what beats me is why Brown stood the old man's insults. He ought to have told him to go to hell and risked not getting a reference. And when Brown himself says he stuck it out because he couldn't bear to leave that weak-chinned Leslie, then frankly I don't believe him."

Wharton nodded. "And there's the other side of the picture. If old Hunt was suspicious of Brown, why didn't he give him the sack? How long'd Brown been with him?"

"Ten years," said Travers.

"He stuck those insults for ten years," commented Wharton. "It's fishy to say the least of it. Had he some hold over the old man, or what?" He shook his head in answer to his own question. "And as far as I'm concerned, Brown's too impeccable. He stands up to insult without moving a muscle. He plots with Charles to get Leslie into a better home. He didn't put dope into the old man's medicine. Hunt did that for himself and what I ought to feel is ashamed of suspecting the immaculate Brown of ever having done such a thing." He shook his head again. "Brown's only made one mistake, and I'm damned if I'm not half afraid to think even that."

"You mean the lie he told about Hunt being ill at St. Raphael?"

"That's it," said Wharton. "Hunt was never better in his life than he was down there. Then, of course, there's the business of the robbery at Peddleby. Nothing can be charged against Brown, but he comes into the limelight."

"Don't you think there may be something important in that suggestion of yours about the unholy alliance between Brown and Charles?" suggested Travers. "If there's hanky-panky afoot two heads are better than one, and an accomplice can always swear to an alibi."

"I know," nodded Wharton. "I've had that in my mind." He frowned in thought for a minute or two, then suddenly turned. "Let's think it out. I'm old Hunt here and you're the nephew. Smith's wide awake in that corner, though he too may have napped. You're opposite and there are the two Olivets in between. Could Charles Hunt or Brown have entered the compartment?"

"I say it's utterly impossible," said Travers. "The risk would have been enormous. Whoever entered wasn't to know that we were all asleep."

"Brown wouldn't have worried about that," said Wharton. "If challenged he'd have had an excuse. Still, I'm disposed to agree. And that puts us up a gum-tree. Not only did someone in the compartment kill Hunt but someone in the compartment also killed Olivet."

Travers nodded. "Whereabouts in the forearm was Olivet's puncture?"

"Here," said Wharton, "in the bottom of the forearm, at the side."

And then Travers hooked off his glasses. Wharton watched the meticulous polishing, knowing that something was coming; and when it came he was incredibly startled.

"I know when Olivet was killed and I know how."

Wharton stared and said nothing. Travers hooked the glasses on again.

"Let me prove it, George," Travers went on. "Olivet was alive all right at the time when the train was entering Dijon station. You'll say that doesn't matter a damn because he was alive hours later. My point is this, however. At that moment I saw him change seats with Hunt. He sat in the corner where you are now. Get up a moment, will you, and I'll illustrate. Here's how he sat, with the window still open, remember. His elbow was on this rest, and the elbow held down the blind and kept it from flapping. *But*, Olivet was only in that exact position for a few minutes. He fell asleep at once, and by the time the train had left the station he had woken up again and shut the window. I suggest that Olivet had that dose of dope jerked into him by someone outside the carriage, and it could only have been while the train stood still in Dijon station, and the position of the puncture proves it."

"By God, you're right!" said Wharton, still staring. "And if that is so, then Olivet shouldn't have been poisoned at all. *It was Hunt who should have been poisoned!*"

"Exactly," said Travers. "Nobody knew of the change of seats, but quite a lot of people knew where Hunt was presumably sitting. The information was common property to the whole train, so to speak. The murderer tried to kill Hunt, but got Olivet instead."

Wharton's face was a mixture of frowns and quiverings. He was egg-bound with ideas and implications.

"But think of the risk," he suddenly burst out. "What you're supposing is that—" He broke off. "Let's get this thing straight. Two kinds of person might have done what you suggest. The first is a person who was not on the train, but laid in wait for Hunt at Dijon."

"That's right," agreed Travers. "The chauffeur, for instance. The man who hasn't an alibi."

"The other class is a person on the train," went on Wharton. "And there I repeat—think of the risk. Say it was Charles or Brown. He had to get out on the platform, duck under the carriage buffers and make his way to the blind side of the line, and then climb up on the step and give an injection. I ask you, is it feasible? And then he had to get down and back to his compartment again without being seen."

"Those railway stations are dark as hell at night," said Travers. "Also, if Brown and Charles Hunt were in alliance, then one could have kept *cave* while the other did the trick; or he could have attracted attention away from the one who was doing the actual injection."

Wharton grunted. "This is a bit too much for me to take in a gulp. I think I'll let it digest for a bit if you don't mind. And when Gallois gets in we'll put the whole thing up to him."

He got down his case and began writing notes and worrying the bone for the marrow which Travers had suggested was in it. Travers had plenty to think of, too. That brainwave had come only at the moment when Wharton had told him the exact position of the puncture mark of the syringe, but however conceived on the spur of the moment, he knew in his heart of hearts that the theory was a sound one. Try as he might, he could find no flaw in it. And then he thought of something else.

"Sorry to disturb you, George," he said, "but wouldn't it be rather a stroke of luck if we happened to be right? I mean, there'd be more flummery got rid of. Olivet could go to blazes. For motives and everything else we'd have merely to concentrate on Hunt."

"Precisely what I was thinking," said Wharton, and went on writing.

Travers resumed his thinking. The train was now approaching the sea again at the end of its long inland sweep, and in a few minutes they would be at Toulon. The sky was clouding for dusk, and his mind turned back to the darkness of that night when he had been in a compartment with two men who would shortly be dead. He tried to recapture something of the atmosphere; something of the dark secretiveness of the gloomy station; something of the slow-breathing quiet of a whole train with its freight of sleeping souls, from among whom certain living and moving souls sorted out themselves and stepped gently into corridors and down to the platform of a station that seemed to have roused itself only for the resented coming of the train and would resume its own sleep when that train had gone.

Travers closed his eyes to make the illusion more real. Now he became more aware of the clickety-click from the rail-joints as his own train tore relentlessly through the night. And now he imagined the first grind of the brakes. There would be the rattling over the first points and perhaps a long whistle from the engine. The train would slow; it would crawl. With those passengers who now bestirred themselves and moved out luggage ready for the descent would be two men whose compartments were strangely handy for the door—one in the third-class of one carriage and the other in a second-class of the next. Each man had only a yard or two to go, and—more important—each had only a yard or two to return.

Travers's eyes were tightly closed. He saw the two get down to the platform and stand motionless for a moment. The station was in darkness. Small groups could here and there be seen emerging from the train. Some would pass the two men, and all would be swallowed up ultimately in the gloom. At one far end of the train a porter or two might be busy with luggage; at the other the engine would be watering. One man would cough or give a sign, and at once there would be only one man on the platform by the carriage door. In a minute there would be two men again; then both would disappear up the steps into the train. One, perhaps, would pause at an open corridor window and hurl a syringe into the darkness...

It was then that Travers opened his eyes again. Something had gone wrong with that mental reconstruction. Charles Hunt was somehow wrong. Why had Charles Hunt seized upon Ludovic Travers, an ordinary occupant of the compartment in which James Hunt was alive and seated, in order to question him about the nature of the spots that had been seen on his chin? Why had Charles Hunt called attention to himself? Why had he asked those questions if it hadn't been in order to obtain information? And if he were really in partnership with Brown he would have known all about those spots. Why, then, question a stranger? And—far more important—there could have been no dissimulation in questioning a stranger as Charles Hunt had done. Nothing could have been in his mind but a desire to get information as to the nature of the spots which he had seen from his peep-hole on his brother's neck and jowl.

The more Travers thought it over, the more he knew that something was wrong. And yet one last thread still held the theory to his mind as a button dangles from a coat. Perhaps Charles Hunt was a mass of nerves that night; witness, for instance, his irritability on the occasion of those two amusing collisions. Perhaps he had so on his mind the oppressing thought of what he had that night to do, that he had been urged by an impulse stronger than himself to speak to Travers, and soothe his nerves by doing so.

Wharton got to his feet and replaced his case in the rack with the remark that it was blind man's holiday. He looked reproachfully at his cold pipe, and then lighted it. Travers tackled him at once with the problems that had come to his mind that last quarter of an hour. The General was in a receptive mood. "I'm inclined to agree with you about nerves," he said. "It's the same psychological twist that makes a man return to the scene of his crime, only here it made Charles Hunt anticipate the crime. He had worked himself to such a state of nerves that he had to talk to somebody about the man he was going to help to kill. That's only a theory, of course, but it's a good theory."

"A curious pair, if it were so," said Travers. "Hunt all nerves, and Brown cold as ice. No wonder he didn't move a muscle when old Hunt sneered at him. His time was coming."

Wharton gave his usual commentatory grunt. "If those two did what we think they did, we've still got to do a little delving into the past when we get back home. All the same, my money's on Ellman. Why, I don't know, but it is."

Travers smiled to himself as he saw the portentous nod. "You're getting keen on this case, George?"

"Perhaps I am," said Wharton. "And I'd have to be, even if I weren't. When the Sûreté Générale ask us for information and help, it's up to us to give the best. People may think that England's down and out, but by God, they're not going to think that about Scotland Yard!"

Travers smiled inside, and with a curious affection. The old General had done his flag-waving with such an earnestness that Travers felt like making some heroic gesture, too. But all he could think of was to switch on the light. Wharton stopped him in the act.

"Leave it off for a bit, will you? I'd like to look outside."

The train was slowing for Toulon, and the lights of the town twinkled in the dusk. Wharton leaned from the open window of the corridor and looked about him. He felt Travers at his elbow.

"Won't be a fair test yet," said Travers quietly. "The station's quite lit up. Lot of people on the platforms, too."

They waited till the train came to a stop, then Wharton went back into his compartment again. He leaned out of the window, and from his own side Travers did the same. Perhaps there had been a fête in the town, for there were quite a few people waiting on the platform across from where they stood. Wharton resumed his seat. "We shall have to wait till we get to Avignon," he remarked resignedly. "The conditions will be better reproduced there."

Travers switched on the light. The train moved on again, and the two sat quietly in their seats. Soon Travers's mind—always more alert as night drew on—began fumbling again with the intricacies of the problem of James Hunt. His thoughts ran on, and he began thinking of how much time he had been spending in railway carriages. He thought of how humorously the idea had struck him when he entered that cinema on the Thursday evening, that a man who had been in a train for hours should choose for recreation a picture which announced itself as "Rome Express." Then he began thinking of the picture, and of continental trains, and—queer anticipation—of Marseilles and how Gallois would soon be making three in the compartment. And then again, with sudden wonder, he jerked upright in his seat, and began feeling for his glasses.

"I'm afraid I've been under a misapprehension, George," he said. "French trains aren't like roads, you know."

"What's this about roads?" Wharton had been half-way to a nap.

"What I mean is this," said Travers, and most apologetically. "On the roads you keep to the right when driving, but the rule of the railway is the same as it is with us: left-hand side all the time."

"But haven't we been working on the assumption?" said Wharton, wondering what on earth he was driving at. "Didn't we have the platform at Toulon on our left hand just now?"

"I know," said Travers, "and that's just the point. When we get to Marseilles we're going to reverse. The engine—or another one—will be hooked on the other end. You're now back to the engine. When we move out of Marseilles you'll be facing it. The next station we draw into after that, *the platform will be outside this window where we're sitting*! While Olivet's arm was being punctured at Dijon, I was staring hard into the corridor, watching Gallois's boots. If the carriage had been light, I'd still have seen nothing."

"You're right," said Wharton. "And how the devil did I miss seeing that?" He thought for a moment. "Then there wasn't any ducking under the buffers or the connecting way to get to the deserted side of the train!"

"There wasn't," agreed Travers. "All the person had to do was to walk along the platform till he came outside this window. The arm of Olivet bulged the blind where he leaned against it. A hand was raised in the dim light, and a thumb pressed home the plunger of the syringe. It was all done as quick as thought."

"Hardly so easy, surely," objected Wharton. "The platforms aren't like ours. They're hardly raised above the level of the line. Whoever did it had to tiptoe up."

"Don't you believe it," said Travers. "You've got in your mind the window as a whole. Think merely of the very bottom of the window where Olivet's arm was. From there to the platform isn't so far. Still, we'll try it out at Marseilles if you think fit—if we draw in with the platform on our right, ready to move off again."

But as it happened they drew in at Marseilles at a double platform, and there was a wait of twenty minutes. Gallois was waiting for the train to come in, and no sooner did he get inside the compartment than Wharton lugged him out again to assist in the experiment. Travers let down the window to its lowest, and placed the blind as it had been that night, and his elbow on it. He was now Olivet, asleep while the train waited in the station at Dijon.

Outside was the subdued sound of voices. Among them, thought Travers, would be the voice of Wharton explaining to Gallois what everything was about. And then all at once Travers felt a prick in his elbow, and he shot his arm away in a flash.

Then he smiled as he put it back again. Wharton had carried realism to the extent of using a pin.

In a couple of minutes the two were in the compartment again. "You were right," said Wharton. "It's as easy as shelling peas. But we noticed you twitched your arm out of the way."

"I wasn't asleep," said Travers, "but Olivet was. Also, if you remember, Olivet did wake up shortly afterwards. We thought it was the draught from the window that woke him, but it may have been what I might call the delayed sensation from the prick of the needle—the itching, so to speak."

Wharton nodded. "That may be true enough. I've had no experience, and I can't tell. But one thing I do know." He addressed himself entirely now to Gallois. "At Dijon it would be wise to ask questions. It is not impossible that someone should have been noticed lingering suspiciously in the neighbourhood of the window. Inquiries, too, about that car. One man would have been asleep in it somewhere while the other—Ellman—did the job."

The two lapsed into French, and there was a ten minute conference. Then Wharton announced that his good friend, M'sieur Gallois, had decided to leave the train at Dijon and carry out certain investigations. It would be daylight then, and there would be no need to worry about waking up.

"And we go on to Paris," said Travers.

"That's right," said Wharton. "The triumvirate splits up."

"And talking of Paris," went on Travers, "did the inspector get any news of the Olivets?"

Wharton glanced at Gallois as if for permission, and then became spokesman.

"They know that the man and woman arrived on the *Paul René* from Egypt the day before they took the train."

"And any news about Madame Olivet? They haven't caught her yet?"

Wharton smiled dryly. "Some of her own pals caught her all right—probably thought she knew too much and might chatter. They caught her all right, as I said—or rather the Paris police did. Caught her in a net."

"In a net?" Travers thought he saw the purport of the meta-phor. But there was no metaphor.

"Yes," said Wharton, spectacular as ever. "A fishing net. They got her out of the Seine last night with a knife wound or two in her back."

CHAPTER XII
HOT NEWS

BY THE TIME the train was drawing in at Victoria there were few details in the case which had not been discussed, and even the earliest discussion had shown that action could be neither prompt nor drastic. Admit Leslie Hunt as a possible murderer of his uncle, then—excluding the dead Olivets—there were four people who could have been concerned in the two deaths, and—far more complex—from those four there might have been every possible combination. In the syringe affair Ellman might have acted alone, but prompted by Leslie. Charles Hunt and Brown might have been the combination, or either of them and Ell-man. And though apparently Leslie could hardly have worked the syringe himself, yet any of the other three might have done that murder entirely alone and wholly unsuspected by any of the others.

Wharton was in a dilemma. Knowing the laws on evidence as he did, he dared not risk a confrontation and a short-cut—and yet he had never been as anxious to deliver the goods. The Sûreté must be shown that Scotland Yard—and the older hands especially—had not lost their cunning. And having talked with Travers, and argued at length, Wharton's mind was at last made up. He had always believed in the wide net and gradual elim-ination, and a good motive was better than a clue. Very well, then: he would dive deeply, swiftly and secretly into the history and antecedents of all his suspects. Out of the information thus acquired there would emerge something on which to base an excuse for an interview. That meant talk—and more information; and once a man talked Wharton had boasted, not without reason, that he was as clay in his hands.

That long code telegram from St. Raphael had been followed by another from Paris. When Wharton reached the Yard he hoped to have in his possession the name and address of a witness who knew the James Hunts at Buxton, and another who had known them—and Brown—at Peddleby. Ellman was being inquired into through his previous job, and a man was on duty at Peddleby to keep an eye on "Marsh View" and its occupants generally. Charles Hunt, Wharton proposed to handle himself. Charles had already brought himself within the law. There would be no difficulty about questioning him.

Palmer was at the station with the Bentley. The General refused a lift; he would rather stretch his legs in a walk.

"Any idea when you'll be wanting me?" Travers asked.

"Can't say," said Wharton. "Depends on what's waiting. Besides, you've got to do something to earn your director's fee."

Thereupon the General had shaken hands and departed for the Embankment. The thanks had already been bestowed, and Travers knew his man well enough to be sure that, for all his secretiveness, Wharton would bring along the news as soon as it passed the test of reliability. But Wharton found no news to impart. His witnesses were not yet run to earth, and one piece of information alone had come in—that Ellman had given in his notice at "Marsh View," and had left that very morning. Wharton was agitated at once. Had Ellman been followed? Was he being watched? Chief-Inspector Norris assured him that everything had been done. When Ellman was wanted, he could be picked up.

Then to relieve his feelings—or maybe to mystify Norris—the General dictated an urgent message for Gallois. He suggested a tremendous effort to follow the course and times of Ellman's car from Avignon to Dijon. Every employee on duty that night at Dijon might be closely questioned. And what about that girl Ellman had met in Paris? Something might have been dropped to her. There was a reminder about the torn-up book on the permanent way, and another about the discarded syringe. Above all, would Gallois send along at once anything whatever that might be discovered.

When Norris had gone, Wharton fussed and fumed for a bit. Then he took off the receiver to tell his wife he would be along in half an hour. Then he changed his mind and made it an hour and a half. An idea had come to him. Two birds could be killed with one stone. Tufnell Park was near enough to Highgate, and he could call on Charles Hunt and then walk through to his own house.

Half an hour later he was at the gate of the house—a three-storied Victorian building with stodgy comfort written all over it. His knock was answered by a dumpy old lady in a black dress. She looked a good-hearted soul. Wharton asked if he might see Mr. Hunt.

"I'm sorry," she said, "but my husband is in bed with a chill. Can I give any message?"

"As a matter of fact, I've come about your late brother-in-law," said Wharton. He was always a great one with the ladies. "If you could spare me a moment or two yourself—er—Mrs. Hunt, is it?"

In a minute he was in a drawing-room, seated in a green plush easy-chair. "I had the pleasure of making the acquaintance of your husband and nephew in Paris," Wharton was saying. "A very sad thing your brother-in-law's death." He caught the look on her face, and added deftly, "in some ways, of course."

There followed a suave explanation of his own presence in Paris, with much confusing reference to inquests, sudden death and the strange ways of foreigners. Mrs. Hunt sat nodding away, and trying to show signs of comprehension. Her husband, Wharton gathered, had told her nothing of his little scrap with the police.

"I understood from your nephew that he was coming here to stay with you," went on Wharton, knowing well enough he was still at Peddleby. "But perhaps he is here."

"No," she said, and the snap of it seemed curious in one so placidly plump. "We're very disappointed in Brown—you know Brown, do you?"

"You mean the late Mr. Hunt's valet," said Wharton, with just the right shade of deprecation to show the gulf fixed between such a menial and Mrs. Hunt herself. "I saw him down at Peddleby where I had to do some business in connection with the death."

She decided that Wharton knew all about everything. "You see, as my husband I expect told you, Brown had been telling us that Leslie was old enough to be his own master; I mean he would be when he was twenty-one. That's why my husband went to France to see him, you know. He ought to have been out of that house years ago. It wasn't right for him to be there with a man like James. No wonder he was what you might call a namby-pamby sort. And there was his health, too."

"Leslie wasn't strong?"

"He was most delicate. I only saw him when we stayed down at Peddleby ourselves, and that was two years ago; but I had the evidence of my own eyes, and I know what Brown's told my husband since." She was settling down to a good gossip, and Wharton was a good listener.

"He struck me as very nervous," he said. "But most people grow out of that when they get to his age."

She nodded. "They used to have an awful bother with him, and only a year or two back. He used to walk in his sleep. Brown used to have to sleep in the same room with him. Once he was actually found wandering in the road."

Wharton clicked his tongue. "Very bad when that happens. Very bad." He leaned forward. "What he needed was a mother's hand, Mrs. Hunt. Somebody to look after him; somebody like yourself."

She was pleased at that. "Well, I do know Mr.—" a glance at the card, "—Wharton, that he wouldn't have been worse off. Leslie favours his mother's side. She was a Wensum, you know—the Suffolk family."

"But I thought Mr. James Hunt's wife was that name," said Wharton, with simulated surprise.

"Oh no; she was a Barlow. Quite well-connected I think. I never met her because there was some trouble at the time and she died, of course, just before James came to Rye."

"Buxton's a long way from Rye," remarked Wharton.

"That's what I said at the time. Still, there's no accounting for tastes."

A kindly old soul, thought Wharton. No malice in her but she likes a chat. Speaks well, too. If only her husband doesn't hammer on the floor, I'll get the family news for generations. And then Wharton became aware that she was still talking.

"I beg your pardon, but what was that you said about Hastings?"

"It was at Hastings we met him," she said. "My husband and I were there for our holiday and we ran into James; you know, so that we couldn't get out of each other's way. Then, of course, Charles spoke to his brother and one thing led to another and finally we spent an extra three days at Peddleby after our holiday." She sighed. "That didn't last long. You'll forgive me for saying it, Mr. Wharton, but James was an impossible man to have dealings with."

"Speak as you find," said Wharton with honest bluntness. "That's my own motto. And about Brown. Do you mean to tell me that he won't *let* your nephew come here?"

"Well—" she hesitated "—that's what it really amounts to and I told my husband as much. Brown's got too much influence over that boy, Mr. Wharton." She nodded darkly. "If you ask me, he's not willing to give up a good home and a good job. Brown's got round him some way or other. I don't like it and I've said so, and if my husband hadn't been ill he'd have gone down there to see about it. There's something peculiar going on, if you ask me. That house gave me the creeps when I was there."

Wharton kept nodding in unison. He was wondering, and wondering furiously, just what questions he could ask to get to the heart of that cryptic suggestion of hers, which, by the dark suspicion with which she imparted it, might have been black magic or even murder.

"You like your nephew?" he began.

She smiled gently. "He's my husband's own flesh and blood." The smile softened and she gave a little shake of the head. "If he'd have lived, our own boy would have been just the same age." Wharton grunted something inaudible and consolatory, then cleared his throat. "That was a long while ago, ma'am."

She shook her head again. "We don't forget as easily as that, Mr. Wharton. That's what makes it hard that now when my brother's dead, we can't have Leslie to live with us." She stopped short and listened. "I do believe—"

The faint noises that had been heard outside now explained themselves. The door opened and in came Charles Hunt, dishevelled and wearing an old dressing-gown. He looked ill, and at the sight of Wharton he looked surprised—but the surprise was too pronounced. Wharton knew that Hunt had got out of his sick bed only because he had been aware of his own presence.

There was a brief chaos, what with Mrs. Hunt starting up in alarm and telling her husband what a silly thing it was he was doing, and making him sit down; and then there was Wharton trying to get in explanations of his visit, and offering his own chair and being told certainly not. But in a minute or so Charles Hunt was seated and his wife had put a rug over his legs, and Wharton was producing the necessary tonic.

"What I really came here for, Mr. Hunt, was to tell you that the whole business about which we met in Paris is now settled. We don't expect that you'll hear any more about it."

Hunt smiled wanly. "Well, I'm very glad to hear it—sir. My wife and I have had a lot of trouble lately over the whole business. It's been very trying."

"I'm sure it has," said Wharton. "And all I trust is that your late brother did the right thing by both of you in his will."

Hunt shook his head and smiled. There was no sneer in the smile.

"We never expected it, sir, and we didn't get it. He left his money where he liked, the same as I shall do mine." Another shake of the head, a more reminiscent one this time. "I don't say that a year or two ago we shouldn't have been glad of the money, but things are better now."

"Then I'm very glad to hear it," said Wharton, shifting to the edge of his seat preparatory to rising. "Independence is the salt of life, Mr. Hunt." There was a mysterious sniffing at the door. A nose nuzzled it open and a little dog of the spaniel type came in. It reared back and gave a whining bark at the sight of Wharton; then circled round to its mistress.

"There now, Charles," she said, "you shouldn't have let Flossie get out."

"I didn't let her out," Hunt began petulantly. Wharton poured immediate oil on the waters.

"What a charming little dog!" He fondled its ears. "What kind is it, Mrs. Hunt?"

"It's a spaniel. A cocker, really. A friend in the country gave it us."

"Beautiful dog," commented Wharton. "Coat like silk. And what ears! And how old is she?"

"Just six months," he was told.

Wharton picked up his hat. "A dangerous age for dogs. You'll have to look out for distemper. We lost our last dog like that."

"Oh, but there's no need to worry about that nowadays," she said. "Our vet told us about it and we had him do Flossie. It's an inoculation. Two doses they have to have, and then they never get distemper—so they say."

"Not *never*, my dear," Hunt corrected snappishly "Ninety-five per cent, effective, so the vet said."

"That's good enough," said Wharton. He stopped and fondled the ears once more. "And what did Flossie think about it? I'm asking you because I'd like to have our own dog done."

Mrs. Hunt smiled. "You must ask my husband about that. I daren't be there. Even then I heard the poor little darling cry out when the vet gave her the first dose—"

Hunt clicked his tongue. "Didn't I tell you that was a big dose? Those were the dead germs he injected. The second dose wasn't anything to be compared with it. Hardly anything at all. The live germs," he explained to Wharton.

"Yes," said his wife, more brightly. "That time she didn't feel the needle at all, even when the vet put it in."

Hunt clicked his tongue again. "Mr. Wharton doesn't want to hear all that, my dear."

"Oh, but I do!" said Wharton. "It's most interesting—" his eye was on Hunt "—when one has a dog of one's own."

Hunt's face was immovable. Wharton held out his hand. "Well, I must be getting along. It's been a great pleasure to see you again, Mr. Hunt. No, don't get up! You've got to look after yourself, you know. You're not so young as you were."

"That's what I keep telling him," said his wife, as she took the outstretched hand. She broke off to speak to the dog which was scratching itself ferociously on the rug. "Stop it, Flossie! Stop it at once."

"They will scratch," said Wharton consolingly. "You can't stop 'em doing it."

"It's those spots again," she explained. "Nothing seems to do them any good." She turned on her husband. "I'm sure I was right, Charles. There must have been something in that stuff the vet gave her. She never was like it before." "Stuff and nonsense," said Hunt. Wharton heard the words none too distinctly for he was already out in the hall, and Mrs. Hunt was saying that her maid had had the afternoon and evening off. Another shake of the hand and Wharton was gone. Mrs. Hunt turned back towards the drawing-room and in her mind was what she would say to her husband—that she had never met a more charming or sympathetic man than that Mr. Wharton. And by the time she re-entered the room, Wharton was passing the open window. It was Hunt who spoke first, and Wharton heard the words distinctly and knew how pettishly they were snapped out.

"And what else have you been telling him?"

Wharton paused for a moment, turned on his heel—then turned again and continued to the front gate. He was shaking his head and puzzling his wits with such complete self-containment that when he looked up and saw the man at the gate he stared at him blankly.

"Ellman, isn't it?"

The chauffeur touched his cap. Something that might have been more than surprise had come over his face. "That's right, sir." He hesitated. "You're the gentleman I saw in Paris, aren't you, sir?"

Wharton was himself again. He smiled hugely, stretching out his hand.

"That's right, Ellman. And what are you doing here?"

The chauffeur gave a little sideways nod of the head. "I left that place, sir, down there at Peddleby. They didn't want me particular and I was a bit fed up."

"Exactly," said Wharton. "But you're not going to work for Mr. Charles Hunt, are you?"

The other smiled. "I didn't even know he had a car, sir. What I wanted from him was an extra reference in case I put in for another job."

Wharton nodded. "Capital! Hope you get a good one. Staying in town for a bit?"

Ellman smiled. "Sister of mine at Highbury, sir. I thought I'd treat myself to a holiday for a bit."

"Nothing like a rest," said Wharton, and shook hands again. Across the road a man with his back to them was looking across at the tiny park and Wharton knew Ellman was in safe hands. But Wharton himself was a worried man as he walked slowly towards Highgate. There was no reason why Ellman should not have thrown over his job. There was no reason why he should not be seeking an extra reference from the Mr. Charles Hunt whom he had met in Paris. Yet it was curious, and more intriguing still was the matter of an injection made so swiftly and surely that the dog had not yelped. And the dog had since been troubled with spots. Most curious—and particularly the spots. Travers had harped on the question of those spots. Nothing in them individually; one man's a rash from the strawberries and the other's the after-effects of atropine. And yet a strange coincidence, and as Wharton shook his head for the hundredth time he recalled from his own experience circumstances that had had other explanations than the purely obvious.

And no sooner did Wharton enter his dining-room than he was looking up the number of his own vet. A moment or two to prepare an opening and he rang him up.

W. Hallo, Millborough; is that you? Wharton speaking. Superintendent Wharton, if you'd like it that way.

M. Oh yes. How are you, Mr. Wharton?

W. Pretty fair. I've got something to ask you, by the way, and it's confidential. That new serum you inject against distemper. Have you had anything to do with it?

M. Oh yes. Why? What's the bother?

W. No bother. The second injection is the active one, isn't it?

M. That's right.

W. And suppose someone stole some of the serum and injected it into a human being; what would happen?

M. (A pause, then a little chuckle). Not very much, I think. I doubt if anything would happen at all. The person might feel a little peculiar.

W. He wouldn't have any spots come out?

M. I don't see why he should. Mind you, I've never had any experience. (Another chuckle). But why not inquire from your own experts?

W. H'm. Perhaps I will. And just one more thing. If a dog has the second injection, will it have a tendency to spots? You know, that perpetual desire to keep scratching that dogs often have?

M. Good lord, no! No reason whatever why a dog should have any skin irritation after it. Of course, I mean if the dog's skin was all right before.

W. Good. That is, thanks very much. Keep it to yourself, will you? Good-bye. Good-bye.

So much for that. Wharton had an excellent meal and then, immediately after it, felt the old restlessness. He told Mrs. Wharton that he was going to the Yard again but he'd be back for supper. Then the sight of his telephone gave him another idea. He found the number of Charles Hunt and rang up the house. Mrs. Hunt answered.

Wharton's tone changed as by magic to a coo. He had thought a lot, he said, of what Mrs. Hunt had done him the honour to confide to him. He was going down to Peddleby on business in a day or so and he had been wondering if there was anything he might do. An old man like himself could often put in a good word with the young. If, for instance, he could influence Leslie in any way, to get him to change his mind about coming to live at Tufnell Park. Just a word of advice and no more, and not in the presence of Brown.

Mrs. Hunt said she would be truly grateful and so would her husband. Wharton cut short her thanks and turned the conversation to dogs. His own would be treated by the vet at once, he said. He intended to lose no more dogs with distemper. And how long ago was it when Mrs. Hunt's Flossie was done? Two months? He would hardly have thought it. To explain away that absurd remark, he made a little more talk. And then a final question—a staggering one. Might he have a brief word with Mr. Hunt? Only a minute at the most, and couldn't the telephone be taken to the bedside?

Mrs. Hunt said she would see. Wharton waited, and as he waited he realized that already some of the bottom had been knocked out of the distemper theory. By no possible combination of circumstances could Charles Hunt have anticipated, two months before, the curious situation that would make possible the killing of his brother by the use of any information obtained from the vet. So much for that obsession about spots. And yet, as Wharton assured himself once again, it was all very curious. Charles Hunt had had experience with a syringe. He had been on the train and had concealed the fact. James Hunt should have been killed with a syringe, and Charles—if only for the sake of his wife and their own dead son—might have resorted even to murder to get his nephew out of his brother's malevolent care.

The receiver buzzed. Charles Hunt was speaking—and speaking timidly. Wharton affected a large joviality. He asked Hunt's opinion of Ellman. Hunt temporized. He knew little of him but he had struck him as a reliable man. Ellman—did the

Superintendent know it?—had called a short time before for a reference and had been given one. So much for that.

"And now a most confidential question," said Wharton. "Let out to a single living soul what I'm going to say and I won't answer for the consequences. This is it. Think back to that Sunday night on the train. What were you doing when the train stopped at Dijon?"

"Doing?" Hunt breathed a bit puffily. "Why, I got out for a bit of air. I was actually on the platform till the train started again."

"Alone, were you?"

"Of course I wasn't." Hunt spoke almost petulantly. "Brown got out with me and we were on the platform together all the time. We got in together—and then I left him and went back to sleep."

"You were together all the time?"

"Yes. Didn't I say so?"

Wharton gave another grunt. "Perhaps you did. But all the same, you went on the platform together and got on the train together, just as it moved off. That's right, isn't it?"

"Absolutely right."

"I see." Wharton was feeling like a boy who has been told the picnic is definitely off. But he had a last idea, if only as an excuse to hang up gracefully. "I suppose you saw nothing peculiar on the platform?"

There was a slight pause, then: "It's very funny you should ask that. Do you know, just as we got on the steps to get on again, we saw something—a man we thought it was—dart under the train."

Wharton's eyes were bulging. "Who saw it first? And where was it?"

Hunt seemed only too eager to tell all he knew. He wasn't sure who saw it first, but he thought it was Brown. There had been a sort of black thing that had disappeared from the platform and had gone under the train or between the carriages. Somewhere about the far end of Brown's own carriage it was—beyond where James Hunt and Leslie had been sleeping.

When Wharton hung up that receiver again, he knew the gods had been kind. The case had narrowed down. Either Ellman was for the high jump, or else the story of a disappearing man was a deliberate concoction between Charles Hunt and Brown; a concoction to conceal their own crime; and in that case there might be a double job for the hangman, and two for the high jump.

At the Yard Wharton found most of what he wanted. There was the name and address of James Hunt's last housekeeper at Buxton. It had been strange that Hunt should have come from a fashionable town to a hamlet as remote from it as he could get. Buxton and Peddleby were worlds apart. At Buxton, with the Peak District on his doorstep, he had been able to indulge in his geological hobby; at Peddleby there could surely be few, or only limited facilities for a hobby of that kind. Why, then, had James Hunt chosen Peddleby? And had Brown been with him then? Or had Brown spoken the truth when he had claimed a service of only ten years? All that, Wharton told himself, he would soon know. Not only was he seeing the last Buxton housekeeper, but the first Peddleby one as well. That would give a continuity. It might also bridge the gap—if there had been a gap.

Those two places which Wharton himself proposed to visit were reasonably close to each other. The first woman was now at Chelmsford, and the second had been located at Cambridge. Both, thought Wharton, could be seen on the following day, and he could be back to the Yard by late afternoon. But that was not good enough. When he returned to the Yard he wanted in his possession certain other vital facts. Travers then must go to Peddleby—and Travers was the ideal man. Brown appeared to have taken to him, and the biggest fool could see when he spoke to Travers that he was dealing with a gentleman and a man of implicit honour. Wharton took off the receiver.

Palmer fetched Travers at once. Travers said he'd be glad to do anything, even to be at Peddleby by ten o'clock. Wharton said he was making a mistake. Hastings at ten o'clock, and then straight on to Peddleby. He himself would see that the solicitors were warned to expect him, and he'd have the doctor rung up, too. Detailed instructions would be sent round to St. Martin's Chambers within an hour.

For the next half-hour Wharton thought hard, and when he took up his pen to write those instructions for Travers, he had a furtive presentiment that he was being bewilderingly mysterious. For those instructions went into three envelopes, and they were marked in red ink as follows:

No. 1. Trend of conversation with the solicitors.
No. 2. Points that must be raised with the doctor. Be tactful, but get explicit answers.
No. 3. Only to be opened *after leaving the doctor.*

And it had been that No. 3 that had given Wharton most thought. It involved a gamble, and it implied an enormous trust in the capabilities and discretion of Ludovic Travers. But just what risks he really was taking, Wharton had no idea, or his sleep that night would not have been the undisturbed slumber that it was.

CHAPTER XIII
CLIMAX!

TRAVERS STOPPED for a moment to glance again at Wharton's instructions, and then entered the offices of Forthright and Hughes. A clerk took his card and showed him straightaway into the private room of Guy Hughes, the surviving partner. The two men ran quick, appraising looks over each other. Travers saw a man of mature years and shrewd level-headedness; the other saw a man who looked like a gentleman, carried his clothes like one, and had the voice and manners of one. Travers took a seat, and Hughes passed the cigarette box.

"What is the particular trouble?" he said.

"I don't know that there is any in particular," smiled Travers. "As the emissary of Scotland Yard I'm merely directed to inquire if there have been any further developments in the matter of James Hunt since Superintendent Wharton saw you last."

The other nodded and frowned. "Of course, if you people would give us a little more of your trust," he said, "we could work less in the dark. James Hunt died a natural death—Superintendent Wharton told me that when he rang me up yesterday afternoon—but it's surely very unusual for inquiries of a confidential nature to be made without giving any information in return."

"We realize that," said Travers. "The trouble is it isn't we who are making a fuss. The death occurred in France, and the matter's out of our jurisdiction, strictly speaking. Only, if the French authorities ask us to give them certain information, all we can do is to go—in the strictest confidence—to those willing and able to supply that information. The French authorities may be satisfied with the manner of your late client's death." He smiled, but the smile was for that fluent and spectacular liar, Wharton. "As for myself, I'm merely here on Mr. Wharton's instructions, to do the best we can to please the French."

"I see," said Hughes. "That seems fair enough. But I don't know that there's anything to tell you. The settling up of the estate is proceeding normally."

"No objections from Charles Hunt?"

"Charles Hunt?" Hughes raised his eyebrows. "How can he dispute the validity of the will? Have you heard anything?"

"Oh no," said Travers hastily. "We merely wondered."

"Mr. Leslie Hunt is selling the house. Perhaps you knew that."

"We didn't," said Travers. "Rather in a hurry, isn't he?"

"I don't know," said Hughes reflectively. "It's not the sort of place he'd be likely to want even if he were staying in England: which he isn't."

Travers looked thoughtful. "Some mention of Kenya, wasn't there?"

"Between ourselves, there's more than a mention," Hughes said quietly. "I shouldn't be surprised if he goes out there almost at once. And I believe Brown is willing to go with him."

"Rather rushing things, isn't it?" said Travers. "And what about affairs over here? Will you have power of attorney?"

"Something of the kind," said Hughes. "If he does go abroad we can always arrange some advance from the estate. Personally, I think it will do him all the good in the world."

"You've seen him quite recently?"

"Yes," said Hughes, and hesitated. "Yesterday morning—and purely professionally. About his will, to be exact."

"His will!" Travers looked puzzled. "What on earth's he making a will for already?"

Hughes smiled tolerantly. "It's a wise enough proceeding. And life's a precarious thing. Not that I wasn't surprised when the matter was mentioned. Our previous experience of—er—that particular client had not been of the kind to make us anticipate such a piece of prudence."

Travers nodded. "You'd care to give us details of the will? Implicitly in confidence, of course."

Hughes shook his head. "Not at the moment. We should have to be given strong reasons for a breach of confidence of that sort. The affairs of the dead and those of the living are very different matters."

"You're perfectly right," said Travers courteously, and prepared to go. "We're most grateful to you for what you've done. And if people of tremendous importance should bother you again, don't lay the blame on me." His smile was so charming and his last few polite nothings so happily expressed that Hughes thought of the brief visit with a curious pleasure at all sorts of odd times during that day.

Palmer drove the Bentley now, and Travers wrote down the substance of the conversation in the lawyer's office. There had been no need to put those leading questions which Wharton had suggested, for Hughes had gone far beyond them of his own free-will. And important as the information was, Travers made no attempt at deduction. He was a carrier pigeon, he thought to himself, and it would be for Wharton to unroll the message and decipher.

He took out the second envelope and re-read his instructions for the visit to the doctor. Certain alterations he judged to be essential in view of what he had already learned that morning, and he noted them for Wharton's information. The doctor's house was found, and the car was drawn up inside the drive and out of the gaze of a possible scrutiny by Brown or young Hunt. A maid showed him in, and he had already caught a glimpse of the doctor peeping through the bow window, where doubtless he had been suitably impressed by the patrician air of the chauffeur and the rakish solidity of the car.

The doctor was a man of about forty; an age when humour is still highly active and yet tempered with some maturity. He took the caller to a comfortable room, and prepared to hear what it was all about. Travers told him the old, old story, with variations. Whatever the doctor knew of English procedure, he knew nothing at all of French. He was mightily curious, all the same, to know what had happened to James Hunt, and Travers had much ado to lie with fluency and conceal with art. And then the doctor threw his own bomb-shell by saying that Brown had been to see him—not professionally, of course—and had told him about what had happened in France. Travers thought furiously, and resolved to be particularly wary.

"Brown remembered all about the spots, then?" he remarked casually.

The doctor smiled. "I don't think Brown will ever forget 'em! Hunt wasn't good-tempered at the best of times, and that house must have been hell for a day or two."

"It was strawberries that caused it?"

"Undoubtedly," said the doctor. "And a surfeit, too, if you ask me. Still, we soon put him right."

"I'm going to ask a very foolish question," said Travers, with a smile which he meant to be shy and feared was only fatuous. "You saw Hunt personally on that occasion? The valet, Brown, wasn't an intermediary?"

"Oh no," said the doctor quickly. "The chauffeur brought a message for me to go to 'Marsh View,' and I went. I saw what was the matter, and sent along at once—by my own man—a bottle of medicine and some lotion."

"Brown didn't know what was in either?" He caught the doctor's look of startled inquiry. "A most important question, doctor, and you'll be told the reason when necessity arises—if it does arise."

"Brown hadn't any idea," the doctor told him. "As a matter of fact he might have guessed the medicine—it was simple enough. Just a white mixture."

Travers smiled. "Epsom Salts flavoured with peppermint?"

"That's it. The lotion, between ourselves, was a sample bottle of some made-up stuff. We're always getting them from firms of repute. I saw it would meet the case, and sent it along." He grinned. "It had to be tried out on somebody."

"You don't remember the formula?"

"I don't. It had a sugar of lead basis, I do remember that, though it wasn't written on the bottle. Whatever it was it did the trick. Even Hunt said it soothed the spots at once."

"Splendid!" said Travers. His half movement in the chair was to indicate that the serious business of the interview was over, and his tone took on a certain flippancy. "And what about your new client? He likely to be a good customer?"

"Leslie?" said the doctor, and shook his head. "I don't know that I'd like to handle a case like his. A specialist is what he wants. Mind you, I think he'll grow out of his nerves now he's his own master. If I'd had to live in 'Marsh View' with old Hunt I'd have had nerves."

"Used to walk in his sleep, didn't he?"

"Yes," said the doctor, and frowned at the recollection. "The whole family history is abnormal, if we could only get deep enough into it." His face brightened. "Still, he's been all right for a year or so now. Brown did call for me to go up yesterday, and I sent up a tonic. That may be only all this worry about the uncle's death, and so on."

Travers nodded. "Yes; a complex case, as you say. The uncle was a hypochondriac, I've been told. But had he any really definite weakness?"

"Oh, yes," said the doctor. "His throat gave him a lot of trouble. I lanced him for quinsy twice, and I wanted him to have his tonsils out, but he wouldn't. Then I got him to adopt that open window business, and I believe he was very much better."

"Tell me!" said Travers, trying to look ignorant. "Does a man's face flush when he has tonsilitis?"

The other smiled. "Not necessarily, only if there's a temperature. Hunt was always very pale."

"I see," said Travers. "And was that what was wrong with him this time, when you advised him to go to the South of France?"

"Partly," said the doctor, and there was a twinkle in his eye. "He was threatened with more tonsilitis—so he thought—and I advised drastic treatment."

"Quite!" smiled Travers, and in spite of the doctor's implication that the South of France had rid him of a nuisance, there was something mechanical about Travers's smile. Through his mind had flashed a picture of the poor devil Olivet lying back choking in his seat, face hotly flushed; and Brown suggesting that the cause of it all was tonsilitis. Travers got to his feet.

"Did the change from Buxton have anything to do with Hunt's throat?"

"The change didn't do it any good," said the doctor. "He was on very high ground there, whereas 'Marsh View' isn't more than forty feet up in spite of the appearance above the marsh. And it's one of those houses that I don't like. It isn't damp, but it feels like it—if you know what I mean. It ought to be a cheerful sort of place, but it isn't to me. It's all gloomy at the back, and there's quite a lot of mist there in the winter—and sea fog, of course."

"I can't say I liked the look of it any too much," hinted Travers. He held out his hand, and there was the usual palaver about the importance of discretion and patience, mixed up with thanks and mysterious allusions. Then the doctor asked if he might look at the innards of the magnificent car, and it was five minutes later before Travers could do what he had been bursting with impatience to do—open that third envelope which held a secret of such importance that it had not to be opened till the visit to the doctor was over and gone.

Palmer made for the inn, where lunch was to be ordered for two, and Travers opened the mysterious envelope. What Wharton had written was this:

"If the doctor said that Brown had knowledge of the contents of medicine and lotion, then make a formal call at 'Marsh View,' giving any excuse that seems likely, and recording any impressions. But if you think definitely that Brown had *no* knowledge of either, then arrange for Brown and Leslie Hunt to be together in the room and first of all hint very strongly that they may be ordered to return to Paris at any minute. When you are asked why, *state clearly the cause of Olivet's death*, even going into details if necessary. Observe the effects on Brown. Then *state clearly the cause of James Hunt's death*, and watch carefully both men.

"If, in your opinion, either man shows signs of being implicated, ring up Rye at once, and simply say that Superintendent Wharton advises precautions to be taken; which means they will keep an extra sharp eye on the house in case either man bolts. Rye know all that. Very many thanks. See you here at four o'clock.

"G. W.

"*P. S.*—In any case, before acting in either way as above, ask Brown confidentially:

1. What did he do at Dijon?
2. What he thought the burglars were after in the safe?"

Travers regarded the note very thoughtfully for a good few moments. What it meant was beyond him, but its instructions were implicit and clear, little though he liked them. And before he went back to "Marsh View" he wrote up the conversation with the doctor so that Wharton might see precisely what had happened.

It was now cloudy and the promise of the earlier morning looked like being rudely unfulfilled. The sun had gone and there was a slight coldness in the July air that threatened rain. From the low ridge the horizon stood startlingly clear and the endless sheep dotted themselves as tiny white specks to the remote distance. "Marsh View," as Travers entered its drive, looked too hemmed in, what with its shrubberies and pines, and as he looked away towards the sea there seemed to be a mist. But it was not a mist. It was a bonfire in the kitchen garden at the back of the house and as he stepped off the gravelled drive he could catch a glimpse, between house and garage, of the fire and the man who was stirring it with a fork. That man was Brown.

Travers told Wharton afterwards that he had no idea why he did so, but he took the bricked path to the kitchen garden and went towards Brown. All at once the man caught sight of him. The fork with which he stirred the embers was held still. He drew back and waited for the visitor to approach.

"Morning, Brown," said Travers cheerfully. "I see you're burning up the rubbish."

"Rubbish is the very word for it, if you ask me, sir," said Brown, and kicked into the glowing fire what looked like a burning book. And as Travers followed the action he saw that quite a lot of books had been burned—or else they were papers of some sort.

"Books?" he said. "Rather extravagant of you, wasn't it? I mean, second-hand books don't fetch much but they do fetch a little."

"These won't, sir," said Brown sombrely. "The fire's the place for them." He looked at Travers. "What they call thrillers; Mr. Leslie used to be mad on them. He used to hide them in the wood there and up in his bedroom and that's what used to get on his mind before he went to sleep."

"You mean that was the reason for his sleepwalking?"

"Partly, sir, there's no doubt. He used to be crafty as a monkey about them, after his uncle stopped him reading them."

"Where'd he get them all from?" asked Travers.

"He used to buy up a whole lot second-hand out of his own money," Brown told him. "Tales about cowboys and crooks and—even murders."

Travers smiled. "Well, there's no enormity about that—I mean if it weren't for his peculiar make-up. I read 'em myself. Besides, he isn't a child. He's a man now."

"He may be to you," said Brown, still with the same foreboding look. "In some ways he never developed properly, not as a normal boy should."

Travers nodded. "Well, you ought to know. And did you burn these on your own initiative or did he give you orders?"

"I talked to him for his good, sir," said Brown, "and he gave me permission to get rid of them. If he hadn't been thinking of going abroad, as I told you when you were here last, I'd have tried to get him to read something better." He seemed to pull himself suddenly together. The fork was stuck in the ground and he stepped back from the fire. "Was there anything particular you came about, sir?"

"Well, yes," said Travers. "Nothing very much, only those French authorities keep harassing us for information and we've got to supply it. This time it's about when the train was in the station at Dijon. I suppose you were asleep?"

"Well, no, sir," said Brown, with the most natural smile in the world. "To tell the truth, sir, I was feeling very hot and uncomfortable in that carriage and I thought I'd have a breath of fresh air, and just as I got to the door before the train had stopped, Mr. Charles Hunt came out too, and we went on the platform together. We talked very quietly, sir, because naturally he didn't want his brother to overhear, and we got back into the train together."

Travers smiled. He was appreciating, and with a vague uneasiness, that Brown and Charles Hunt each had a perfect alibi. "Well," he said, "the French won't get much satisfaction out of that!"

But Brown was thinking of something else. "By the way, sir, something peculiar happened that they might like to know. Mr. Hunt and I both distinctly saw what looked like a man who got under the train from the platform."

"Really!" Travers's eyes goggled. Here was news for Wharton. And he had suddenly the same thought that had come to the General. "Who saw the man first?"

"I think perhaps I did," said Brown. "Yet I wouldn't like to say, sir. It was one of those peculiar things you both see at once. We thought it was a luggage thief."

Travers nodded. "Most interesting—and I hope it'll please the French authorities. And talking of thieves, do you think your own burglar here had any idea of anything special in the safe?"

"Anything special?" The lines ran across his forehead and he gave a quick look. "In what way do you mean, sir?"

"Oh, I don't know," said Travers airily. "Just anything special."

Brown shook his head. "It was just a chance thief, if you ask me. He found the safe and he opened it—and had some good luck."

"Precisely," agreed Travers. He made as if to go on, then stopped. "What's your opinion of Ellman?"

"Ellman?" Brown frowned again. "He was just the ordinary type, sir. Specious, and a bit of a rogue."

"How do you mean?—in the strictest confidence, of course."

"Well, I know personally he worked the old petrol trick, sir. Getting garage hands to give a receipt for more than was put in the tank. An old dodge that, sir." He smiled reminiscently. "I once knew a man who—who got caught like that."

Travers suddenly wondered. There had been something strange in the statement. Was it Brown himself who had been caught? Or, more fantastic, had Brown done the catching? But he merely smiled at the reminiscence. "And Mr. Leslie Hunt, Brown. Is he in?"

Brown smiled sardonically. "He's in the late master's study, sir. All those geological chippings and things that the late Mr. Hunt got together, he's going to dump out there in the wood. If they'd have burnt they'd have gone on here."

Travers nodded again. "Ask him if he will see me, will you?"

He followed Brown round to the front, and was shown into the dining-room. Somehow he felt singularly uneasy. It was not altogether that childish revenge which young Hunt was taking on his dead uncle, or the pessimistic saturnity of Brown, or the fact that the rain was now falling and the room where he was dark; it was none of those, and yet it was all of them that gave him a feeling of disquietude. And there was the message he had to convey, and the effect it might have on the two who heard it.

Travers sat in that room for ten minutes before he heard steps on the stairs. When he looked round, Leslie Hunt was entering the room. His face was pale and that was strange, for his normal colour, as far as Travers remembered, had been of the pinky type. Travers rose at once, and gave his best smile.

"Good morning, Mr. Hunt. My name's Travers. Perhaps you remember me as a fellow passenger in the train."

Hunt licked his lips as he held out a nervous hand. Brown hovered by the door, and then with a quick explanation came over.

"If you'll pardon me, sir, I'll shut this window. The rain's coming in."

The two stood watching him and Travers's heart began to beat fast. He gave a little clearing of his throat.

"Don't go, Brown, will you? I'd like to speak to both you and Mr. Hunt if you've no objection."

Brown shot a look at him, and at his master.

"Do sit down, both of you, won't you?" smiled Travers, and took a seat himself. "I shan't keep you very long. I ought to say first that I'm not here in a private capacity. I represent the police authorities."

Leslie Hunt stared fixedly at him, and there seemed to be no drop of blood in his face. Brown stood intent with never a flicker of an eyelid.

"For instance," went on Travers, "I rather gathered, Mr. Hunt, that you were thinking of going abroad in the near future."

Hunt began to stammer something. Travers, now desperately self-conscious, was afraid he was going to burst into tears. The look on his face was the same that had trembled on it in the train that evening when his uncle had rated him. Brown's voice cut in. "You mean, sir, that we shouldn't be allowed to—to go out of the country?"

"Yes—and no," Travers told him. "The orders I'm instructed to convey to you are that you must both hold yourselves in readiness to proceed to Paris at a moment's notice. You may be required to give further evidence in the matter of the death of the Frenchman, Monsieur Olivet."

Leslie Hunt gave a quick gasp of what might have been relief; then he wiped his lips with his handkerchief. Brown's eyes narrowed slightly.

"Olivet? The one I asked you about, sir? The one who had something the matter with his throat?"

Travers nodded. "That's the man. He was murdered!"

There was a look of quick interest from young Hunt. Brown looked puzzled.

"Murdered, sir?"

"Yes," said Travers. "A dose of atropine was injected into his forearm with a syringe."

Brown craned forward slightly. "A dose of what, sir?"

"Atropine," repeated Travers. "A highly poisonous drug."

Brown shook his head. "Never heard of it, sir. And how did it all happen, sir, if I may ask?"

His manner was so utterly natural that Travers saw no point in pursuing that particular line any further. He smiled dryly.

"That's what the French authorities want to find out. Still, there's something far more important than even that, which may mean both of you going back to France."

"Indeed, sir?" broke in Brown.

Travers nodded, and his eyes went from one to the other of them. "You will most certainly be required to tell all you know about the death of James Hunt."

Brown kept his level-eyed look. It fascinated Travers, and for the life of him he could not turn his own eyes away.

"I understood that that inquiry was finished, sir."

"You mean you thought your late master died a natural death?"

"And didn't he, sir?" Brown's eyes narrowed.

Travers shook his head. "Not a natural death, Brown. He was killed. Stabbed with a hatpin!"

Leslie Hunt's eyes were goggling. Brown seemed to thrust himself forward, and his words came as a torrent.

"That was the dream, sir. He said he did it in his dream." He shook his master by the arm. "Pull yourself together, sir. It *was* only a dream, sir. It couldn't be true."

His voice rose to a shout. He leaned back to Travers, and his face was convulsed.

"He dreamt he did it. In a dream." He whipped round again, and it all seemed horribly grotesque as he shouted. It was like a man who rouses a drunkard to tell him some dreadful thing; something that he must hear; something that has to get through the fuddled brain into clear consciousness. And then Travers saw the flop as Leslie Hunt went down in the chair. Brown had his arms round him in a moment, and his voice was suddenly and strangely quiet. "He's fainted, sir. It's been too much for him."

Travers gave a foolish shake of the head as he followed Brown out of the room and up the stairs. In the bathroom was an arm-chair, and the limp body was laid back in it. Brown went to the corner cabinet.

"If you keep an eye on him, sir, I'll see if I can get him round."

He mixed a dose of what was obviously sal volatile. Travers lifted the head, and Brown tried to get some of the liquid down. He shook his head.

"I'll get him on his bed, sir. Perhaps you'll bring a towel, sir, and wet it in the cold water."

They worked on him for five minutes before he opened his eyes. As soon as they fell on Travers they closed again, and he gave a sort of moan. Travers didn't like the look of him, and he told Brown so.

"I've seen him like this before, sir," Brown told him. He got an eiderdown from the wardrobe drawer and laid it over the body of the scarcely conscious boy—Travers could hardly think of him as a man—and wiped the perspiration from his forehead. Then he made signs to Travers.

"He'll be better in a few minutes, sir. We ought really to leave him quiet."

Travers tiptoed from the room with Brown at his heels. But as soon as the door was closed, Travers had to speak.

"Don't you think you'd better get the doctor to have a look at him straightaway?"

Brown's eyes narrowed again. There seemed to be something menacing in the way he spoke.

"I don't think so, sir, if you'll pardon me. If he doesn't recover, as I think he will, then I'll have the doctor fetched."

"Have your own way," said Travers curtly. "Only, don't blame me if anything happens."

"Nothing will happen, sir," said Brown quietly. "I know what I'm talking about, if you'll pardon me." But he still stood between Travers and the door.

Travers looked him in the eye. "Don't keep using that parrot phrase. It's not a question of pardon—it's a question of responsibility. And now what was this you were telling me down there just before he fainted? That story about a dream?"

Brown's attitude changed miraculously to one of humility. His shoulders sagged, and a look of pain came over his face.

"He told me about it this morning, sir, and I wouldn't believe him. I said it was one of those books of his he'd been reading that had got it into his head, and I thought I'd made him see sense, and that's why I burnt all those books."

Travers stared. "You mean he dreamed he killed his uncle with a hat-pin?"

"God forgive me, yes, sir," said Brown solemnly. "Only, if what you say is true, sir, it wasn't a dream really. I mean it was a dream, and if he did it he didn't know what he was doing."

"I see." Travers nodded heavily. Then he flashed a quick look at the valet. "You believe his story? He didn't kill his uncle deliberately?"

"I believe him," said Brown quietly. "I've known him longer than you have, sir. He's done some queer things in his sleep. He wouldn't harm a fly otherwise."

Travers looked away. Things had happened too suddenly and too overwhelmingly. He moistened his lips as he thought.

"All the same, you'd better see that neither you nor he leaves the house, Brown," he said at last. "Is there anybody you can send for the doctor?"

"Not a soul in the house except ourselves," said Brown. "The women left yesterday, sir. Ellman, the chauffeur, went, too."

"Right!" said Travers. "You stay here, and I'll see the doctor." A sudden thought. "You're not on the phone?"

"I'm afraid not, sir. People who know us, sir, phone to the inn, and they come and tell us."

Travers left him, and hurried off for the Bentley. All he realized was that he himself was in a dilemma. His place ought to be with Hunt, to hear his own statement when he came round, and yet Wharton had been most insistent on four o'clock in town. And perhaps at that very moment Brown was in the bedroom putting new words into Hunt's mouth—*just as he had seemed to put into his mind that story about a dream.* Then Travers thought what might be done. He would arrange with the doctor to telephone him on the journey back to town—say at Sevenoaks—and he would use the doctor's phone to deliver that message to the Rye police.

CHAPTER XIV
CATASTROPHE!

WHARTON GOT GOING early that same morning. The Yard saw him at eight o'clock inquiring anxiously for any news from Gallois. But there was none, and he set out for Chelmsford. A fast car with a good driver landed him at Colby Hall at ten o'clock. It was a large house with spacious gardens, and Mrs. Cheerly, he thought, must have risen in the world since acting as housekeeper to the Hunts at Buxton. In any case, he left the car by a side shrubbery, and went round to the back door. Ultimately he was shown into the butler's parlour where he found a quietly-mannered, competent woman of late-middle age, who was obviously very much at a loss to know either who he was or what he wanted.

The first piece of information Wharton gave her frankly, and he soon gathered that she had read of the death of James Hunt. After that he wrapped up the reason for his visit in so much high-sounding verbiage that she probably connected him with solicitors and surviving relatives, who could only be entangled from the grip of obstinate French officials with her own good help. But whatever she thought, she talked freely enough.

She had spent seven years with the Hunts. Mrs. Hunt was a younger woman than her husband, and she came of good family—at least, so it was understood. Mrs. Cheerly always got on with her very well indeed, and as Mrs. Hunt was never strong, in course of time the housekeeper had become virtual mistress. James Hunt was a queer sort of man with a biting tongue, though, as Mrs. Cheerly said, his bark was worse than his bite. He doted on his wife, who, for all his occasional irritabilities, could twist him round her little finger. There had been one child—a boy—that had died a few moments after birth.

"Was that while the nephew, Leslie, was there?" asked Wharton.

"Oh, no," she said. "Leslie came the year after that. The year after the War. What I thought was, the reason they adopted him was to make her forget about her own."

"No doubt," said Wharton. "He'd be seven years old then. They sent him away to school?"

"Not away," she said. "He used to go to schools quite close. Mrs. Hunt didn't like him being away."

Wharton nodded. "And there was a valet in those days?"

"A valet?" She smiled. "Mr. Hunt didn't keep a valet. There was me and the two maids, and a chauffeur-gardener. Of course we used to have a woman in for rough work sometimes."

"Naturally," said Wharton. "And why was it the Hunts came to leave Buxton?"

"Ah!" she said, with a meaning nod of the head. "There was a mystery about that I never quite got to the bottom of."

"A mystery," repeated Wharton, with an enigmatic nod of his own. "Perhaps I shall be able to explain it for you. What was mysterious exactly?"

"Well," she said, "there was something peculiar about the whole thing. It was in the March—the year after Leslie came— when we first heard about it, then Mr. Hunt gave us all notice. He was very kind about it and said he was sorry, and I must say he gave everybody a very good reference; and he said, of course, he'd never have dreamt of parting with me if he hadn't been going abroad."

"Abroad?"

"Yes," she said, "and that's the peculiar part about it, because when poor Mrs. Hunt was lying sick, and I looked after her a bit while the nurse was out of the room, she told me they were going right away to the south of England."

"Which is just what they did do!"

She nodded. "That was funny, wasn't it? And not only that; to show how small the world is, the sister of one of the maids went to Rye and got friendly with someone at that Peddleby place, and that's how I found out that Mr. Hunt had been putting me off with a lot of lies."

Wharton clicked his tongue to signify his horror of lies and all wickedness. "A remarkable thing, as you say. What on earth did he want to put you off like that for? And as soon as he got down to Peddleby he went and engaged a new staff exactly like the one he had got rid of so unnecessarily at Buxton. Very mysterious."

"You see," she went on, "even his wife's death didn't make any difference. The end of the month they were supposed to go away, and she was took ill suddenly in the middle of the month. A heart attack it was. I remember we stayed on till the day after the funeral, and the same day as we left, the removal vans came along, and next day the house was empty and up for sale."

"Something fishy somewhere," said Wharton, and really meant it. "I thought perhaps I might have explained it, but I can't. It's beyond me. Unless, of course, you ever ran across Brown."

But a description of Brown produced nothing. She remembered nobody of the type or name who had been employed at Buxton. She had never heard the name mentioned by either of the Hunts, or any of the maids. Wharton asked a few more general questions, and then said he'd have to be going.

"Funnily enough," he said, "I'm just about to interview at Cambridge the housekeeper who was your successor at Peddleby. If anything interesting turns up, would you like to hear it?"

"I would, very much," she said. "I hate mysteries, don't you?"

"I do," said Wharton. "At least, when you can't get to the bottom of them."

He refused the wine and biscuit she wished him to have against his journey, gave her the most charming of thanks, and pushed off again in the car. It was exactly noon when he knocked at the door of that large, detached, Victorian house known as "Montguichet," on the Royston Road. Mrs. Ayton, the housekeeper, was a woman of about forty-five; alert, affable and informative.

Wharton tried the prescription as before, and when she had gulped down the plausible dose, added a sweetener to the effect that he had just seen her predecessor in the service of James Hunt. She received the information with so little curiosity that he knew Hunt had made no mystery when he engaged her. And then he knew why. Leslie was the connecting link between Buxton and Peddleby, and there was little use in Hunt's lying about Buxton when his nephew might at any minute boyishly blurt out the truth.

The disclosures of Ellen Ayton were made slowly at first, but became positively garrulous as the minutes went by. She said she had obtained the Peddleby post through an agency. She had then seen Mr. Hunt personally, and had been responsible for the engaging of the two maids. But Brown, the gardener-chauffeur, had already been at "Marsh View" for a fortnight when she first saw the place herself.

"Gardener-chauffeur?" said Wharton. "That's queer. Only a month ago he was gardener-valet. There was a special chauffeur."

"Oh, yes," she said, "that was after the accident."

Wharton pricked up his ears again. He had never heard of any accident, he said. And then she confessed that her own ideas were rather hazy, but as far as she remembered, the facts were that the car had at the time been proceeding from Peddleby to Rye, Brown driving and his master inside. According to Brown's story, something had gone wrong with the car at the top of Rye Hill, and he got out to attend to it. By some unaccountable slipping of the brakes the car had moved off and before Brown could get to it, was careering down that terrific slope. Two hundred yards down it caught the high bank with a crash and overturned. Luckily, however, James Hunt had leaped just as the car gathered speed, and he got off with cut knees and a broken arm. Had he remained in the car he would have been smashed pretty badly.

"And Brown didn't get the sack?"

"Well, it wasn't really his fault," she said.

"All the same," smiled Wharton, "Mr. Hunt didn't raise his salary!"

"Oh, no," she began, and then made a curious pause. She seemed to be thinking back, and she gave a reminiscent nod of the head. "It was very funny about those two," she went on. "I don't know how Brown stood it, the way he used to get spoken to. I know I wouldn't have put up with it myself."

Wharton nodded. "I've gathered something of the kind. Any violent scenes were there?"

She hesitated again. "There was something very funny—so I thought at the time." Her voice lowered. "I reckon Mr. Hunt got into his head that Brown meant to kill him in that accident. Don't tell anybody I said so; but I thought it at the time, and I've often thought about it since."

Wharton leaned forward confidentially in his chair. "What made you think that?"

"Well," she said slowly, "it was something really that I heard. After the accident it was, when the master got about again. I happened to be in the room above where him and Brown were and the bottom window was open, and I heard what you might call high words, and I couldn't help listening. I heard Mr. Hunt say: 'You'll never kill me like you killed—' and I didn't catch what it was he said Brown had killed. And then Brown said something, and Mr. Hunt he said: 'You're afraid of what I've got under lock and key.' I heard that as distinctly as I hear you in that chair. And that was all I did hear, because Brown shut the window downstairs. And when I got a bit—well, a bit more friendly with Brown a month or two after, I let out what I'd heard, and Brown said he'd been talking about the accident, and what he meant by Brown being afraid of what was under lock and key was the reference of his previous master which said something about another accident Brown had had with him."

Wharton smiled sarcastically. "Pretty fishy, wasn't it, for an explanation?"

"That's what I thought," she said. "Brown said if Mr. Hunt liked to put the accident he had with the other man and the one he had with Mr. Hunt into his testimonial, nobody would ever employ him again as a chauffeur."

"And did Mr. Hunt employ him again as a chauffeur?"

She smiled. "Oh, no. That was when Brown was brought into the house to do odd jobs and serve at table, and so on. Mr. Hunt got a special chauffeur, who had to help in the garden, too."

Wharton nodded. "And how did you get on with Mr. Hunt?"

"Oh, not so bad," she said. "The work wasn't hard, and it suited me all right. What I didn't like was the way he sometimes treated Brown and his own nephew, and when I couldn't stand it any longer I gave in my notice. Then he raised my wages—the second time that was—and I stopped."

What Wharton set himself then to do was to analyze the precise position of Brown in the house, and Mrs. Ayton's reactions to him. The task was too difficult. The housekeeper seemed to have liked Brown, and at the same time to have mistrusted him. There was something funny about him. It was not that he was stand-offish, for that was only during the first weeks after her arrival at "Marsh View"; but there was always something in Brown's background that kept him apart. All she ever gathered about his past was that he had been a chauffeur-gardener before, and yet as a chauffeur he had failed, and as a gardener excited risibility in the new chauffeur-gardener who worked alongside him, though he soon picked things up.

And then again, Brown, for all his reserve and his secrecies had a good heart. He went out of the way to help her and the maids, and once when one of the maids scalded herself and the doctor was not handy, Brown saw to her himself, and he blushed when the doctor told him how well he had bandaged, and so on; though all that Brown had disclosed on that occasion was that he had belonged to an Ambulance Society in his younger days. Brown was well educated, too, for he used to read the paper through of an evening, and would often explain things to the staff, who gathered that his people had come down in the world.

"And what was Leslie Hunt like?" Wharton asked.

She thought for a moment. "Oh, he was all right. Not a boy you could get fond of, though I must say he and Brown got on well together. I didn't like him much. He was sort of peculiar; got a screw loose somewhere, I used to say, though Brown wouldn't believe it."

Though Wharton stayed on for another quarter of an hour he got no more marrow from the bone. The rest of the chit-chat were merely cumulative—snubs and sneers which Brown took calmly from his master; the incipient nerves and sleep-walking of Leslie Hunt; and the gradual dislike of the house and its occupants which came over the housekeeper till, as she said and could not explain, if she had stayed any longer she would have gone mad. Wharton himself admitted that she had done well to remain there for four years.

It was one o'clock when he left the house, and the hour's talk had been broken by brief absences when the housekeeper left him to see to the progress of the lunch. He lunched at Cambridge himself, note-book on the table beside him, and as he ate he tried to fit into his own dossier of Brown the facts which he had learned in the last few hours. The whole seemed sufficiently startling.

Not only did the new information fit into the vague theory which he had begun to formulate; it did still more: it began to suggest motives to bulwark that theory. Brown was a peculiar character—there was no denying that—and a lot of evidence stood below his name in Wharton's dossier to prove it. But what the new evidence showed was that Brown and James Hunt, *taken together* were two strange men. What was the bond that held them together? Why had Hunt kept Brown in his employ after that attempt to murder him? And why was Hunt still employing Brown years after that, although he still thought that Brown might murder him—as was shown by those sneering remarks of his which he made to Travers about the lotion and people getting hanged by the neck? Was Brown blackmailing Hunt? But that couldn't be, since Brown was always the under-dog and Hunt the sneering, tongue-lashing master. Then had Hunt blackmailed Brown? But that couldn't be, since a master cannot blackmail a man who had nothing to give. Then had the two been partners in some unholy enterprise which kept them tied snarling to each other like two dogs lashed by the tails? And there again Wharton shook his head, for Brown had done no sneering. He had been in Hunt's power, and that power could only be broken by death; and even after death there remained that *something under lock and key* which still was to keep Brown in his place and make him suffer for a murder from which it had not deterred him.

Wharton saw now the reason for that supposed burglary at "Marsh View"—the reason which had been only vaguely in his mind when he had asked Travers to put to Brown a certain question. Hunt's keys had not been available, but Brown had by some means made a duplicate. He had hurried back to England to open that safe and remove the document that might betray him. The line of action against Brown was, therefore, to clap him by the heels, if necessary, and use the burglary charge as a hold-on till a major charge might be brought.

But could a major charge be brought? Wharton knew the idea was preposterous. Unless Charles Hunt had been Brown's confederate, and Charles Hunt's evidence could be broken down, then Brown had an unassailable alibi. Brown did not use that syringe. And yet—there was a mystery about Brown, as even Mrs. Ayton sensed. Where did he come from when he arrived at "Marsh View"? Who was his former employer? *Who was it that he had killed?* And how had Hunt become aware of that killing?

It was then that Wharton made a sudden resolve. If Hunt and Brown knew each other before Brown came to "Marsh View," then surely it must have been at Buxton, where Hunt had spent most of his years. And Brown's name in those days would not have been Brown, though Hunt's was still Hunt. Then why not let Mrs. Cheerly cast her eyes over Brown to see if she recognized him? Wharton nodded to himself in satisfaction when he thought of that, and with the nod came a confirmatory thought. Mrs. Cheerly—the housekeeper who had suited so well—had been dismissed at Buxton simply because Brown—whom she knew under another name—was to join the household at Peddleby.

Wharton frowned as he looked at his watch. He had lingered over his lunch, and it was now two o'clock. An hour to get to Chelmsford; half an hour with Mrs. Cheerly and her employers, and that meant well over half an hour late for the interview with Travers at four o'clock. Wharton who prided himself on his punctuality, saw no way out of it but to send a message for Travers to stand by.

Travers, who also made a fetish of punctuality, arrived at the Yard a quarter of an hour ahead of time. He was not in the least annoyed when he received Wharton's phone message, because there was something he wished to do, and half an hour would be ample time in which to do it. Within fifteen minutes he was at his bookseller's in Oxford Street, inquiring for a thriller which was called "Murder at the Sal—" and had on its gaudy jacket a splay of pink like the rising sun of Japan.

Madgery knew Travers extraordinarily well, and he was only too anxious to please. First of all the book itself was run to earth, and its full name was "Murder at the Sales." No other publication of recent years had a title that would fit on to that truncation of "Sal—". But when the book itself was brought, there was a difficulty. The jacket was gaudy enough, consisting of a futuristic study of dummy models in a window, but there was no sign of the rising sun of Japan.

"That's curious," said Travers, and then had an idea. "But this is a half-crown edition. Mightn't the jacket of the original seven-and-sixpenny be different?"

Madgery looked inside the cover, and then shook his head. "This is, as a matter of fact, the original edition of last year, with the cheap price printed over." And he exhibited the circular label stuck over the original price.

Travers had another idea. "Sorry to be a nuisance, but could you possibly tell me a book which has that rising sun business on its jacket? I believe two words on it were 'Mystery' and 'Murder.' Also I'd judge it to be fairly new, because the jacket I saw was quite clean."

Madgery put an S O S through to all departments. The result was more astonishing still. All that turned up was a "Short History of Modern Japan," and its jacket was a sun with pink-streaked rays the very spit of those which had covered the book that young Hunt had read in the train. Travers had a good look at it, then all at once put it down and began hooking off his glasses.

"That is the chap I want," he said to Madgery. "My bat eyes rather put me wrong. The words I saw were 'History' and 'Modern,' not 'Mystery' and 'Murder.' I'll take the thriller as well."

He ran his eye over the stodgier book during the short run to the Embankment, and there seemed nothing in it that bore even remotely on the Case of the Three Strange Faces. In Wharton's room a cup of tea was brought to him, and he sat looking through the thriller. And though he had no time to do more than skim it, he could see that it was well-written, and that its plot was out of the common.

The detective hero seemed to be a woman of charm and some social standing who had come down in the world, and was employed by one of the big stores as an anti-shoplifting detective. The first chapter presented her pleasantly and sympathetically at the moment when the doors of the store were opening on the first morning of the greatest bargain sale that London had ever seen. The second chapter showed the swirl of eager and mercenary entrants; seething through the departments by the mere press of numbers from the rear. And of all the crowd one person was behaving strangely, and upon her fell the eyes of the lady-detective. Then there was a shriek, and what looked like an altercation. One woman was accusing another of wearing a *hat-pin* too prominently, so that her face had been scratched. And at that very moment Travers heard the General's feet in the outside corridor.

Wharton came bustling in with a smile in lieu of greeting. "Just heard from Gallois," he said. "They've experimented on the train, and find that injection business was easy enough. And they think they can prove the car left Dijon shortly after the train. The devil of it is they've got nobody who saw anything suspicious going on on the platform." His eyes fell on the book which Travers had hastily closed, and he squinted at the title.

"Hm!' Murder at the Sales!' I just got that from Gallois, too. And what about your day? Get anything important?"

Travers began at the wrong end first, and told him what Brown had said happened on the Dijon platform. Wharton pretended an enormous surprise. Travers, duly gratified, went on to what happened at "Marsh View," and the curious haste of Leslie Hunt to make a last will and testament. Wharton never took his eyes off him till the last word was said. Then he flopped down in the chair.

"Killed him in his sleep, did he? That lets young Hunt out of it. Half the case is gone." He clicked his tongue. "My God! what a catastrophe!"

"But surely," began Travers mildly. "I mean, the fact that Brown appeared to put words into the other one's mouth; even the fact that young Hunt himself may now swear they're true, doesn't mean that it can't be proved otherwise. Leslie almost certainly murdered his uncle, and Brown was shielding him."

Wharton shook his head. "We'd have to bring in medical experts. Juries don't like experts. I don't know why, but they don't—at least, the sort we'd have to bring in."

"You mean psycho-analysis experts?"

Wharton shrugged his shoulders. "Something of the sort. There'd be the question of hypnotism." He looked up quickly. "You thought Brown was trying to hypnotize young Hunt?"

Travers shook his head. "I didn't. What I thought was that he was trying to put an idea into his head." His eyes suddenly opened. "I say—I've got a terrific idea! Suppose, for instance, young Hunt really stabbed his uncle and confided in Brown. Brown might have blackmailed him then into making that will, and if so, the will should be in his favour. *But*, when I suddenly sprang the hat-pin business on the pair of them, Brown saw that young Hunt looked like going to confess to me, and so he gave him the cue to pretend it had all been a dream."

"I see." Wharton scowled. "It's the devil of a tangle. Brown didn't use that syringe. He didn't try to kill old Hunt. And he doesn't strike me as a blackmailer." Then all at once his eyes opened. "If what you say is true, do you realize what might happen? If young Hunt's made a will in Brown's favour, then—" He shook his head portentously. "I don't like it. I don't like it at all."

Travers began polishing his glasses. "Let's keep a sense of proportion, George. Brown wouldn't think of murdering Leslie. We must have got it all wrong. The will may leave the money to Charles Hunt."

Wharton gave another ponderous shake of the head. "Wrong or not, I don't like it. I feel like going down there myself— straightaway. Still," and he brightened up, "I'll go down first thing in the morning and hear what this Dreamer's got to say for himself, and I'll get your friend Lambry to go with me, and we'll also see the doctor. Anything else of importance happen?"

Travers began all over again at the right end, and spread out his notes before the General's eye. He was just concluding the account of his visit to the doctor when the bell rang at Wharton's elbow.

"Hallo!" said Wharton, eye still on Travers's notes. Then he stared. "Yes? Superintendent Wharton speaking. Yes. Carry on."

He seemed to be listening with his breath held, and his eyes scarcely dared to blink. He sat for two good minutes like that, and then snapped into action.

"Right! I'll be down there quick as the car can bring me. How long? Just over two hours."

He gave a curt good-bye, banged the receiver back, and turned to Travers.

"I said young Hunt was out of it, didn't I?"

"Well, I think you did," Travers ventured.

"I was right," said Wharton. "He is out of it—for good. He committed suicide about an hour ago. Brown found him dead in his bedroom. Prussic acid."

CHAPTER XV
WHARTON IS SURPRISED

WHARTON'S CAR took the party down, and Travers, who wished to finish his examination of "Murder at the Sales," sat in front with the driver while Wharton and Menzies, the police-surgeon, sat behind. In a traffic jam at Lewisham, Travers joined the other two.

"Well," said Wharton, "what'd you make of it?"

"I think I've found out the mystery of the two books," Travers told him. "Leslie was playing that old trick on his uncle which some of us used to play at school. I mean he was using the jacket of a perfectly serious book as a blind for the one he was really reading. If you remember, old Hunt had expressed his opinion of thrillers, and so his nephew used the little device of the 'History of Japan' jacket to cover 'Murder at the Sales.'"

"And what about the book itself?" asked Wharton pertinently. "Had it a murder by means of a hat-pin?"

"It hadn't," said Travers, but by no means apologetically. "It did have that little fracas between the two women on account of one of them having too prominent a hat-pin. That turned out to be a staged affair so that a confederate could do some lifting during the confusion. The hat-pin thereupon became a sort of side-track to lead the reader up the garden, so to speak. The real murder was committed by a dummy; you know, one of those lay figures on which clothes of various kinds are draped." He caught Wharton's incredulous look. "Not a real dummy, of course. Someone posing as a dummy."

"Damn clever," said Wharton bitingly. "And where's it get us?"

Travers smiled modestly. "I think it gets us a long way. Leslie Hunt had that hat-pin episode in his mind. Then, later on in the evening, what should happen but something of the sort in real life. I honestly believe he thought the Olivet woman was going to stab his uncle. I put it to you, therefore, no wonder hat-pins got so on his mind that he dreamed about them."

"I see all that," said Wharton. "So does Menzies. But it doesn't satisfy me that young Hunt woke up in the night, found in his hand a hat-pin which had fallen from the rack, and then went to sleep again and actually killed his uncle under the impulse of a dream."

"It's not too improbable," said Menzies, who took a delight in ruffling Wharton's feelings. "People have done strange things in their sleep. Besides, from what I've gathered, he hated his uncle like hell, and he must have thought of polishing him off long before he read that book in the train."

Wharton shrugged his shoulders. "Why worry? He's dead himself, isn't he? A jury won't have to worry their heads over him." He nodded. "What worries me is the immaculate Brown. Brown loved young Hunt like a father—so he says. See the point?"

He whipped round so suddenly with that question that Travers recoiled. "I'm afraid I don't—unless he really *was* his father."

Wharton grunted. "There are more unlikely things than that. But you're a man of some penetration—"

"Thanks!" cut in Travers.

"And I'd like to put the question to you direct. And to Menzies as well. Under what conditions could the immaculate Brown have murdered Leslie Hunt and got away with it?"

Menzies got out his pipe and thought under a pretence of indifference. Travers made faces to himself. Both gave it up.

"Think again," said Wharton. "Think of what that Mrs. Ayton told me. Think of M. Pajou of St. Raphael."

That let out Menzies, who knew nothing of either suggested recollection. Travers puzzled his wits again, and once more gave it up.

Wharton shrugged his shoulders again. "Later to-night I may have to put that question to you again. And, by the way, what was that you were telling me about Brown and the gerund?"

"The gerund?" Travers smiled. "What I told you was that Brown was capable of speaking perfect English, and I believe you rather sat on me."

"Come, come," said Wharton. "I might have been absent-minded, perhaps, but supercilious—no I Still, what precisely *is* a gerund?"

Wharton protested that he was in earnest. Menzies offered his own definition.

"If I remember right, it's like this. You say, 'I don't like *your* hat!' You wouldn't say, 'I don't like *you* hat.' In the same way you'd say, 'I don't like *your* singing,' and not, 'I don't like *you* singing,' or, 'singing songs.'"

He looked at Travers for confirmation. "That's well put," Travers told him. "Singing in 'singing songs' is a noun or gerund."

"I'll take your word for it," said Wharton. "And that makes Brown out to be a man of considerable education, does it?"

"Either that or a man who has had much direct experience of the speech of cultured people."

"I see," said Wharton, and looked not displeased. But he went off at a tangent. "Where are we now? Somewhere near Sevenoaks?"

The front gates at "Marsh View" were closed, but a constable was on duty. Quite a number of people were round the front door, and the local inspector came forward to meet them.

"Where is he?" Wharton asked at once.

"Upstairs," he was told. "We haven't touched anything."

"Right!" said Wharton. "You coming, Mr, Travers?"

Travers shook his head. Once before he had seen a death by cyanide poisoning, and it had taken him weeks to forget it. Wharton and Menzies went through to the stairs, talking with the county surgeon. Brown was seated in the corridor, and another constable was on duty outside the bedroom door.

"We asked Mr. Brown to be here in case you wished to hear the evidence yourself," the inspector said.

Wharton nodded. "How are you, Brown?" he said. "Still more trouble for you?"

Wharton's manner was so sympathetic that Brown could only shake his head and say nothing. The four went through the door. Wharton and the inspector stood aside after the first look, and Menzies and his colleague examined the body. Young Hunt in death was grotesque rather than horrible. His eyes bulged, one of his hands clutched the sheet at his side, and there was an absurd sort of stain along his mouth and chin. The sheet was stained, too, where the dregs of the poison had trickled from the glass which lay on the carpet at the far side of the bed where doubtless the convulsions of the dead man had kicked it. Menzies drew back.

"Seems clear as daylight," he said. "You any suggestions?"

The county surgeon said he had none, except of course that there should be a P.M. Wharton suddenly cut in:

"What about the local doctor? Did he—?"

The words were cut short by the opening of the door, and there was the constable showing the doctor in.

"Ah, here you are," said Wharton briskly. "Doctor Popland, isn't it?" He went on talking through the handshake. "What did you actually do to this chap when Mr. Travers called you in this morning?"

"As a matter of fact, I didn't see any need to do anything," Popland told him. "I did give him a little more sal volatile, but that was more for effect than anything else."

"He was all right then?"

"Well, not exactly all right. I'd say, not very wrong. He'd undoubtedly fainted, but that was nothing very serious in one of his medical history. Also, he'd had a lot of worry recently. I gave him the one tiny dose, and told him to lie where he was for a bit. Then I told Brown afterwards to see how he was in half an hour, and then get him to have some lunch. Brown said he would, and he'd also get him to go out in the car, and Brown was to fetch me if anything serious happened. I told Mr. Travers all that when he called me up from Sevenoaks this afternoon."

"Let Brown come in for a moment," said Wharton.

The valet entered with a quick glance round at the crowded room. Wharton tackled him at once.

"What happened precisely after Doctor Popland left this morning?"

"You mean—" He hesitated.

"That's right," said Wharton. "What happened to the one who's dead on that bed?"

"Well, sir," began Brown, "as I've already told the inspector—"

"I know you've spoken to the inspector," said Wharton patiently. "We're not trying to muddle you or catch you out in anything. All I want you to be good enough to do is to forget what you told the inspector, and tell *me* what happened."

"Well, sir," went on Brown again, "I did just what the doctor said. I set the lunch table. Cold mutton we were going to have and salad, and there was some tinned fruit salad I'd got at Rye. When the half-hour was up, I roused Mr. Leslie, and he came down after going to the bath-room. He had a little lunch, sir, and some lemonade with it—as you'll find, sir, if you have to make an examination of him."

"I expect we shall," said Wharton, taken aback at what had been an amazing remark. "Carry on, Brown."

"Then after the meal, sir, while I cleared things up, he read the paper and smoked a cigarette or two. I suggested that either I should drive him out somewhere, or he should drive himself, but he wouldn't do either. He went upstairs again, and then he came down and went out towards the garden. I didn't see him again till three o'clock, sir, when I went to the garden to look for him, and as he wasn't there I went up to his room to look through the window because, as you can see, sir, it gives a view over the garden and the path through the wood. That's when I found him, sir, and I at once informed the doctor and the police."

"Where'd he get the poison from?"

"Undoubtedly from the shed, sir. There's always some there. All the dangerous stuff is kept on a shelf by itself above the door; weed-killer and stuff for wasps' nests."

"Nothing else happened previously? Nothing at all?"

Brown frowned in thought. "Well, sir, a message came from the phone at the inn that Mr. Hughes was ringing up from Hastings, and would like to speak to Mr. Leslie. I slipped over and said he wasn't very well, and I took the message myself, and met Mr. Leslie coming down to lunch."

"What was the message?" asked Wharton.

"Only to say that the letter had been destroyed, sir."

"Letter? What letter?"

Brown shook his head.

"I haven't any idea, sir. I merely gave the message as directed."

That was all that Wharton wanted from Brown at the moment. As soon as the door closed on him, the inspector began complementing the valet's evidence.

"It was all right about the poison," he said. "Ellman, the late chauffeur, got it at Rye, and signed the book in the usual way."

"What about prints on the glass?" Wharton asked him.

"We're all ready to do that now."

Wharton nodded. "Then if these people are ready to get him away, you might make a start. I'm going along to the local inn for a bit."

The police ambulance was drawn up outside, and when Wharton came out Travers was regarding it contemplatively. He agreed with Wharton that a quick meal would be a good idea. It was a good while since lunch, and it might be longer before there was a chance of supper. Wharton gave his impressions of the bedroom as they strolled along. Travers could find no flaw in the case for suicide.

"The only thing is the bed," he said. "Why should he be lying on the bed if he wanted to drink poison?"

"Suicides are queer folk," said Wharton. "But what struck me was not so much the fact that he was lying on the bed as the way he was dressed. His jacket was over the back of a chair, and he had on a cricket shirt open at the neck. I asked Brown about how he was dressed at lunch, and Brown said he had his jacket on. Presumably, therefore, he had it on when he went to the tool-shed to get the poison, and presumably he had it on when he went to the bath and got the glass and the water in which the poison was to be dissolved. Why, then, did he take off his jacket when he entered the bedroom?"

"Don't know," said Travers. "Perhaps he took it off while he lay on the bed to get his courage to the right point. And after all, everything else was all right, wasn't it?"

"Oh, yes," said Wharton dryly. "Everything else was all right. Now will you order a meal of sorts while I do some telephoning?"

It was ten minutes before the General was back, and Travers was already at the table. Wharton nodded amiably at the ham, and beamed at the pot of tea.

"What about staying over the night?" he said to Travers. "Any minute something might turn up which you'd have to corroborate."

"If you think it at all necessary," began Travers.

"That's all right then," said Wharton. "The room's all ready, and the landlady's fixing you up with a nightshirt!"

Travers was forced to smile, not at the nightshirt, but Wharton's assumptions. The meal was well on the way before he ventured to ask what the programme was.

"First thing in the morning we see that solicitor," Wharton told him. "Then we get back here in time to parade Brown in front of the Buxton housekeeper. Ellman is being brought down here, too. If nothing happens, we shall probably go back to town, and there'll be a ways and means conference, where some genius will suggest that we dive deep down into Brown's past life, and Ellman's, and James Hunt's!"

Travers frowned slightly. "A mere suggestion, but wouldn't Brown be prepared to tell you something about himself if he were approached in the right way?"

Wharton smiled sardonically. "You forget that Brown never makes a mistake. I *did* have a word with him—just now. I was offering private condolences, and I said, 'You always struck me as too good for this kind of work. What did you do before you came here?' He made no bones about telling me. He'd been in Australia, doing much the same thing; only, he added something like this. 'It's a part of my life which I don't look back on with any pleasure, and I'd rather not talk about it, if you don't mind.' See the point.

Travers smiled. "He was telling you very tactfully that he knew the laws of evidence, and suggested you should mind your own business."

"Exactly!" said Wharton. "Also, though Brown didn't know it, he was confirming some of the evidence I got this morning. Mrs. Ayton said he was a dud gardener. If he'd never done any gardening in England he undoubtedly was."

"You believe the Australia story, then?"

"I believe every man," said Wharton virtuously, "till I catch him out in a lie."

"And what about that lie Brown told when he said James Hunt had been ill at St. Raphael?"

"That was a first let-off," said Wharton; "every man's entitled to one chance. Besides, Hunt may have been ill after all."

Travers gave it up after that. The meal came to an end, and the two went back to "Marsh View" again. They inspected the tool-shed where the red tin of weed-killer stood on the shelf above the door and a bottle with a red label was wedged into the shelf corner. Wharton sniffed the cork from a distance, and Travers caught the almond smell. When they got to the house again the inspector reported that the prints on the glass were those of the dead man only. And he showed Wharton a diagram to prove that the prints were naturally placed and not such as might have been superimposed by a second person after death.

"That's all right, then," said Wharton. "I suppose, by the way, the house was under observation all the afternoon?"

The inspector indicated Travers. "Fifteen minutes after this gentleman rang us up, we had two men here. One was this side and one that."

"And Brown didn't leave the house?"

"He didn't."

"He wasn't seen going out to the garden? To that tool-shed, for instance?"

The inspector pulled a face. "That'd be asking too much, sir. You can see for yourself. Unless you come right inside the drive you can't see what's going on in the grounds."

Wharton grunted, then changed the subject. "I suppose you don't know by any chance where the two maids and the house-keeper went after they left here?"

"I know where one of the maids is," the inspector told him. "Brown might know where the others are."

"Brown's the last person I want to ask," said Wharton, "so don't mention anything to him. And where's this maid?"

"She's with a sister of mine at Bittlesham," the inspector said. "I got her the job as soon as I knew she was leaving here."

Wharton took the address and said he might do worse than pay a quick visit. The village was nearer Rye than Hastings, and it would not be dark for well over an hour. So Wharton's chauffeur was sent to the inn for a meal, and Travers drove the car. When they found the cottage Wharton asked him to come in.

The maid was not Sussex bred, but a Londoner in type; pert in tongue and yet sufficiently unintelligent to answer questions without seeing too much of their imports. Wharton asked her about conditions at "Marsh View," and then put the direct question about Ellman.

"I didn't like him—not much," she said.

"Any particular reason?" asked Wharton winningly.

"Well," she simpered, "he was a bit fast. He took too much on himself."

"Exactly," said Wharton. "And a smart girl like yourself naturally attracted him. And did you ever hear him say anything about his master?"

"Oh—er!" she blushed for the exclamation. "Once he did, when he'd been ticking him off. He said he'd like to do him in."

"You mean—murder him?"

She nodded. "Yes, and he called him—something dreadful. I wouldn't repeat, but something beginning with 'b'."

Wharton's eyebrows raised themselves in horror.

"He wasn't like Mr. Brown," she went on. "He was very nice, he was."

"How nice?" smiled Travers archly.

"Well, he did things for you. Sort of was—well, nice. Once I had indigestion, and he gave me something for it. Took it away at once, it did."

But Wharton's other questions were unanswered. She had no information on the relationship between Ellman and Mr. Leslie, and nothing new to impart about Brown and Leslie, either. The whole affair had taken no more than ten minutes, and when they came out of the house, Travers made a suggestion.

"Seems a pity now we're so close to Hastings not to see that chap Hughes at his private address. I believe he said he lived somewhere near."

Wharton agreed and went back to the house to inquire if anything was known. Mr. Guy Hughes, it turned out, was quite well known. His house was less than five minutes' drive away, on the Winchelsea Road.

And when they drew up outside the house, which stood well back from the road, sounds of revelry were coming from it. Wharton made a grimace, and as he and Travers rounded the short drive, there were the Hughes family having a dance of their own on the lawn to the music of a loudspeaker. Hughes looked more sheepish than surprised when he caught sight of the two visitors, but he gathered that something serious was in the wind, and he took them into the house. Wharton told him the news. The lawyer seemed horrified to hear of Leslie's death—so horrified and upset, in fact, that Wharton, as Travers knew, was knocked out of his stride. Wharton had certainly been intending to give Hughes the full length of his tongue; as it was he toned things down.

"I have an idea, you know," he said, "that if you'd have told Mr. Travers the contents of his will, there wouldn't have been this new disaster. Keep that to yourself, by the way."

Hughes began a defence. It would have been unpardonable to give away a client's confidences without implicit assurances.

Travers could see that what he wanted to say was that he could betray confidences only to someone of staggering importance—like Wharton himself—and not to a comparative nonentity like Travers.

"That's all right," Wharton told him, "but you can't very well have any scruples now. Who gets his money?"

"Brown gets it," said Hughes. "The will, I ought to say, was a home-made one, and only shown to me for an opinion whether it was in order—which it was. Naturally I made no comment. I ought to tell you, though, that it contained a very fulsome kind of acknowledgment. Brown is referred to as 'my only real friend.'"

"Perhaps he was," said Wharton enigmatically. "And while I'm on the subject, Charles Hunt may look you up to-morrow. As the only relative, he ought to be down in the morning—if he's well enough."

He added an explanation about Charles Hunt's cold, and then said he would have to be getting along back. Hughes accompanied them to the car, and it was just as Travers was pushing out the clutch that Wharton thought of something else.

"Without inquiring too closely into still more private affairs, didn't you call up Leslie Hunt from the inn this midday about a letter?"

"That's right," said Hughes. "I did. It arose out of what you told me yesterday on the phone, that his uncle's death was perfectly natural."

Wharton frowned. "What *is* all this mystery? I rang you up and told you his uncle's death was natural?" Some vague premonition was coming over his mind that, like many another honest liar, he was being caught in his own camouflage.

"Well, there's no reason why you shouldn't know all about it now," said Hughes. "It was some years ago—ten or thereabouts—that James Hunt entrusted us with a letter, duly sealed, with instructions that if he died an unnatural death it was to be opened and, if not, it was to be destroyed by us. Leslie Hunt himself was aware of its existence because he asked me about it when I last saw him. I told him I could not destroy till I was satisfied, and then when you rang me up yesterday and I asked you, and you said the death was a natural one, I decided to destroy. But I didn't." And there Hughes looked at Travers triumphantly. "I decided to wait till Mr. Travers came this morning in case anything fresh had happened. Mr. Travers will recall that I particularly asked about James Hunt's death, and he confirmed your statement. Thereupon I destroyed the letter in the presence of the necessary witnesses."

"And quite right, too," said Wharton, with a heartiness that was probably the best effort of his histrionic career. He nodded once or twice. "Then we'll see you at the inquest? Eleven o'clock at the inn."

Travers's hand went to the gear lever, but Wharton thought of something else.

"Oh, Mr. Hughes, what did you assume were the contents of that letter?"

"I assumed nothing," said Hughes stiffly. "It isn't my place to assume. As I told you, on the outside of the envelope it said that it was only to be opened if he had died an unnatural death."

"And what'd you think when you were given it?"

"You'll pardon me," said Hughes, "but it isn't my place to think. It was a definite instruction given by a client, and I thought no more about it. Also that client was a peculiar man to get on with. The envelope was placed in his box with other papers, and the rest you know."

"Perhaps you're right," Wharton admitted grudgingly. "And when did you see Leslie Hunt about his uncle's will?"

"I got a telegram from him on the Saturday afternoon," said Hughes. "It was quite unusual, but I went to see him on the Sunday morning as requested."

"And he made his own will on the following morning," commented Wharton. "Quick work, that." He smiled grimly. "I suppose Brown hasn't been to see you about making *his* will?"

"I know," said Hughes, and looked rather uncomfortable. "It's a most remarkable affair. Brown inherits thirty hours after the will was made. Still, there we are. Facts are facts." He looked up. "Anything else I can do for you?"

"I don't think so," said Wharton, and somewhat limply. "See you to-morrow, then, before the inquest begins."

Travers got the car going. All at once a faint blush stole over his face and pinked his ears. He shook his head gently.

"George, the way of transgressors is hard."

Wharton glared. "Don't go hurling your lumps of Scripture at me. All the same, how were we to suspect the existence of anything like that letter?"

"Lord knows," said Travers consolingly. "Only, it strikes me that before this case is over we're going to wish pretty damn hard that we'd kept to the straight and narrow path."

"You keep this car to the crooked and narrow road, and let me think," was Wharton's curt rejoinder.

CHAPTER XVI
ZERO HOUR

THERE WAS SILENCE for a minute or two. Wharton, as Travers for all his flippancy knew, had gone through a bad quarter of an hour. He had decided—and probably rightly—that James Hunt's murder should be kept a secret, except in so far as it had been used by Travers himself in the presence of Brown and Leslie Hunt. Now, in a few hours' time, Brown would take the stand at the inquest, and his evidence could only reveal that Wharton had taken a risk—an unpardonable thing when that risk failed to justify itself. Then there was the question of Hughes, who would naturally be more than indignant at having been led into committing a breach of trust. Travers uttered that last thought aloud.

"You'll square Hughes all right, George," he said.

Wharton grunted. "Perhaps I shall. All the same, there's only one way to satisfy him about that letter, and that's to be in a position to tell him what was in it."

Travers whistled dolefully. "That's a tall order, George!"

"Maybe," said Wharton. "Brown's our only stand-by. Mind you, he didn't do the murder—at least, he didn't do it alone. And, talking of that murder, don't let's get muddled. What turned out to be Olivet's murder was really Hunt's murder by poisoning. The hat-pin business was Hunt's murder by stabbing. What I'm stating is that Brown didn't poison Hunt, unless Charles was in league with him."

"I know he didn't," Travers agreed consolingly. "But what are you driving at, George?"

"Merely this," Wharton told him. "Brown *ought* to have done the poisoning. If we take that housekeeper's evidence as implicitly correct, then Brown had already killed one person, and James Hunt knew it. Further, it isn't too absurd to suppose that the car accident was a first attempt by Brown to kill James Hunt. Again, James Hunt knew all that, and he had presumably in his safe a letter which, if Brown ever succeeded in killing him, should get the said Brown hanged by the neck. That was why Brown faked the safe burglary—to get the letter." Wharton shook his head. "Just think of Brown's feelings when he opened the safe and found the letter wasn't there! He must have had a few minutes' concentrated hell."

"All the same," said Travers, "if we agree—as we do—that Brown wasn't concerned in the poisoning, why take all this bother over him? Finding the murderer is the chief thing—and damn Hughes and his letter?"

Wharton shook his head. "Brown intrigues me. There's something in Brown which keeps nagging at me like a rotten tooth." He clicked his tongue. "Take that house. There's been something frightening going on there for years. There's been an evil spirit in it; something fermenting; something coming to a head. It's rotted and seethed, and it's come to a head. And why?" He answered his own question. "What held that house together was James Hunt. He dominated it, and as soon as he died, then all this happened."

Travers found nothing to add; his ideas on "Marsh View" were those of Wharton. There had been the perpetual, mysterious hostility between Brown and his master; hostility that had once before ended almost in murder. Even to the last, when Hunt had entered Pajou's shop, murder had been in the air. And between the larger opposing characters of Hunt and Brown had been the spineless, nervy and not wholly sane personality of Leslie; bullied and sneered at by his uncle, and moulded perhaps by Brown for his own peculiar ends.

"What are you going to do about it, George?"

"First thing in the morning I'm seeing Brown," said Wharton, and he added to himself: "I'm trying a new line of approach, and I think he'll talk."

"I'm sure he will," said Travers hopefully. "Brown's coming not too badly out of all this business, George. The paper of which he was afraid is destroyed, and he's got enough money to live like a fighting cock the rest of his life."

Wharton merely grunted. "Just pull up a minute. There's something I'd like to think out before we enter the village. About that fake burglary. Even if Brown made false scratches, the fact remains that he had a key and opened the safe with it. Then why did he fake a burglary at all? Why didn't he merely open the safe and abstract the letter?"

"I haven't thought about it," Travers told him. "What's your own solution?"

"Well, as I see it, there's two answers," said Wharton. "Hunt may have laid some trap or other. Can't you imagine him torturing Brown? Can't you hear him say that what a pity it is that Brown can't open just that one little door and get free of the letter?—he knowing all the time that the letter wasn't there. Imagine him laughing and saying to Brown, 'And even if you do open the door you'll have a most unpleasant surprise. Everybody'll know it.' That's why I think Brown went to work the wrong end first. He probably scratched the lock before he used the key. And the other reason why Brown had to fake a burglary was because Brown knew that somebody else was aware of the envelope being in the safe. Leslie knew, for instance, though that puzzles me still more. Brown oughtn't to have feared Leslie."

Travers clicked his tongue. "Damnable when you come to think of it. Old Hunt would tell Brown to be careful how he dusted the picture for fear the safe should be scratched or hurt. 'Be careful, Brown,' he'd say. 'There's something very precious inside there.' Then he'd gloat when he saw Brown flinch." He shook his head. "Somehow I'm not sorry he was murdered."

Wharton went off at a tangent. "How did Ellman strike you?"

"As a man—well, not so badly," said Travers. "You're definitely assuming, by the way, that Ellman was the man whom Charles Hunt and Brown saw duck beneath the train?"

"If I were, I wouldn't be worrying my head," said Wharton ironically.

"Don't be fractious, George," Travers told him. "You'd still have to prove it to the satisfaction of a jury."

"I know." The General pursed his lips. "Still, I'm seeing Ellman to-morrow morning, and I'm seeing Charles Hunt. There'll be Mrs. Cheerly here, too, though she's a forlorn hope."

"Pardon the pessimism," said Travers, "but if nothing arises out of to-morrow, George, then how do we carry on?"

"Well"—Wharton was hating too early a disclosure of his plans—"I may have something up my sleeve. I'm going to get right down to the history of Brown. We've just agreed that that house was rotten and demented. Two of the characters are dead, but one's left. Find out all about Brown, and the rest may follow."

Travers nodded. "I agree, George. But suppose Brown—as the law allows—refuses to open his mouth. How are you going to find anything out?"

Here was a chance for the spectacular. Wharton produced his notebook, thumbed the pages over and stopped at the one that was headed "Thomas Brown." Then he wrote something at the bottom of the already crowded page.

"Here we are," he said. "If everything goes wrong, this is what I'm going to do. And as a perfectly sporting proposition, I'll show you this page to-morrow as soon as the inquest's over. I'm having a gamble that a certain theory I've formed is all right. You agree?"

"Of course I agree," smiled Travers. "It's a sporting proposition, as you say; but your theory can't possibly be wrong."

Wharton glared. "Oh? And why can't it?"

Travers chuckled. "Because I know you too well, George. You're not going to show me that theory of yours unless you're plumb certain it's right."

It was practically dark when the car drew up outside "Marsh View." Most houses that have trees and shrubberies enclosing them, thought Travers, are gloomy and depressing in autumn and winter, when everything is damp with dew or rain, and yet in summer those same green, enclosing masses give an effect that is cool and umbrageous and pleasing. But "Marsh View," it suddenly struck him, was not like that. Its trees and encircling green were strangling and choking things that stifled even on a July day, and in winter would oppress with a gloominess that would gnaw at nerves and vitality. No wonder James Hunt had been a hypochondriac and his nephew the furtive, nervy thing that he was.

The inspector emerged from the gloom of the drive, and came over. He conferred with Wharton for a bit, and then the General suggested that Travers should go on to the inn with the car, and he'd be along himself later. Menzies was having a solitary drink in the private room when Travers entered, and he promptly stood the newcomer one.

"Everything satisfactory about cause of death?" Travers asked him.

"Aye," said Menzies. "We might all as well go home, for all they'll need now is the same old gramophone record."

"Gramophone record?" Then he smiled at his own obtuseness. "You mean the same old verdict by the jury."

"That's right," said Menzies. "I'm laying twenty to one."

"But not to me," smiled Travers. "I suppose, by the way, you didn't find any spots on him anywhere when you did the P.M.?"

"What sort of spots?"

"Like those his uncle had after eating the strawberries."

Menzies shook his head. "His skin was as clean as a baby's. The sort of chap who shaves once a week only." He rubbed his own stubbly chin. "There's always something peculiar—what I might call eunuchy—about those smooth-skinned ones. Give me a hairy man."

"You ought to have seen Olivet," Travers told him.

Then Wharton came in; stood the company a final drink, and heard what news there was.

"I wish to God we could get hold of that silver," he remarked to Travers, as they said good night on the landing. "Then Brown'd have to speak."

"You mean the silver Brown took out of the safe when he faked the burglary?"

"That's it," said Wharton. "The inspector got Brown out of the house to-night, and brought him over here for a drink while his men hunted the house and the gardens. Nothing doing!"

"Well, cheer up, George," Travers told him. "There'll be better luck to-morrow. And I'll be with you at breakfast."

"Then you'll have to be up early," said Wharton, "because I've ordered it for half-past seven."

It was just before nine that following morning when the landlord ushered Brown into Wharton's private, downstairs room. It was a perfect July day. The window was open to the garden, and the three easy chairs were shrewdly placed. Travers was putting aside the newspaper; Wharton was adjusting those old-fashioned spectacles that always gave him the appearance of a harassed paterfamilias.

"Take a seat, Brown, will you?" he said quietly. "Looks as if we're in for another fine day."

"Yes, it does, sir," said Brown, and took the middle chair. His manner was assured and uncannily natural.

"We've asked you here to help us," went on Wharton. Travers offered first cigarettes, and then his pouch. Wharton waited till all three pipes were going.

"As I was saying," he went on, "we want you to help us. *And* we want to help you."

"To help me, sir?"

"Yes," said Wharton quietly. "To help you. Scotland Yard mayn't be quite the omniscient place that novelists suppose it, but it has a habit of finding out things. What it has found out in this particular case, I may tell you later. It depends on yourself."

He smiled engagingly. "Shall we have a heart-to-heart, man-to-man talk? Just the three of us? And entirely without prejudice?"

"Without prejudice?" He hardly gathered the full import.

"Yes," said Wharton, "without prejudice. No statement to be taken, and nothing to be used as evidence." A deprecatory smile. "Not, of course, that there's likely to be any question of evidence."

Brown's eyes narrowed slightly, and he moistened his lips. "What precisely was it you wished me to talk about, sir?"

"What?" Wharton grimaced. "Well, we'd like you to tell us precisely why you endured your master's insults for years, and still remained in his employ; why it was that he had the idea you were trying to murder him; why he had a letter about you to be opened by his lawyers in case he *was* murdered, and why you—knowing precisely what was in the letter—faked the burglary to get that letter from the safe." He leaned across urbanely. "I think that's all, Mr. Travers, isn't it?"

"I think it is," said Travers gravely. "Unless, of course, Brown cares to add where he placed the silver."

"Exactly!" Wharton nodded in agreement. "Where Brown put the silver."

Brown rose slowly from the chair, and four eyes watched him. But he only went to the empty fire-place and knocked out the pipe. When he sat down again he was nodding as if his mind were made up.

"Entirely without prejudice then, gentlemen, I'll tell you what I know. It'll be hard to believe, because you've got the whole business topsy-turvy. And it's going to be hard for me to tell the truth because my sole witness is dead."

"You mean James Hunt?"

He shook his head. "Oh, no, sir. Leslie would have been my witness. I loved that boy, sir; I always did. There was something in him—something undeveloped—that woke what I believe has been called the paternal instinct. I got to think of him as my own son. That was why I stood his uncle's jeers and insults."

"But why should he have insulted you at all?" asked Travers.

"Why, sir? Because he was made that way. He had a warped, venomous mind. He hated me because I loved the boy, and the only reason why he didn't dismiss me was because he liked to have me there to jeer at and hurt. I was a sort of chopping-block for his tongue."

"I see." Wharton nodded comprehendingly. "But why did James Hunt reproach you one day with having already killed somebody?"

Brown shook his head. A look of pain seemed to pass quickly over his face. "He only took me on originally, sir, because I was down and out, and humbled myself to him. He happened to discover, sir, that I'd been involved in an accident where my former master was killed."

"You mean, you'd misled him?"

The same look of pain. "Yes, sir; that's what it amounted to. The fault wasn't mine, though I was blamed. It was in Australia, sir, and beyond what I've said I'd rather not think of it again. It's hard to think back—sometimes."

"Yes," said Travers. Something like a vague surge of affection for Brown was coming over him. "But what about the letter?"

Brown smiled wanly. "That's where you've been wrong, gentlemen. That letter concerned Leslie, and not myself. James Hunt taunted me with the letter because he could hurt me through the boy." He caught Wharton's look of overwhelming surprise. "I'll explain, sir. Even as a boy, Leslie had those sleep-walking fits, though we hushed it up. Also he had what's called homicidal tendencies with it, and some years ago his uncle woke up just in time to find him in the room with a knife. After that I slept with the boy, and even then he once escaped me in his sleep, and got at his uncle again. It was about Leslie that his uncle wrote that letter. That was one of the holds he had over him. If he were killed, he said he would see that Leslie was brought to justice, and he'd prove in the letter that he had been perfectly sane."

Wharton's brain was beginning to reel. He wanted to fit things in, and he wanted to hear more. Travers's voice came in.

"Yes, go on, Brown. Tell us what happened after I left the train."

The valet nodded. "After you left the train, sir, Leslie saw his chance. There were two keys of the safe on his uncle's chain, and I took one. Leslie insisted that I should fake a burglary"—he smiled sadly—"his mind was always full of those thrillers, sir. So I got away at once and faked the burglary, as you said. The letter wasn't there—but I put the silver in the water tank in the attic."

"Yes?"

"Then as soon as Mr. Leslie came back he was in despair. He arranged that he should sound Mr. Hughes, and we discovered all about the letter." He smiled, and as he did so became aware of the perspiration that trickled slowly down his cheek, and wiped it away. "It was like a voice from heaven, sir, when Mr. Hughes told me that the letter had been destroyed."

"Yes," said Wharton, "I expect it was. And yet immediately afterwards, Leslie committed suicide."

"Can you wonder, sir?" Brown asked that almost fiercely. "Think what he'd been through. He knew he'd killed his uncle in his sleep. He'd thought the letter was going to betray him." He made as if to go on, but the words wouldn't come.

Wharton clapped him on the back. "Thank you, Brown. We won't trouble you any more. Only, keep your mouth shut. You will say nothing to the Coroner about how James Hunt was killed. That's to be a secret between us three. You'll say that Leslie committed suicide because he'd been upset over his uncle, and he was that sort—which is true. Is that understood?"

"Perfectly, sir." He hesitated. "And if I might thank you, sir?"

Wharton held out his hand. "Nothing to thank me for. We'll see you again after the inquest."

"Sorry," smiled Travers, "but just one insignificant question. We know why Ellman left, but why were the servants all cleared out so quickly?"

"Quickly, sir?" He shook his head. "Well, you see, he was anxious for his liberty, sir. He was getting some money from Mr. Hughes, and he was thinking of going to a London hotel and taking me with him as valet and seeing a bit of what he called life. He didn't want to go to his uncle."

"Thank you, Brown. I think that's all." He smiled friendlily. "I shall probably see you later."

The door closed on Brown. "Poor devil!" said Travers, and shook his head gloomily. Then he chuckled. "You've got yourself nicely out of that hole with Hughes."

But Wharton refused to smile. He was mopping his face with his handkerchief, and he was worried.

"Everything's wrong. Hellish wrong. I'm sorry for Brown, and I oughtn't to be." He shook his head. "Just shows you how circumstantial evidence can be all wrong. Yet I don't know." He shook his head again. "There's something very queer. Brown's all wrong. The more he's right, the more he's wrong!"

Travers looked up quickly. "How is he wrong?"

"I don't quite know—yet," said Wharton. "I've got to think things out. No, I won't. I'll see Ellman—if he's here. Something may turn up out of that. And if nothing turns up over that Cheerly business, we'll have Brown in again, and we'll turn his story inside out. We'll have the local doctor in, too."

"You don't disbelieve Brown?" asked Travers, vaguely hurt.

"Not necessarily," Wharton told him, "only something's wrong, and where, I don't know. And now for Ellman."

But a new rôle was required for Ellman, and Wharton took off the spectacles. The chauffeur came in gingerly enough, and the look on Wharton's face was not helpful.

"Sit down, Ellman, will you?" The voice was coldly official. "There's something we've got to talk about."

The chauffeur fidgeted nervously with his cap. "You mean about the inquest, sir?"

Wharton shook his head. "I very much doubt if you'll be required at the inquest after all. We may have had you down here for nothing. Still, as you *are* here, we may as well tell you something. You may have to go back to Paris. The French authorities aren't satisfied about your statement with the car."

"Surely there's something you can remember that will help determine the time you were at Dijon?" suggested Travers.

"I've already told 'em everything, sir," protested Ellman. "There's only one thing I've thought of since, and that's about the bugle."

"What bugle?" asked Wharton quickly.

"A bugle—a lot of bugles—what we heard as we were coming in," said Ellman. "My friend—the Frenchman what I told you about—he heard it too; sort of in his sleep. It was just as I was passing a place like a barracks."

"Probably be the cavalry barracks," Travers told Wharton. "If so, it'd be a special réveillé for early morning manoeuvres."

"I'll rush an inquiry through at once," said Wharton. He let a beam of joviality spread over his face, till he was sure the jocularity would ring true.

"I suppose, Ellman, you never felt like murdering old Hunt?"

Ellman shot a look, then grinned. "Many a time I did, sir."

A look of indescribable archness came over Wharton's face. "But you didn't do it?"

Ellman grinned again. "No, sir, I reckon I didn't."

That virtually concluded the interview. Ellman was bidden to stand by in case he was needed for the inquest, and Wharton went out with him. The message to Dijon had to be rushed through, and the next interview prepared for. Travers felt singularly perturbed as he thought of the interview with Charles Hunt. That business of the distemper injections had struck him, too, as a strange coincidence, and there was the matter of the spots which had since attacked the dog. Charles Hunt's presence might be necessary at the inquest as sole relative of the deceased, and yet Travers knew that Wharton would have had him down—as he had had Ellman—in any case. And now Brown was out of the poisoning affair, and Ellman had the chance of an alibi, was Wharton going to spring a dramatic surprise and make an arrest? Was that what was written at the foot of the page in the General's note-book?—the page which was to be so sportingly exhibited when the inquest was over? And then voices were heard outside—the voices of two men and a woman—and the door opened.

Wharton did the introductions. Charles Hunt seemed taken aback when he set eyes again on the long-shanked, blundering Englishman of the train. He was looking most unwell, and in spite of the weather he had on an overcoat, and a muffler was round his neck. Travers ventured on a word or two of sympathy. Hunt admitted that his nephew's death, and the manner of it, had been a terrible blow. "I can't understand it," he said, with a shake of the head. "Just when he had everything, he goes and does this. It isn't right somewhere. It isn't right."

"Human nature's a queer thing," said Wharton consolingly. "And he was a strange character himself, you'll admit that."

Hunt shook his head again. "Well, he's gone now. When I go, that'll be the last of us."

Wharton turned his attention to Mrs. Cheerly. It must have been a shock to her, he said, to hear of the tragic death of one whom she had known as a small boy. But there would be no need for her to view the body. All he wished her to do was to sit well back in the room with one of his own men—not Mr. Hunt; that might cause some wonder in Brown's mind—and watch Brown while he gave his evidence; and as soon as she had made up her mind as to whether or not she had seen him before, she was to leave the room, when her escort would bring her back to where she was at that moment.

Wharton's man was sent for, and Mrs. Cheerly left. There seemed to be considerable excitement in the neighbourhood of the inn, with people and cars arriving. It was on the stroke of the hour and Wharton glanced at Hunt.

"I'm having a seat reserved for you next to Mr. Hughes, your late brother's solicitor," he said, "so if you can spare us a minute or two to answer some questions, we'd be very grateful."

Hunt said he'd be only too glad. Wharton produced his notebook.

"When you asked Mr. Travers in the train that evening about the spots on your late brother's face, were you genuinely asking for information?"

"Why, of course I was," said Hunt. "Brown sent me a note to my hotel saying the party had decided to go back on the so-

and-so train, but he didn't say why. That worried me rather, and I was most perturbed when I saw what was the matter with my brother. I admit that Brown told me about it later on the station at Dijon."

"Naturally you were worried," agreed Wharton. "And when Brown left for England that Monday, did he have the keys given him?"

"The keys?" Hunt thought. "I wasn't there, of course, but I understood they were given to my nephew last Saturday when we all left."

"Then how did Brown get in the house?"

Hunt smiled. "The housekeeper and the maids were back already. They'd been away on a long holiday on board-wages, I understood. The housekeeper had her own keys."

"Of course," said Wharton. "How foolish of me. Oh, one little thing, Mr. Hunt. I think I got you clearly over the telephone, but just to make sure. Brown and you were together all the time on the platform at Dijon?"

"Oh, yes," said Hunt, and then looked rather puzzled. "Just why are you so particular?"

"Merely a question of certain times," said Wharton airily. "The French keep bothering us for information." Then he smiled roguishly, and dug Hunt playfully in the ribs. "In other words, suppose the French people ask if you had a perfect alibi at Dijon, I could tell them you had?"

"Well, yes." Then the smile faded. "But alibi for what?"

"Just my little joke," said Wharton, and chuckled hugely. Then his face straightened. "But to be more serious. This, Mr. Hunt, is far more important." He leaned forward impressively. "When you were staying here during that brief visit some two years ago, did your brother mention to you any document of a private nature—other than his will—that he was leaving behind?"

Hunt made faces, and he thought. He chewed the words over again, and made more faces.

"Something happened one day when he was pulling Brown's leg—"

Wharton looked surprised. "Pulling his leg?"

"Yes," said Hunt. "That seemed to be a trick my late brother had, of chipping Brown unmercifully. Why, I don't know—or what it was about. Some private joke between the two of them; though Brown didn't seem to think it much of a joke. I mean, he never laughed like my brother did."

"Yes?" said Wharton, craning still farther forward. "And what was the joke on the one occasion you remember?"

Hunt made still more faces as he thought back for the exact words.

"Well," he said, "as far as I remember it was something like this. My brother had fetched something from the safe and locked it again—or put something back, I forget which. Anyhow, I happened to mention the word *safe*, and Brown happened to come into the room at the time, and my brother looked at Brown and told me to keep quiet—told me playfully, as it were. He said he and Brown never dared to mention the word *safe*, as there was something most important in it. He said, 'Isn't there, Brown?'—like that. Something it was, he said, that meant quite a lot of difference to Brown."

Wharton cut in. "You're sure he said it to *Brown*?"

"Oh, yes," said Hunt. "He distinctly spoke to Brown, and said 'you.' I guessed it was his will, and I asked him why he didn't keep it at the bank or his lawyer's, and then he said, 'No, that would never do, Brown, would it '?"

Wharton drew back his chair. "Thank you, Mr. Hunt. We're most grateful to you for the information, and time's getting short or I'd ask you for more. I hope to see you again after the inquest. And now, if you come this way, there's a side door which will save you going round. You'll be shown to your seat."

Travers watched them from the door of the room. He heard the side door open, and caught from inside it the sound of Brown's voice. And he still felt that quick, exciting sense of something desperately imminent. Wharton would not have been so friendly with Charles Hunt unless he had something to conceal. But when Travers looked at Wharton again he was closing the door on Charles Hunt, and then he stood by it for a moment listening with lowered head. Then he came back to the room. He peered at Travers over those same antiquated glasses which he had donned for Charles Hunt's benefit.

"Well, it's what you Army people used to call zero hour."

"Yes," said Travers aimlessly. His heart was again beginning to quicken in a most ridiculous manner, and he put his hand to his ribs and felt it with a sudden, instinctive movement. And as he did so he had an extraordinary idea; so extraordinary, in fact, that he hooked off his horn-rims and began polishing them.

CHAPTER XVII
OUT OF THE PAST

BUT TRAVERS KEPT that sudden thought to himself. The moment was hardly ripe, and perhaps there would never be any real need to refer to it. When he glanced at Wharton, there the old General was, calm as one might have imagined Napoleon in the same circumstances, making himself comfortable in the chair and preparing to look through the newspaper.

Travers stoked his pipe, lighted it and promptly let it go out. There were a dozen things about which he had to think. What was going to happen about the fake burglary now Wharton had passed his word that Brown's confessions should be without prejudice? And what had Wharton seen wrong in Brown's story? As far as Travers could see, it fitted in with the precision of a set of ball-bearings. Melodramatic, of course, particularly that part about a boy walking in his sleep and appearing in his uncle's room with a knife. And yet, Travers knew himself as far from a mental expert, and such things rang reasonably true. And what precisely had there been in that one main question about the letter which Wharton had put to Charles Hunt? James Hunt, as Travers saw it, had spoken *to* Brown because it was Brown's feelings he wished to hurt. And, though time had been short, as Wharton had remarked, why had Charles Hunt been sent into the inquest room with no end of possible questions unasked?

Then, just as Travers was asking himself the question as to who really had done the poisoning murder, he became aware that Wharton had dropped the newspaper, and was listening intently from his chair. There was a sound outside in the passage, and Wharton flew to the door.

By the time he had it open, there was his man with Mrs. Cheerly. Her handkerchief was to her eyes, and she was sobbing quietly. Never had Wharton so rejoiced at the sight of tears. He patted the housekeeper on the back as if he had been her father, and motioned frantically to his man to clear out of the way so that he might have her to himself.

"There now, there," he said. "You've been upset. It's been very trying for you. There now, there."

He led her gently towards the easiest chair. The sobs gradually ceased, though she kept dabbing at her eyes. Travers loomed above the pair of them, and he was bursting with curiosity. Then he was told to push the bell, and as soon as the landlord came in, Wharton ordered his famous panacea—a pot of tea.

"A nice cup of tea will do you good," he said, and Travers smiled at the delicate blending of sympathy, concern and restrained eagerness. "And what was it that upset you so badly?"

"Everything all came back so," she began, "and then I got thinking of poor Mrs. Hunt and everything—" The handkerchief went to her eyes again, but only for a moment. She smiled drearily. "I'm sure I'm looking a fright. Do you think I might—"

Wharton cut in hurriedly, and he smiled with the obsequiousness of an Armenian who offers a carpet.

"A fright? My dear Mrs. Cheerly, if you'll pardon the truth from an old man, there are some people who couldn't be that under any circumstances." He bent down over her as she simpered faintly. "Now just compose yourself for one moment and tell me. Did you recognize him—or not?"

Her face became alert at once. "Yes, I did! I thought I knew him as soon as I saw him, only I couldn't remember where, and then when I heard him begin to speak, I knew him at once. But he had altered though."

Wharton made a movement of impatience. "Yes, but who was he?"

"*Doctor Barlow—Mrs. Hunt's brother.* That's who he was."

Wharton closed his lips. He pursed them. Then he grunted.

"Doctor Barlow. Hm! And Mrs. Hunt's brother. You saw him at Buxton, eh?"

But now the natural inquisitiveness that she must have been feeling got the better of her. She had to put a question of her own first, and she put it impulsively.

"Oh, Mr. Wharton, do tell me. I'm simply dying to know. How is it he's like this?"

"Like this?" repeated Wharton. "Oh, you mean, why is he a valet? Well, you see, people often come down in the world till they're glad to do anything."

Travers saw the lameness of the explanation, and was not surprised at the way she took it.

"Yes, but being valet to his own brother-in-law I And after him keeping his own valet, too."

And as Wharton raised his eyebrows, in came the landlord with a huge pot of tea, and three cups.

"Excellent!" said Wharton. "I don't know that I can't do with one myself." He fluttered the landlord away, and saw to the pouring out himself. Travers had a cup, too, for the good of the cause, and drew in his chair to make the party complete.

"So he had his own valet once, did he?" said Wharton. "And how long ago was that?"

The gist of her story was this. Doctor Barlow had been abroad, and had not been back in England long when he paid a visit—a week-end—to his sister. He had bought a practice in London, and Mrs. Cheerly thought it was Kensington. Mrs. Hunt was very fond of her brother, anybody could see that; and no wonder, for he was what Mrs. Cheerly called very nice. He always spoke nicely to you when he met you on the stairs or anywhere, and was not a bit stuck-up. He must have had a remarkably fine practice because he came down in a superb car driven by his chauffeur-valet, who had only just been engaged and could, therefore, give no gossip about his master. (Mrs. Cheerly said that with a distinct tone of regret.) As for general impressions and the little gossip she had picked up, all Mrs. Cheerly could add was that Mr. Hunt had definitely objected to the valet's being in the house on account of the maids, and his wife had laughed him out of it. All the same, Mrs. Cheerly had himself heard him petulantly ask why her brother needed a valet at all. However, that was not said, of course, in the presence of the doctor, who had seemed to get on well with his brother-in-law, though, as Mrs. Cheerly admitted, he was very much a bird of fine feather in that comparatively humble aviary.

That visit was in 1914, and in the autumn. The following Christmas, Mrs. Hunt spent a week-end in town with her brother, and came back with a tale of the glories of the town establishment. The following March Mrs. Hunt had a serious illness, and went into a nursing home. Shortly afterwards Mr. Hunt informed Mrs. Cheerly—quite casually and arising out of some reference—that the doctor had sold his practice and gone abroad again, where he was helping the Government in the War. Some long time later, Mrs. Cheerly happened to ask him if the doctor had ever returned to England, and she was told that he had not.

"That word *abroad*," said Wharton. "Think back and try to remember. Did you ever have any reason to connect it with Australia?"

Oh, no, she said. "You see, we thought it was somewhere to do with the War. Somewhere like France."

"Of course," said Wharton. He got up rather thoughtfully, and pushed the bell. The landlord came in.

"Will you see that Mrs. Cheerly here, and also a Mr. Hunt, have anything else they require." He tapped his chest to indicate that the bill was his affair. "And perhaps your wife will look after Mrs. Cheerly herself in a minute or two."

"Any lunch for you two gentlemen, sir?"

"Sorry, no," said Wharton. "We have to return to town in a very few minutes."

And as soon as the landlord had gone again, Wharton held out his hand to Mrs. Cheerly. "I may not be seeing you again to-day. It's been a great pleasure meeting you, and we're most grateful. My man will take you back to Chelmsford entirely at your own convenience." His voice lowered. "I needn't impress on you the fact that on no account must you breathe to a living soul the discovery you've made this morning!"

He drove the point home, and there seemed to be no risk of the news getting out. Travers shook hands with her, too, and followed Wharton out to the passage.

"We'd better get our things together," the General said, "and then I must phone Norris." He began to mount the stairs, and then on the first landing, halted and took out his note-book. He found the page, jabbed his finger on something at the bottom, and thrust book and finger beneath Travers's nose.

"You asked me what we should do if she couldn't identify him. There's the answer."

Travers gave a quick polish to his glasses, and read:

"N.B.—*Go through all cases of men struck off the Medical Register prior to* 1920."

Five minutes later the inquest was over, and Menzies would have won his bet. A quarter of an hour after that, Wharton and Travers were on the way back to town in the car in which they had come down. Somewhere behind them Ellman and Charles Hunt were following to Scotland Yard, and Travers, when Wharton had made the arrangements, had wondered why. But now Travers was rather enjoying the experience of sitting at ease in the comfortable saloon. Wharton spent his time as far as Tonbridge in writing notes, and as soon as he put his papers away, Travers took the first opportunity he had had of tackling him.

"How did you arrive at that amazing conclusion of yours that Brown had been struck off the Register?" he asked.

"I don't say he has," temporized Wharton. "That's got to be seen when we get to town and have a look at what Norris has ready for us."

"You know what I mean, George," smiled Travers. "Why did you think so confidently that he'd been a medical man?"

The General looked amazed at Travers's ignorance. Travers, who knew a lot of what was in Wharton's mind and preferred to hear the story in the General's own words, gave a little shrug of the shoulders to admit that he was a fool.

"There were five separate and unimpeachable witnesses," said Wharton. "The first one was yourself. You told me that when Olivet was lying ill, Brown—who was in the corridor outside—suggested to you that he had tonsilitis. Now that was a most peculiar remark. What would an ordinary person have said?"

"I don't know," admitted Travers. "Perhaps that Olivet was ill."

"Exactly!" said Wharton. "The ordinary person would have said—bearing in mind the symptoms that Olivet was displaying—that it *looked as if he had something wrong with his throat.* But Brown called it tonsilitis, because he wished to throw you and everybody else off the scent. Already he knew—though perhaps not quite why—that somebody had poisoned the wrong man."

Travers's eyes bulged. "Somebody? You mean Ellman—or Charles Hunt?"

"That remains to be seen," said Wharton dryly. "But, to go on at where I left off. If you say to me: 'Oh, yes, but Brown knew all about tonsilitis since his master was a chronic sufferer from it,' then I retort by saying that if Brown based his judgment on what he had seen in his master, then he was all wrong. Olivet's face was a fiery red. *Hunt's face—as the doctor told you himself—was always very pale.*"

Travers delivered himself of a Whartonian grunt. "That's right enough, George." He smiled. "I don't mind your doing that devil's advocate stunt of yours if you deliver the goods like that. And who were the other witnesses?"

"Pajou is the star witness," said Wharton. "Assume that Brown knew—or did not know; it makes no difference—the precise contents of that bottle of medicine which Popland gave Hunt when he had spots in England after eating strawberries. The fact remains. Brown imposed his own formula on Pajou. It was not Popland's formula. It would have been remarkable if Brown *had* discovered what Popland put in the bottle; and if he had, he diverged from it when he had that argument with Pajou.

In the same way, Brown was able to discuss with Pajou the nature of the proposed lotion."

Travers frowned. "Yes, but aren't all sorts of medical prescriptions public property?"

"I'm glad you asked that," said Wharton. "I was most anxious, if you remember, that you should ask Popland if Brown had any idea of what was in the medicine bottle. It was purposely a most unusual question, and it should have provoked various unusual answers. Popland might have said that Brown had asked what was in it. He might have said that Brown often had a chat with him and showed interest in medical matters. Brown might have said that he had had thoughts of becoming a dispenser. In other words, I hoped that the doctor's answer would betray that Brown had medical tastes and knowledge, and I could have put that evidence with what I knew from you and Pajou. The evidence the doctor *did* give you was sufficient for me to authorize you to inform Brown about the murders. That evidence was that Brown did know quite a lot about medicine; enough to know—without Popland's aid—suitable prescriptions for a rather rare case of spots."

"Yes, but what about my objection that chemists often publish prescriptions, and Brown might have seen these particular ones?"

"I've answered that already," Wharton told him. "Chemists only publish things that are common and things that will sell. They don't publish prescriptions of *rare* things, like remedies—internal and external—for spots caused by the eating of strawberries. And if it comes to that"—he switched round in his seat—"tell me this. You're a man of marvellous memory. Give me a prescription for one of the commonest ailments—disordered liver."

Travers thought and thought. A possible cure he could give, but not a prescription.

"That's all right, then," said Wharton. "My argument's admitted. Then there's the evidence of Mrs. Ayton and the maid I saw last night, about Brown taking an interest in ills and ailments. And lastly, there's my own evidence."

"What is that?" asked Travers. "I don't remember it."

"It was when Menzies and I were looking at Leslie Hunt's body," said Wharton. "Brown gave evidence about what had been eaten for lunch, and said we'd see for ourselves that that was correct *if we had to make an examination of him.* You see the point? Brown couldn't help giving us a hint, and yet he had to disguise it in layman's language. The man in the street wouldn't have known anything about stomach content. Brown slipped out that he did know something, and at the same time his instinct made him wrap up the words as he thought a layman would use them. But it wasn't the words that struck me—it was the fact that Brown had the knowledge."

Travers nodded. "That seems conclusive enough, taken in bulk. But why shouldn't you have assumed that Brown was a chemist? I mean to say, that he had been a chemist in his younger days."

Wharton smiled dryly. "You ask that—after combining with Menzies to prove to me that Brown was a man of superior education? Do chemists know all about gerunds?"

"They might," said Travers. "That is, here and there one might."

Wharton swivelled round again. "Besides, there's something else. Now I'm not an utter fool—"

He said it with such false modesty that Travers had to laugh. "That's delicious, George. Do go on. You're not an utter fool. And what then?"

"What then?" repeated Wharton. "Well, I can use my eyes and form opinions. I've met all sorts in my time." His eyes twinkled. "People like yourself, for instance. I had my own views about Brown, though I didn't publish them. Brown had at some time been a gentleman. I got that into my mind, and there was no dislodging it."

"You ought to know," Travers told him perfectly seriously. "I respect your judgment, George, though I try—somewhat unsuccessfully—to pull your leg."

"You agree that the evidence pointed to the fact that Brown might have been a doctor?"

"Well"—somewhat grudgingly—"yes. Bearing in mind, of course, the other peculiarities of the case. That Brown occupied a strange position in the Hunt household, for instance, and that he was tied in some inexplicable way to old Hunt."

"But you agree?"

Travers wondered at the insistence, but said he agreed.

"I'm glad of that," said Wharton, "because I've kept back the strongest piece of evidence of all; evidence on which Gallois will most certainly secure a conviction."

Travers opened his eyes. "A conviction against whom?"

Wharton smiled exasperatingly. "That remains to be seen. But the evidence itself is very dear to your own heart. Now think it out for yourself. I've got to make some quick notes arising out of what we've been saying."

"Dear to my heart," said Travers. "I ought to know it?"

"You do know it," said Wharton, already balancing his note-book on the attaché case and preparing to write.

But as the car came to Westminster Bridge, Wharton put the notebook away. He was looking a bit restless. Never, he confided to Travers, had he been so curious to know the history of a person as he was to know all about Brown. He was first out of the car at the Yard, and Travers followed pantingly on his heels. Chief-Inspector Norris was at Wharton's desk when they entered the room, reading something typed on a quarto sheet. Travers shook hands, and was unaffectedly glad to see him again.

"Any news?" burst out Wharton.

"Inspector Gallois is coming over to Croydon by air-liner this evening," said Norris.

Wharton was already turning over the pile of newspapers at the desk.

"Got what I asked for?"

"Everything's here, sir," Norris, unruffled as ever, told him. "This is C.R.O.'s stuff, and this is a précis of the case from all sources."

Wharton picked up the précis and began to read. His eyes flew along the lines, then he gave one look at the newspaper which lay at the top of the pile. What was on it Travers could not see, except that it was probably the general news page with a photograph at the side. And then Wharton's hand went over the photograph as if to hide it from view.

"Norris!" He spoke so sharply that the inspector gave a little start. "A Charles Hunt and a chauffeur named Ellman are due here now. If they aren't here, wait for them, and show them up at once. Let Hunt in first. And get me through to Peddleby—now. Make sure the local police are the other end."

But no sooner was Norris's head outside the door than he was popping it in again.

"They're now coming up, sir."

"Right!" snapped Wharton. "Send Hunt in, and keep the other. And get me through to Peddleby, quick."

Travers, heart racing furiously, drew back to the far corner of the room. In came Charles Hunt, looking about him with the slow curiosity of a man who finds himself in an unusual place for the first time. Wharton forced his own face into geniality.

"Here we are again then, Mr. Hunt. Take a seat. And I won't keep you more than a minute or two."

He took his own seat behind the desk, and when Hunt had settled himself and looked up, it was into a pair of desperately searching eyes.

"Mr. Hunt, I want you to do me a great service. If ever you thought hard in your life, I want you to think hard now. Think back to that moment when the train was slowing down into Dijon station."

Hunt thought so hard that he closed his eyes.

"You're there," said Wharton. "Brown joins you by the door. You whisper. You go down to the platform. The air is sweet and cool, and it's dark everywhere. You begin to stroll along. *And which way do you stroll?*"

Hunt's brow furrowed in thought. He remembered. It was in the direction of his brother's compartment that they strolled.

"Right!" said Wharton. "Keep thinking hard. You are now strolling on. *When did you stop—and why?*"

Hunt's mouth gaped. He sat up in the chair.

"Why—how'd you know we stopped?"

"Never mind that," snapped Wharton impatiently. "Tell me what happened."

"Well," he paused to think again, "we were going along when all at once Brown stopped me and pointed to a light up on the hill. He asked me if I saw it, and he said that one day he'd tell me something interesting about it. Then we turned back towards the carriage door again."

"Talking very quietly, were you?"

"Well, yes," admitted Hunt. "Whispering, in fact."

Wharton came round. "Just get up a minute, will you? Wasn't Brown nearest the carriage, like this ...? I thought so. And wasn't it his left arm which went over your left shoulder, like this, while he pointed with his left hand ...? I thought so. And you didn't feel his free hand—his right hand—doing anything?"

"Why, no," said Hunt. "What should he be doing?"

Wharton smiled. "I don't know. Scratching his head—or anything. Still, that's all, Mr. Hunt, thank you. The car will take you right home. In case we should want to see you again to-night, you might be so good as to remain at home." He hustled him to the door and into Norris's arms. Travers heard the "No, I don't want Ellman yet," and then the General was shutting the door again. He flew over to the telephone.

"Hallo! Am I through to Peddleby yet? ... Oh, I am ..." He glanced over at Travers and then settled to the phone again. "Oh, yes. That you, Inspector? ... Brown tucked up at home all right? ... Yes, put him under arrest at once, and hold him till I get there.... Charge of fake burglary. The silver's in the tank in the attic. ... Yes, at once, please. And report here all correct.... Good-bye!"

He hung up the receiver. Travers came across.

"I say, George, you're not going to arrest Brown for that. You gave your word."

"I know I did," said Wharton unblushingly. "I promised immunity from disclosures. But he didn't tell us he stole the silver. *We* told *him* he had done it. Besides, anything's fair in a case of murder."

"A case of murder," said Travers slowly. "I rather gathered that much." His eye fell on the *Sunday Worker*, and Wharton beckoned for him to move round. Travers peered at the photograph, then whipped off his glasses and gave them a quick polish. Looking at him was the face of Thomas Brown. Beneath were the words:

DR. DAVID BARLOW—THE ACCUSED MAN.

CHAPTER XVIII
TRAVERS CONCLUDES

WHARTON DROPPED BACK into his chair, and picked up that précis which Norris had made. Travers peered over his shoulder and read it too.

David Barlow disposed of a good practice in Biarritz, and purchased one in Kensington. He was very well qualified, and was the author of two medical works, one of which—"Manual of Toxicology and Medical Jurisprudence"—was much in use in the medical schools.

Wharton jabbed his finger on the title of that book, looked up meaningly at Travers, and then resumed his reading:

After he had been in Kensington a few months he attended a Mrs. Miller, widow of a Colonel Miller, Indian Army, retired. She was a woman of about sixty and somewhat eccentric, and Doctor Barlow gained her confidence. It appeared that he had gifts of money from her at various times, some of which paid off the balance due for purchase of the practice. A year after he first attended her, she died suddenly from heart trouble, and he signed the certificate. It was then found that deceased had left a will by which Doctor Barlow benefited to the extent of twenty-three thousand pounds—virtually the total of the estate.

The relatives of the deceased woman made inquiries, employing a private detective agency. Startling discoveries were made. One of the witnesses purported to be a footman who had been killed in action since the time of the presumed signing, and the prosecutor claimed that his signature had been made after it was known that he had been killed. The other witness—a maid in the employ of the deceased—confessed that she had signed in the presence of Doctor Barlow and the deceased, but had neither seen the deceased sign, nor the other witness sign. Moreover, Doctor Barlow had given her a hundred pounds to keep her mouth shut.

Doctor Barlow received a sentence of five years, and was later struck off the Register. Mr. Justice Beauchamp, when passing sentence, said that Barlow's act had been undoubtedly due to living beyond his means, and to the gambling and betting mania which had possessed him. He added also that if Barlow had not already made restitution of his own free will of the monies he had obtained from Mrs. Miller prior to her death, the sentence passed would have been much heavier.

Wharton jabbed his finger down again on that last sentence. The rest of the précis was merely the names of the two prisons in which Barlow had been confined and the date of release, but Wharton sat on frowning over it all as if to extract the very last morsel of confirmation of his own theories. Travers began turning over the newspaper files.

"Anything you want particular, sir?" asked Norris, who had just come in.

"Well—er—yes," Travers stammered slightly. "I rather thought Barlow must have killed that Mrs. Miller, and I was trying to find an account of the exhumation of the body."

"What's that about the body?" said Wharton, looking up.

"Mr. Travers was wondering if Barlow killed that Mrs. Miller *off* to get her money," explained Norris. "As a matter of fact, sir, he didn't. Another doctor confirmed that it was heart all right. Not that it wasn't hinted at during the trial that Barlow might have helped the heart along, so to speak."

Wharton nodded as he got to his feet.

"Anything else you want, sir?" asked Norris.

"I don't think so," said Wharton, and gave a tentative smile. "You seem to have given us all we're likely to digest for a bit. And talking of digestion, have some tea sent in as you go out, will you? It seems the devil of a long time since breakfast."

And as soon as the door closed on Norris the tentative smile became a chuckle, and the General rubbed his hands. "Well? There's life in the old dogs yet—eh? This is going to make Gallois think a bit."

"Yes," said Travers, "it's good work, George. All the same, I wish that housekeeper hadn't given us a short cut by identifying Barlow. He'd have been a bigger feather in your cap if you'd found him out by going through the list of men struck off the Register, as you'd intended, and you certainly would have found him out."

"Well, I might," said Wharton modestly. "Still, we're not going to tell Gallois *how* we found out all this," and he waved at the pile of papers on the desk. "A little mystification won't do him any harm."

Travers began fingering a copy of the *Sunday Worker* and shook his head at it. "One thing I can't understand, George. I wonder why this Barlow story wasn't super-front-page stuff. It's sensational enough, even for the *Worker*."

Wharton had a look, and then pointed out what the real front page stuff was. A big offensive had been on in France, and the pages blazed with it. No wonder the Barlow story had been crowded out.

"What's more," said Wharton, "you can bet your life James Hunt took jolly good care that the servants at Buxton didn't see anything. If they had seen the case and thought there was some connection between the Doctor Barlow they knew, you can also bet that Hunt had an answer all ready for them. Not that it matters to us."

Wharton watched the arrival of the tea tray, and drew up the two chairs. "I suppose you're in no particular hurry?" he said to Travers. "I'd like to go over the preliminary report for Gallois."

Travers knew what that meant. Wharton was proposing his old game of trying it out on the dog. Not that Travers minded; he was only too anxious to fill in certain gaps, and as he took his cup of tea from Wharton, he set the ball rolling himself.

"I know now that all that yarn which Brown handed us out this morning, George, was pure hokum. Brown never was a chauffeur in Australia. And therefore I can't understand that reference James Hunt made when he taunted Brown. I must call him that; it doesn't seem right to call him 'Barlow.' You know what I mean, George; when he accused him of killing somebody. Did James Hunt know in some way that Brown had killed Mrs. Miller? Was that also in the letter?"

Wharton shook his head. "Hunt could never have known that. It wasn't Mrs. Miller he was referring to. You know how sergeant-majors are supposed to taunt recruits. 'You may have broken your mother's heart, but you won't break mine.' That was the kind of thing."

"Yes," persisted Travers, "but whom had Brown killed?"

"That'll all fit in in a moment," said Wharton, as he brought out his notebook.

Travers shrugged his shoulders resignedly. "And did Brown do the killing off his own bat? Or is Charles Hunt implicated at all?"

Wharton looked at him with pained amazement. "Charles Hunt hadn't anything to do with it. Brown didn't need a confederate. All I got Charles down to the inquest for was because he was the only surviving relative. He had to be there."

Travers smiled ironically. "You don't get away with that, George. Up to the very last moment you thought there was something in that dog-distemper affair. You had Charles Hunt nice and handy in case anything turned up from the visit of Mrs. Cheerly that might incriminate him as well as Brown."

"Well, two strings to a bow are better than one," said Wharton imperturbably. "And now, if you like, I'll give you my version of the whole case as I shall give it to Gallois. It's only a rough outline, and the more holes you pick in it the better. First of all, we assume that as soon as the trouble arose, James Hunt was summoned to London. His brother-in-law's Counsel probably told him that it would certainly be discovered that the monies Brown had had from Mrs. Miller were intended by her as loans and not gifts, and if restitution were made, the inevitable sentence would be less heavy. Thereupon Hunt, for his wife's sake, *paid that money out of his own pocket*, since Brown hadn't any himself. I suggest also—and we can prove it by interviewing Brown's Counsel—that Hunt extracted from Brown not only a receipt but a promise—and a most binding one—to repay. Those documents, together with accounts of the subsequent trial, were the contents of that envelope which Brown had to obtain by hook or crook—and which, as we know, he did try to obtain.

"Mrs. Hunt, as we also know, was so distressed that she fell ill, and was removed to a nursing home. Hunt told Mrs. Cheerly that the doctor had gone abroad again. The years went by, and the time came for Brown to be released. Mrs. Hunt begged her husband—whom, you may remember, she could twist round her little finger—to give her brother a home. Hunt said it could only be done if they went right away to where none of them were known, and finally that was agreed on. The staff were dismissed, and then, at the very last moment, the tremendous worry of it all brought on the illness from which Mrs. Hunt died. We may assume that on her death-bed she made her husband swear that he would not break his promise to shelter her brother.

"Hunt, then, had lost his wife. He always had a bitter tongue and a warped nature, but what he felt now we can imagine. He loved his wife as he loved nothing else, and it was Brown who had killed her. Think of him, then, meeting Brown at the prison gates. See the two men alone when they got to 'Marsh View.' See Hunt scowling venomously. See the cynical slit of his mouth as he gives Brown the shock of his life.

"'Why isn't my sister here?' Brown says.

"Hunt tells him: 'Because she's dead—and you've killed her. And, by God! you shall pay. You forged and robbed in order to throw your money about on chauffeurs and valets. Now try what it's like to be a menial yourself. You had my money to make your sentence shorter, and you've signed your name to pay it back. Very well, then. You shall work it off in my service. If you attempt to bolt, I'll follow you and expose you, even if you get to hell's gates. I'll tell the world who and what you are, and I'll make your name stink. And in case you think you can clear by killing me, let me tell you that I've drawn up an account of everything, and if the doctors are not satisfied that I've died a natural death, they'll set the law on you.'"

Wharton, carried away by the intensity of the imaginary scene, smashed his fist down on the table. The dancing of the crockery restrained his enthusiasm.

"Well, how's it working out?" he said to Travers.

"A.1 and copper-bottomed," Travers told him. "Let's have some more."

"The rest is easy," Wharton went on. "Hunt began a new life in his new home. His daily amusement was to torture Brown with diabolical ingenuity and inventing new ways of baiting him. He made Brown a menial, and he kept him under. The embitterment, as I might call it, grew, and it became an influence that hung right over that damnable household. I should say that Hunt even hated Leslie because he was a reminder of his dead wife. If he didn't hate him, he despised him. As for Brown, he stuck it out because he could do nothing else, but all the time he was working out plans to get rid of Hunt. The motor accident was his great chance, because that might be assumed in a way to be a natural kind of thing. But when it failed, Hunt had him closer than ever, because you can bet he put an account of that accident with the other accounts in the envelope, and he took good care to taunt Brown with it."

Wharton paused to light his pipe. "Still working out right," said Travers. "But what was that important evidence you were holding back on me about Brown's being a doctor?" He smiled. "Pardon the gerund."

"Oh, that," said Wharton, rather too casually. "Well, let's go on to the real crime. I'm going to assume that Brown brought the strawberries to the table knowing the effect they'd had on Hunt the previous time. Brown's mind was always running on what I might call toxicological grooves. He was always wondering how he could poison Hunt and get away with it. If Hunt—who was a greedy feeder—ate the strawberries, Brown thought he saw his chance. *Only a doctor could have seen the peculiar combination of circumstances that made that chance.*"

"Yes, but why did you insist that I ought to have known all about it?" objected Travers.

"Well, you certainly ought to have known," Wharton told him bluntly. "You had a hunch about *spots*, and you didn't believe sufficiently in your hunch to act on it. You knew that *two men had spots, and both died*. You suspected a connection, and there was a connection. The fact that one had spots before death and the other after death made it all the more easy, especially as soon as you yourself discovered that Hunt and Olivet were the same person! I mean by that, of course, that it was Hunt who should have been poisoned and suffered just as Olivet did."

"I think I'm beginning to see," said Travers slowly. "Still, carry on with the story, George."

"Let's go on with the crime," said Wharton. "It was easy enough for Brown to get a syringe and of the size he wanted. Anybody can buy one. I say also it was easy enough to get the atropine, and once Gallois has a photograph of Brown, I'm betting he hunts every chemist and doctor round St. Raphael till he knows where and how Brown got it. Very well, then, Hunt ate some strawberries and spots developed. If he'd stayed at St. Raphael or gone home by car, he'd still have been killed in the same way. As it was, he went by train. Brown gave him the injection at Dijon, and it's been proved that it was an easy enough thing to do. It even succeeded with Olivet, who hadn't had a sleeping draught as Hunt had!

"You yourself admitted that Brown had nerves of steel. Brown had to have nerves of steel to push home that plunger with the right hand while he distracted Charles Hunt's attention with the left. As for that man who was supposed to slip under the train, that was all bunkum. Brown said: 'Look! did you see that?' and, of course, Charles Hunt would admit he saw something. Perhaps there was something—a shadow, perhaps—that he did see. However, Brown gave that injection at Dijon and then waited calmly till the morning, or when he should be sent for to his sick master. He needed those steel nerves when he knew that in some unaccountable way he had poisoned the wrong man. But he kept his nerve even to the extent of suggesting to you that

Olivet had tonsilitis, and there he damned himself. It was Hunt who should have had that constriction of the throat, and Brown could have explained it away as an illness from which Hunt had repeatedly suffered, and Leslie Hunt—and Charles, if necessary—could have supported him. And if spots had appeared—as they often do after atropine poisoning—they wouldn't have been noticed on Hunt, since he already had the other spots which had been caused by eating the strawberries. It was when I saw the beauty of the plan that I knew the poisoning must have been done by somebody with special medical knowledge."

"I see that now," said Travers. "All the same, Brown must have known that there would be an inquiry."

"He had a perfect alibi as things happened," cut in Wharton. "Remember that Brown expected also that the same strawberry spots would conceal the puncture mark of the needle. And on the face of it, in any case, how could he possibly have been concerned with the death of a man in a closed compartment which he couldn't possibly have entered? The French authorities recognized that when they allowed him to go on to England, and kept back only the chauffeur and the two Hunts."

"Yes," persisted Travers, "but suppose the death hadn't taken place in the train, and Brown hadn't his alibi. What about the inquiry then?"

"I see it like this," explained Wharton. "Brown knew France, and he thought he knew the French. He had every confidence in himself and the plan, and he had what most people have—a sneaking, insular sense of superiority where foreigners are concerned. Brown had staged things so that he himself—as the dead man's personal servant—would be the principal witness. He also knew he could rely on Leslie for confirmation sufficient to convince a lot of foreigners who couldn't possibly have the same knowledge as himself. No," and Wharton shook his head, "Brown ran one risk, and one only."

"You mean the document?"

"Precisely!" said Wharton. "Brown must have managed at last to get a duplicate key to the safe where he imagined the document was, and that was probably the beginning of the whole damnable scheme. I'd say he'd have found some means to bring out spots on Hunt's skin even if the strawberries hadn't been eaten."

"No syringe was found at Dijon?" Travers asked.

"Not that I've heard," said Wharton. "You bet Brown threw it where it will never be found. In the same way, there's no telling where he had the duplicate key made. He may have made it himself from an impression. Still, that's Gallois's business. All it's up to us to do is to give the main facts." And there he gave a most peculiar look. "I wonder what sentence he'll get."

"Not much of a one if it's only a question of killing Olivet, and not intent to kill Hunt."

Wharton shrugged his shoulders. "I'm betting he gets off with a couple of years. Then we may have a go at him ourselves."

Travers stared at him. The stare relaxed. "You mean over the death of Leslie?"

"That's it," said Wharton, with a gusto that seemed to Travers perfectly ghoulish. "Remember the question I asked you and Menzies? What were the conditions under which Brown could have killed Leslie with impunity?"

Travers frowned. "I remember all right, but I still don't see it, unless it has something to do with Brown's being a doctor."

"The very thing," said Wharton. "Mind you, what I'm going to say will probably never be told to a jury. There isn't a shred of real evidence. All the same, I say that it's circumstantial and deductive evidence of the very best kind." He stoked up his pipe again as if determined to enjoy his own theories.

"Let's take Brown and Leslie Hunt. When Brown saw Hunt dead in that train and knew he had not died from atropine, he knew there was something fishy about the death, all the same. When the train left, after you and the other occupants of the compartment had lost it, Brown and Leslie were left alone with the corpse. Brown knew Leslie inside and out. Do you mean to tell me that Brown didn't know that Leslie had something on his mind? Of course he knew. And why shouldn't Brown, with the corpse entirely at his disposal, have made a quick examination? He might have thought of hat-pins and found the puncture mark. He may have told Leslie, who thereupon accused Madame Olivet. Still," and Wharton shrugged that all away, "that doesn't so much matter. What matters is our knowledge of Leslie Hunt and his nerves and his conscience. Brown got more and more suspicious as soon as Leslie got to England. Perhaps he put on the father attitude. 'Tell me all about it,' and so on, but in any case I suggest that Leslie had to confess to somebody that he killed his uncle on a sudden impulse. Brown didn't care two snaps of the fingers for Leslie. He told you he liked the boy because it was an excellent excuse to explain away why he stayed on in the Hunt household, and as soon as Leslie confessed, then Brown had him! He said he'd see him through if he did what he was told. Brown burnt the books which an inquisitive inquirer might discover were a likely cause of putting murder into Leslie's head. He also had a will made in his own favour.

"But when you came along yesterday and blew the gaff, by showing you knew all about the two murders, Brown had to act. He couldn't rely on Leslie. Leslie might squeal, and tell all about his confession, and the reason he made the will. He might have told you that Brown had put him up to asking Hughes about the letter. So Brown staved you off with the yarn of a dream, and then he killed Leslie. He had to kill him. It was inevitable—and it was childishly easy."

The General paused for a moment to see the effect of that grand climax.

"And why was it easy?" he went on. "For these reasons. It isn't unreasonable to suppose that just as Brown had done some private doctoring of the servants, so he'd also done some occasionally to Leslie. But leaving that out, and merely saying that there was a confidence about Brown where medicine was concerned, that'd explain it alone. Or leave that out, too, and you'll admit that Leslie trusted Brown implicitly. Very well, then. Here's what I think happened after you left 'Marsh View' yesterday morning.

"Leslie was cheerful again at lunch, because Brown told him everything would be all right. Brown was cheerful himself, because the letter had been destroyed. Leslie had lunch, as Brown said. We know that's true, or Brown wouldn't have challenged us about the stomach content. After that, Leslie fretted himself unwell again, and of his own accord or on Brown's advice, went to lie down on his bed—hence the jacket over the chair. Then Brown mixed the cyanide and brought it up in a glass *on a tray*, in his capacity of manservant. He had mixed in one glass and poured into another glass, and he used the tray to avoid prints. He came into the room and in his paternal capacity spoke somewhat like this: 'Hallo, not asleep yet? Well, drink this. It's a very special pick-me-up the doctor's just sent round. Gulp it down straight away. Don't stop to smell it. Hold your nose and swallow it down. It'll make you sleep. And," concluded Wharton, "it certainly did!"

"Yes," said Travers. "And perhaps it wasn't a bad thing that it did. But you'd never dare go to the Director of Public Prosecutions with a case like that, George. No jury'd ever convict. You'd be laughed out of court."

"I know," said Wharton, decidedly regretful. "The evidence is all hypothetical, and you and I know it's good evidence, though a jury'd never convict on it. Still," more hopefully, "if we have time we can work it up. Brown'll be a long while in jail."

Travers suddenly shook his head, and there was something of pain in the gesture, so that Wharton wondered if he were feeling the strain of the last few days. But it was not that.

"Aren't you ever satisfied, George?" he said. "Can't you let that poor devil Brown rest for a bit? If he does get off with two years, even then he'll get more than that. All his past will be dragged into the light again. And when he comes out from where the French send him, what will he have to live for? Every man's got the right to have something to live for. Brown did a wrong thing years ago, and he paid for it. Then he had to go on paying for another ten years and more while old Hunt tortured him. And now you want to go at him again, though you've only an unsubstantial theory to work on."

Wharton snorted. "You're too soft-hearted. You always were. We've argued that out before."

"Maybe," said Travers, "but there's another point. If Leslie killed his uncle with malice aforethought, then Brown merely saved you people work, and did an act of justice in killing him."

Wharton smiled wryly. "The law doesn't accept deputies. And there's a good deal you're conveniently forgetting. Brown wasn't the mute martyr you make him out to be. He'd a right to repay James Hunt that money, and his conduct certainly killed his own sister. And he tried to smash up Hunt in that car accident, and but for the fact that Olivet got the dose instead, Hunt would have died in that terrible agony with which Olivet died. Only a fiend could kill a man with atropine." He snorted again. "And when you talk about Brown having nothing to live for, you're forgetting something else. When he comes out of jail he'll have twenty thousand pounds—the twenty thousand that Leslie left him. Nothing to live for? My God!"

Travers flushed slightly at that home-thrust. "Perhaps you're right, George. I'd forgotten that. Still, somebody's got to have it."

"Charles Hunt ought to have it," said Wharton. "He's not at all a bad old chap when you get to know him. And his wife's a very nice old soul, and both of them independent enough to tell James to keep his money, though they could have done with it."

"Travers smiled as he picked up his hat. You've got it rather wrong, George. If you ever prove that Brown killed Leslie—and you won't—all that'd mean would be that Brown wouldn't inherit."

"I don't care a damn who gets it so long as Brown doesn't," said Wharton grimly. "And you're going now, are you? Like to see Gallois when he comes?"

"Very much," said Travers. "I'll be in all the evening. Bring him along for a bit."

"I will," said Wharton. "That'll be the end of another case—thanks to yourself."

Travers smiled. "Rubbish, George. I did nothing except be there." He smiled down again. "Don't trouble to get up. I'll find my way out. And I'll expect you both later."

Wharton watched him with a look that was remarkably like affection. Travers opened the door, and he opened it slowly. Then he turned and regarded Wharton in a queer sort of way. There was something whimsical in the look, and something quizzical and something ironical.

"Sorry to rake up things again, George," he said, "but about your anxiety that Brown shouldn't inherit that twenty thousand. If you could really prove that Leslie murdered his uncle, then Leslie couldn't inherit—and therefore Brown couldn't."

Wharton frowned in thought, and he wondered why Travers was regarding him so amusedly.

"We'll never do that," he said. "The evidence is even more flimsy than if we were trying to prove that Brown killed Leslie."

Travers shook his head, and he was still smiling. "You forget things, too, George. That wouldn't be a murder trial. Leslie Hunt is dead, and you don't judge the dead. All there would be, would be an application to the Courts to have the will set aside. Circumstantial evidence would have more weight than in a murder trial, and you've got plenty of circumstantial evidence to bring forward in support of the theory that Leslie Hunt murdered his uncle."

"Hm!" went Wharton. "He sat convenient for the hat-pin, and he had a motive for the murder. Also there was that book which he destroyed in case it should be brought against him as evidence—suggestive evidence."

"There's better evidence than that," said Travers.

Wharton thought again. "I don't see it. What is it?"

Travers smiled. "You've done an awful lot of leg-pulling recently, George. Only a few moments ago you were telling me airily of something I ought to have known. You ought to know one more reason why Leslie Hunt killed his uncle."

"Oh, ought I?" said Wharton, and thought again. Then he shook his head. "Well, I'll be a fool for once, and give it up. What is it?"

"*For once* is good," said Travers. "Think again, George. It's to do with spots. Those spots you told me I ought to have known about."

"Damn the spots!" exploded Wharton.

Travers came back from the door, and stood by the desk, where his tall, lank body towered above the face of the General that almost glowered at him from the chair. Travers's eyes twinkled behind the horn-rims.

"When we were back there at the pub, George, and things began to happen, my heart began to race, as it always does. It raced so hard that I felt it to reassure myself it wasn't going to burst. At that very moment I had an idea."

He picked up a pen from the rack, and held it towards Wharton.

"Here's a hat-pin, George. I want you to imagine you're going to stab me clean through the heart. It's life and death to you to do the job well. It's very dark, but I've got on a white waistcoat. Don't be afraid, George. Remember, you hate me like hell. Now then, clean in the heart!"

Wharton sat frowning away as he balanced the pen. Then he leaned forward, and the nib touched Travers's waistcoat.

"There," he said. "That's where I'd strike."

"Too high," smiled Travers. "Remember my elongation, George. Experiment on yourself. Try it out."

Wharton's hand went to his own left ribs, and he began to feel. Travers suddenly laughed. "You haven't any spots, have you, George?"

Wharton sat up. "What do you mean?"

"Well," said Travers, and now his face straightened, "wouldn't anybody have thought you were scratching yourself?"

Wharton stared. "You mean—?"

"Yes," said Travers, "that's what I mean. Leslie Hunt had made up his mind to kill his uncle when he went into the lavatory to destroy that book. He, too, wanted to know exactly where to strike. He probably tested himself in the lavatory. When he came out he had a sudden panic in case he'd forgotten again, and once more he fumbled to be dead sure of the position of his own heart. And I saw him do it, and thought he was scratching himself because he had spots. But he hadn't any spots—and that's why we ought to have known he killed his uncle."

"You're right," said Wharton. He looked down at his note-book, and shook his head morosely. Then he nodded once or twice to himself.

"If you'll swear to that, Brown certainly won't inherit," he began. But when he looked up for the answer, Travers had gone. Wharton blinked, gave another grunt or two, then pushed the bell for Norris. Then he felt the tea-pot, and seemed surprised to find it cold.

Norris coughed gently as he came in. "Pardon me, sir, but what about that chap Ellman? Do you want him now?"

"Want him?" Wharton glared. "Of course I don't want him. Thank him, and tell him he can go." A smile flickered at the corners of his mouth. "Wish him luck, and tell him to drive more slowly in future. Oh, and send me in a stenographer—and another pot of tea."

His face straightened as he sat down again at the desk. Then all at once a look of humorous wonder came over it. His fingers moved up to his ribs. He began to fumble. He smiled to himself as he found the right place and felt his heart stolidly beating.

THE END

Printed in Great Britain
by Amazon